GASLIT

Books by Megan Davidhizar

SILENT SISTER
GASLIT

GASLIT

MEGAN DAVIDHIZAR

HARPER FIRE

First published in the United Kingdom by Harper Fire,
an imprint of HarperCollins *Children's Books*, in 2026
HarperCollins *Children's Books* is a division of HarperCollins*Publishers* Ltd
1 London Bridge Street
London SE1 9GF

www.harpercollins.co.uk

HarperCollins*Publishers*
Macken House, 39/40 Mayor Street Upper
Dublin 1, D01 C9W8, Ireland

1

Text copyright © Megan Davidhizar 2026
Cover design copyright © HarperCollins*Publishers* Ltd 2026
All rights reserved

ISBN 978-0-00-861703-5

Megan Davidhizar asserts the moral right to be identified as the author of the work.

A CIP catalogue record for this title is available from the British Library.

Set in Adobe Caslon Pro by HarperCollins*Publishers* India

Printed and bound in the UK using 100%
Renewable Electricity at CPI Group (UK) Ltd

Conditions of Sale
This book is sold subject to the condition that it shall not, by way of trade or otherwise, be lent, re-sold, hired out or otherwise circulated without the publisher's prior consent in any form, binding or cover other than that in which it is published and without a similar condition including this condition being imposed on the subsequent purchaser. No part of this publication may be reproduced, stored in a retrieval system or transmitted in any form or by any means, electronic, mechanical, photocopying, recording or otherwise, without the prior permission of HarperCollins*Publishers* Ltd.

Without limiting the exclusive rights of any author, contributor or the publisher of this publication, any unauthorised use of this publication to train generative artificial intelligence (AI) technologies is expressly prohibited. HarperCollins also exercise their rights under Article 4(3) of the Digital Single Market Directive 2019/790 and expressly reserve this publication from the text and data mining exception.

Find out more about HarperCollins and the environment at
www.harpercollins.co.uk/green

*For my kids,
because I will always believe in you*

1

December 31

People say pain can't kill you.

I think they're lying. I might actually die tonight. Or at least be forced to stop living.

But I've worked too hard taming my hair into curls and meticulously perfecting my eyeliner for a migraine to keep me home. My fingers slip on the dress zipper, but I'm fine.

Tonight will be spent with the one friend who hasn't deserted me. We'll meet at her house and drive with her parents through the city. At the dock along Lake Michigan, we'll board the private yacht for her mom's work party. Waiters will serve fancy hors d'oeuvres we don't know the names of, while we drink mocktails and laugh at the old men on the dance floor. Because after weeks of planning, that's how people who are fine get to ring in the new year.

I can still go. It's not that bad.

I can ignore it. Hide it.

The heartbeat in my brain.

The slow, throbbing pulse. The methodical punch to the right side of my skull like a metronome.

Mom knocks on my door before poking her head in. 'Ella, aren't you leaving to—'

She doesn't have to ask why my eyes fight to stay open against the light, why my jaw clenches in pain.

She knows. She doesn't even look surprised.

'Come on, let's get into bed.' She gently drapes an arm around my shoulders.

I shrug her off and grab my stilettos, the new ones I bought on sale to match the dress. They'll pinch my toes and kill the balls of my feet with their four-inch heels. I'll regret wearing them instantly and feel the pain well into tomorrow, and it will be worth it.

I shove my foot inside and fumble with the straps. 'I'm fine.' My voice is strong, well-practised at deceiving.

One shoe secured.

'I'll get your meds.'

I wince at her volume, which isn't loud but feels like a jackhammer. 'I already did. Ten minutes ago,' I bite out, shoving the left strap against the buckle and failing to get it through. 'I don't have time for this.'

I need to get to Sierra's house in fifteen minutes. After missing her Christmas party and too many dance lessons, and spending so many hours in a doctor's office or isolated in this room, I deserve this. I will get there.

Mom takes a deep breath and flips off the lights.

I hate the relief it brings, hate the confirmation that she's right and this migraine is settling in fast and strong.

No. I'm fine. I'm going. Sierra and I will stay up way too late and—

'I'll get the ice pack.'

'I'm not staying.' My voice cracks like a traitor. 'It's not bad. I can still go.' Please. *Please.* My hands quiver in the dark, and I can barely see, but turning on the lights will hurt more. 'Sierra is counting on me and once I get this stupid strap in – ugh!' I rip off the shoe and hurl it across the room, wishing it would break the mirror above my dresser, hoping the crash will wipe away the pain creeping in, or at least distract me from it.

But it hits the wall with a heavy thunk and falls to the floor, doesn't even have the decency to leave a mark. No visible evidence of its crime.

Mom huddles beside me again, and I repeat, 'I'm fine, I'm fine.'

But this time I don't push her away. Like a puppet whose strings are now properly attached, I let her guide me over the accessories littering my floor: my headband with pink feathers and the year in glittery numbers on top, my sunglasses with the matching lenses. I don't resist when she seats me on the bed, removes my shoe like a broken Cinderella who won't be watching the clock strike midnight. I don't fight her when I lie down and she pulls a blanket over me like a child.

Because I desperately want my words to be true.

Two hours later, I pick at the sparkly pink fabric against my pale thighs, trying to imagine some other event on my calendar that might require this many sequins. Not likely.

'It's okay you couldn't make it,' Sierra says on the video call, her Kentucky accent coating the words with warm sugar, making them even sweeter.

I fold the blanket on my bed and return it to the closet before grabbing the rest of my care kit: ice pack, washcloth, eye mask, meds and water bottle.

Of course the migraine would subside in enough time that I could have enjoyed the party, but I missed my ride to get there.

When the migraines come, they creep in like a fog, a dull haze at the edges, sometimes blurring patches of my sight before the pain sets in. When it does, I'm not able to do anything except lie in my bed, fight off nausea, and pray for sleep to rescue me from the throbbing of my brain.

Thanks to my migraine tonight, Sierra sits on the boat alone, surrounded by more luxury than I imagined. The private airline knows how to throw a party.

'It's not okay. Aside from missing an epic New Year's with my best friend on a dinner cruise, now you have to endure your mom's work party as the only one on board who isn't allowed to drink.'

She stirs her blue mocktail with a toothpick, careful to avoid the cherry stuck on the end. 'If you left now, you could still get on the boat before we leave the dock.'

'My first experience driving in Chicago probably shouldn't be on one of the biggest party nights of the year.' Her hopes don't help erase my disappointment.

'Fair. Would your parents bring you?'

'Doubt it.' Sierra knows about my mom's car accident seven years ago. She almost died and spent months in recovery and has been nervous about night driving ever since. 'Besides.' I check the time. 'Doesn't the boat leave in like thirty minutes?'

'You know I would throw myself in that lake as an anchor if it meant getting you on board.'

'Thanks, but save the polar plunge for tomorrow.'

'Are you out of your mind? I am not submerging this head in freezing water simply to feel a thrill.' She scrunches her twist-outs, pouting, but then drops her hand and turns serious. 'Better to miss tonight than our recital in two weeks.'

'Definitely.'

Like I get a choice. My migraines could take dance from me too, including the recital we've been preparing for the past six months.

'You sure you're okay?'

I smile too bright. 'Absolutely. I'll be fine. Look, Oreos.' I lift the package I keep at the bottom of my care kit, a reward for making it through another episode.

'Hear, hear.' She raises her glass. 'To not controlling the disruptions in our lives, but controlling our reactions to them.'

The still-dim light of my room hopefully hides my cringe at her dad's therapy-speak sneaking in again. One thing's for sure: next time I'll fight harder. These migraines will not tear apart my life, no matter how hard they try. I toss the once-cool washcloth into the hamper.

Sierra's mom mumbles something in the background and

Sierra sighs. 'I have to go. Apparently there's some other pilot I *have* to meet.'

'Go have as much fun as you can.'

'Won't be much without you!' She waves, her brightly painted nails practically glowing.

Mom hovers in the doorway as I hang up.

'I thought I heard you talking. Feeling better?' She runs a hand along her dark, slicked-back ponytail, swiping for stray hairs that aren't there.

'Yeah.' I pull a shirt off the floor before she has a chance to point it out. I could call some of my other friends – if I can still call them that – to crash their New Year's Eve plans. I haven't spoken to them much since winter break started. Kayla claims I've 'pulled away'.

She's not wrong. But she's also not brave enough to ask why. Or doesn't care.

That's another reason I hate cancelling tonight. I don't want Sierra to think I'll always bail, that I'm not worth inviting in the first place. She lives in another county, so seeing each other outside of dance doesn't happen very often, but since my school friends already ditched me, I won't have anyone left if Sierra does the same.

'I forgot to tell you,' Mom says, 'about your next doctor's appointment.'

My phone buzzes, a perfect distraction. 'Aunt Julie's calling.'

Mom ignores the interruption while my phone continues vibrating in my hand like a timer reminding me this conversation could be over. 'Well, it's on the third at ten in the morning, which means you—'

'Have to miss dance.' We say it in unison, except Mom says it with hesitation and I say it with irritation. Of course the appointment can't be rescheduled.

'I know you hate that, but—'

'I'll let Madame Leheller know.' I answer the video call. 'Hi, Aunt Julie.' Her wild curls and infectious smile take up nearly the whole screen, but a little head manages to peep up in the corner, straining against a seat belt in the back seat of the car. 'Joey!'

He holds a hand up to his mouth like a radio and says, '*Crrrr*, this is your captain speaking. Please keep your hands inside the plane at all times.' Then he screams and waves like one of those inflatables outside a used car dealership.

'Happy New Year's Eve.' I laugh, pretending to get six-year-old humour.

'That's actually why I'm calling,' Julie says, biting her lip. We have the same blue eyes, the ones I got from my dad, Julie's brother. 'We've had a change of plans.'

'Oh?'

Mom sighs in the background, like she expects last-minute changes from her sister-in-law. Honestly, the fact that Julie has plans feel like a feat given her usual live-in-the-moment lifestyle.

'Joey and I were headed to Blake's for the evening. You remember him, right?'

Julie's latest boyfriend. They've been together longer than

most of her relationships – if you can call them all that. But Blake stands out because he's one of the few who's stuck around long enough to meet the family, and he actually has a stable job.

'Yeah, he was nice!' He let Joey be his partner when we played euchre the day after Thanksgiving, and never got mad at his mistakes – though I'm pretty sure he bet money on me and Joey's older brother Chris losing the next game . . .

'Well, he just called to cancel because he's not feeling well, thinks it's that bug going around. He sounded miserable on the phone, and I'd like to check in on him or bring him some chicken soup or something.' She notices a smear of purple paint on her forearm and scratches at it. 'But I'd hate to expose Joey to that or ruin his New Year's – he's been looking forward to staying up till midnight for the first time – and Chris drove to his friends' right after we left. I'm picking up a few things for tonight before heading to Blake's, but I don't want to call Chris home and—'

'Julie. I'd love to come babysit Joey.'

'Wahoo!' Joey squeals in the back seat. At the same time Mom says, 'Ella . . .'

Julie strains to be heard over Joey but hardly stifles her laughter at his excitement. 'I hate to ask or have you cancel plans—'

'Nope.' I pull my feathered headband from the floor and pop on the pink sunglasses. 'I'm all dressed up with nowhere else to go!'

'Ella—' Mom says again.

'Ooh, you do look divine! Can't wait to see it in person. We'll finish up at the store and then meet you at our house in say, forty minutes?'

'I'll be there!' I hang up to the tune of Joey singing 'Ella Bella is the bestest!' to his own little melody.

Mom doesn't hesitate. 'Are you sure you're up for this?'

The question grates me. 'The pain is gone.' Mostly. Yeah, there's still pressure behind my right eye, but since I didn't have any say in cancelling on Sierra, choosing to watch Joey feels like regaining my balance after a series of pirouettes. 'Chris shouldn't have to miss out on his plans to babysit his brother when I'm already missing out on mine. I want to do this.'

Aside from that, I want to help Julie after everything she's done for me. She moved in with my family before Joey was born to help after my mom's accident. Mom still feels guilty for the months she missed out on 'being a mom', as she puts it, while recovering.

Julie was never one for housework, but she knew what my older brother Sean and I needed: she let us have ice cream for breakfast while Dad drove Mom to physical therapy. She played The Floor Is Lava and built forts with us when Mom was resting in the afternoon. And late at night when I was feeling bad for being the reason Mom was on the road that terrible night, Julie hugged me and declared, 'You're stronger than you know.'

Mom shifts her weight. 'It's already dark out.'

'I've driven to their house about a million times. I'll call if I need anything.'

She wrings her hands like she's about to dial Dad for reinforcements.

'Don't I look better?' I shimmy so my sequins sparkle, and she can't help but laugh.

A crack in her defences.

'You're not actually going to let Joey stay up till midnight, are you?'

'It's whatever Aunt Julie says.' So there will be sparkling grape juice, confetti, noisemakers and no bedtime.

'Those country roads get so dark . . .'

I straighten my spine. 'I'll keep my brights on.'

'And call me when you get there.'

Is she saying what I think she's saying? No sudden movements. 'Of course.'

'And Ella?'

'Yes?'

She opens her arms for a hug. 'Have fun with him.'

I give her a squeeze. 'It'll be a night we never forget.'

2

December 31

I strain to see beyond the glow of my headlights. Mom was right: it is very, very dark.

Julie, Chris and Joey live out on a practically dirt road. The houses are spaced so far apart that all the mailboxes have to be on one side of the road, and there are no streetlights. Towering pine trees and dense woods hide most of the houses, so unless you know where to turn, you'd miss them completely.

My cousins' place was probably nice fifty years ago, with the sprawling yard that made us feel like we were in our own little world when Chris and I screamed down the Slip 'N Slide every summer. The house itself has been added to several times, so it's a bit like a jigsaw puzzle. The uneven floors and bedrooms aren't quite square and are definitely not equal in size, but somehow every time I'm there I . . . fit.

When I finally pull into their driveway, the front door is open but no lights are on. Weird. I expect to see Joey racing out to greet me, but no silhouette appears in the doorway. All is still, like a forgotten painting.

The hair on the back of my neck stands on end as I put the car in park and hop out.

I'm sure everything's okay. They must be inside playing a game or Joey forgot to close the door.

But then why is it so dark?

I quicken my pace.

Aunt Julie wouldn't leave before I got here, right? Certainly not without closing the front door.

Unless someone broke in. And the intruder's inside.

No. That's ridiculous. Who would be all the way out here in the middle of nowhere? I'll walk inside, and Joey will jump out to scare me before he collapses in a fit of giggles, and all will be fine.

Except I'm almost to the door and there are no voices or music or any sound at all.

I run up the steps.

'Aunt Julie?' I call, crossing the threshold, the open door inviting me in. My hands fumble for the lights, but the switch isn't where I expect. Before I can check the other side of the door, I'm nearly knocked back by a noxious odour dripping through the air.

Something's wrong.

The sulfuric stench of rotten eggs presses against my throat, choking me. I don't want to inhale another breath. I know that smell.

Gas.

The house reeks of it.

Before I can retreat to the fresh air, the pale moonlight streams through the window, and across the room, I see them.

Two crumpled bodies are tangled in a heap at the bottom of the stairs. Still. Completely still.

'Chris! Joey!' I race to their sides.

They're splayed out on the floor. Neither one of them is moving, their eyes closed.

'Joey!' I shout again, flipping him over. The little boy's eyes don't open. His wavy brown hair flops to the side just like his arm. 'Joey, wake up!' I shake him, but no response.

His head lolls to the side. My first cry escapes. We were supposed to play Connect Four tonight. I was supposed to let him win, and he was supposed to laugh until he slid off his chair.

'Joey!'

I shake Chris and nothing. I thought he wasn't going to be home tonight.

'Chris! Wake up!' No response.

Oh no, oh no. Oh, God, help them. I have to help them.

'Aunt Julie!' I screech, her name scratching at my throat on its way out.

Where is she? Is she home?

But then another smell reaches my nostrils. Rancid. Vomit. There's a mess next to Chris on the wooden floor.

Oh no.

I have to get them out of here.

'Aunt Julie!' I scream again, my voice hoarse, and I almost gag on the smell. 'Help!'

I spin, as if she'll jump out from her bedroom down the hall, as if she hadn't noticed the smell or heard them fall and will appear to make it better like she always does.

Instead, I see her by her bedroom. Most of her body remains hidden behind the doorframe, but her hand is extended, delicate fingers curled up from the worn carpet, as if she's reaching out for help.

'Oh, God. Help me. Help me.' I call it into the silence, a prayer for any kind of miracle to appear.

But there's only me. Me and the three of them, quiet and still.

'Hello? Are you still there?' A muffled voice breaks through the hush. Chris's phone sits a few feet away, like he dropped it on his fall to the floor. 'Hello?' a voice calls through the phone again. 'This is an emergency operator. Is everyone all right?'

I snatch the phone off the floor. 'Help, please send help. My cousins. They're unconscious.'

'There was a young man who called, and said he smelled gas in the house—'

'He's here. I think there's a gas leak and—'

'Miss, I need you to stay calm and exit the house. Get out of there.'

'Yes, yes. Okay, get out.'

But not without my cousins.

I scoop Joey off the floor with ease, his too-short Spider-Man pyjama pants clinging to his limp legs. I sway on my feet, nearly losing my balance. My head is light, from panic or lack of oxygen or a rush of adrenaline, I don't know. I tug on Chris's wrist, hoping to pull him along the floor. 'Come on,' I cry.

'Are you out of the house, miss?'

'Almost,' I grunt, straining against Chris's weight, pressing the soles of my feet into the floor while I try not to drop Joey.

Chris is too heavy. *I'll be back*, I silently promise, Joey slipping in my arms. He has to be okay. He has to.

'Miss? What's your location? We're sending help.'

By the time I recite the street address, I've reached the threshold, cradling Joey. Outside, I swallow great gulps of fresh oxygen. My chest feels tight and my head hurts. Is it a regular pain or from the gas?

'Joey,' I yell again, laying him on the partially frozen grass. 'Joey!' As still as a corpse. 'He's not breathing.'

'Help is on the way,' the woman on the phone says. 'Stay where you are.'

But Chris is still inside. I can see him. And Julie. I know she's down the hall. I can get them out. I won't let them die.

I race back inside and reach Chris first, wedging the phone between my ear and shoulder, trying and failing to drag Chris by the wrists. 'My cousin,' I grunt, heaving him backwards, but he barely moves. 'I have to get him out.'

He's too heavy. I can't move him on my own.

'Miss, you need to exit the house immediately. Do not turn on any lights or appliances. A single spark could ignite the house.'

'I can get him.' I shift to pull from under his armpits.

I stumble. The phone clatters to the ground.

'Miss?' the distanced responder calls.

My shoulder hits the wall. I'm dizzy. Lightheaded.

'I'm here.' I snatch the phone and give Chris a mighty heave, dragging him as far as I can. I'm almost to the door. Almost outside. A breeze from the cold winter night wafts in, bringing fresh oxygen into the space.

'Miss, you need to leave the house immediately. Paramedics are on their way.'

'No. Time,' I huff.

I step down, careful not to trip, dragging Chris to the grass, next to Joey's still body.

Please let them be okay. Let Julie be okay. Let Chris be okay. Let Joey be okay. The lump in my throat makes it hard to breathe even with the clean air pouring into my lungs. I vomit on the grass between Chris and Joey.

'First responders are on their way. Are you safe?'

'I – yes, but my aunt.' The last word comes out as a screech. I step away from Chris, wiping my mouth on my sleeve and facing the door.

Julie.

I need to save her.

She needs me.

'My aunt—' I repeat, stumbling towards the door, picturing her still lying on the carpet, angelic hand extended, ready for me to drag her to safety too.

'Do not enter the home again.'

'I can get her. I can.' The smell hits me before I reach the doorframe.

'Miss. Gas leaks are extremely dangerous. Wait for help. Do not enter that house. Get away from the area.'

Sirens wail in the distance. Someone's standing across the road, a dark figure. I want to call out for help, but the world shifts. The figure flees. I fall to my knees, stomach rolling, head pounding. The rescue team is coming. They'll get here in time.

Chris and Joey have to wake up. The phone drops from my hands.

Julie will be rescued. My vision blurs.

I did everything I could.

Help is on the way.

3

January 1

The fluorescent lights flood the hospital hallway as I scan the room numbers along the wall. The reality of last night hasn't quite travelled from my mind to my heart, like a shield has gone up to prevent me from feeling the full depth of that pain, allowing only a few drops of it to penetrate at a time.

When the paramedics arrived at the house, they immediately began working on Joey and Chris in the front yard, gently pushing me aside, strapping them onto gurneys. I never saw Aunt Julie. They loaded us into the ambulance before she was taken out of the house.

The smell of the hospital makes me want to gag. It wasn't noticeable when a doctor was evaluating me in the ER, but now that they've cleared me and I'm walking through the wide, bland halls under the sterile lights, the scent has grabbed my senses and won't let go, won't release the memories of being here so many times before. The whiffs of harsh antiseptic whisper, *You'll be back again and again and again.*

I shouldn't worry about that right now, not with one family member lying in the hospital bed and another . . . another . . .

My shield breaks. I'm no longer floating through the hall like a string ties my head to my body; I'm thrust against the wall by the force of the memory.

If only I had shown up sooner, taken deeper breaths from outside, something . . . then I could have saved everyone. I should have done more . . . tried harder . . .

I suck in a breath like I'm coming up from the bottom of a pool and straighten my back. I can't fall apart. I won't.

Focus on something else, anything else, like Julie taught me.

The reason I left the hospital room: the cold pop numbs the fingers of my right hand. The candy wrapper crinkles in my left. My family needs me and I need to get back to them.

It's no wonder I don't register the guy coming around the corner, nearly bumping into him.

'Excuse me,' I say, taking in the man with the precisely groomed grey beard and thick brows. Even though I haven't seen him in months, recognition strikes. 'Dr Mullins.'

'It's fine,' he says. His tone is polite, but his expression reveals the truth: he doesn't recognise me.

Why should he? He probably sees hundreds of patients in a week. He doesn't have time to connect with each one. He hardly has time to listen.

He didn't listen to me.

Or at least, that was how I felt.

At first I didn't want to tell Mom how severe the pain was becoming – she worries enough as it is – but once the migraines interfered with school, causing me to miss days or come home early, there was no avoiding it.

At my first appointment, I told Dr Mullins about my migraines, the ones that have been coming back for months. They creep in with an aura, a weird dizziness that makes it difficult to see straight and a tingly feeling that's hard to describe other than I know it when I feel it and it's always accompanied by a sense of dread. The pain can be excruciating, too severe to sleep, to do anything other than lie in a cool, dark room and pray it doesn't make me throw up.

They're worse than any lingering effects from the gas leak, and my family doctor couldn't find a reason or pattern behind them. So when I sat in his office, I hoped Mom was right and Dr Mullins could make the pain disappear.

I was wrong.

Dr Mullins was quick to dismiss me and ask my mom about pressures I'm facing at school. He assured us it must be stress from my AP classes. It was like he didn't believe the pain was as intense as I claimed, as if I was being too dramatic by missing school, like I was lying about how I had to cancel plans with friends regularly, couldn't even look at my phone to respond to them. He assumed I wanted to get out of my assignments instead of barely being able to get out of bed. My complaint of being unable to eat was ignored.

He didn't believe me. Instead of asking if we had questions, he scribbled some notes and told me to drink more water, exercise more often and get more sleep.

Out the door with a flourish, and now here he is again, in a rush to get away.

I need to return to the room, deliver this food, be with my family, but something stops me.

The pain hasn't disappeared, and none of his suggestions made a dent. Another doctor looked me and my parents in the eye, stayed an extra minute to be sure we weren't too hesitant or rushed to ask our questions. I want him to know how much of my life has been taken from me these last few months and he couldn't bother to listen.

But saying all that out loud would show how much he hurt me.

'Sorry,' he says, somehow able to slow himself enough to consider me instead of rushing to wherever he's headed. He appraises my curls that must be a bird's nest by now, my sequin dress that still sparkles despite everything that's happened. 'Do I know you?'

'Yeah,' I said. 'Ella Forrester. I came to you two months ago for my migraines.'

What would he say if he knew I pulled two people from a house last night? Would he think I was lying? Exaggerating? Would he rush by anyway?

'Oh, right,' he says, but I don't believe him. He doesn't remember me at all. Two months? How many other patients has he seen in that time? I hope he helped them more than he helped me. 'It's nice to see you,' he says, stepping aside to continue on his way. My answer must have satisfied that small itch of recognition.

'You missed it,' I say, the words coming out like the accusation they are.

'Excuse me?' He glances back, almost as if he's not sure I was really speaking to him.

'Another doctor diagnosed me with a brain tumour last month. You missed it.'

He stops in his tracks. His mouth gapes. He remembers me now, an apology stuck in the back of his throat.

I hope he chokes on it.

I march down the hallway with my head high. If he didn't remember me before, he won't forget me now.

Aunt Julie would be proud.

When I round the corner, my parents are at the end of the hall talking to a doctor. Probably about what to do with the body.

The one that's already lying in the morgue. Cold. Stiff. Alone.

I should have been there sooner. I should have done more.

My parents were notified before the ambulance left the house, and they met us here shortly after. Mom told the doctor my full medical history as soon as she arrived, right after she raced to me and rubbed her hands over my head, wiping hair from my cheek. Dad hugged me too but didn't say anything.

The doctor said aside from nausea and a mild headache, I should be fine.

As if those symptoms aren't a part of my life already.

Twelve hours ago, my diagnosis dominated my worries, taking up more than physical space in my brain. Twelve hours ago, I wanted Julie's phone call to distract me from hearing the reminder about my next appointment.

Now I'd give anything to go back, to not have death being the thing to sweep the tumour from my thoughts.

When I walk in and see Joey curled up in a chair, I should be relieved he's alive. His dark hair's a tangled mess. His eyes stay empty, his body oddly still for a kid. But even though his heart is pumping and his lungs are breathing, the life in him? That's gone.

It might as well be on a slab in the morgue next to his mom.

Chris lies on the bed. The nurse says he should make a full recovery, that he was awake for a little while – long enough to tell them how he came home from his friend Alex's house, smelled the gas, found his brother and his mom on the floor, and called 911 – but he's fallen asleep or they gave him something to knock him out, I'm not sure which.

Why he came back, I don't know. Why the gas took him out faster than it took me, I don't know. He's alive, yet all I can think about is the one who didn't make it.

Julie's death shouldn't have shocked me. I was there. I saw her on the floor. I should have known she was already dead. But I still didn't believe it until the doctors said the words aloud.

They tried to explain what condition my cousins were in, but I didn't hear anything else for a few hours. The news of Julie's death devoured me whole, leaving me to swim in the darkness of knowing I might have saved her.

If only we'd agreed to meet at her house sooner . . . or not at all. What if I had asked her to bring Joey to my house instead?

At least I will only be able to imagine her delicate frame on the gurney, a mask pressed over her face, the straps squashing her wild hair. I won't have to know it, replay it every time I try to fall asleep. I can still think of her as the woman who bought me my first concert tickets when I was thirteen, the person who only ever made waffles if they were covered in sprinkles. Her smile, her sparkling eyes, her warm hugs . . . those will be the pieces of her I carry with me—

No. Focus. The cold of the pop in my left hand, the crinkle of the candy wrapper in my right.

'Are you hungry yet?' I place the candy bar on the table and crack open the pop for Joey.

He blinks. He hasn't eaten anything since we arrived, hasn't slept. He's just . . . staring. He looks younger than his six years make him.

Chris, on the other hand, has aged from seventeen, like his body knows he's an orphan now and beyond the world telling him he needs to grow up, he's forced to. His brown hair is dishevelled; a slight shadow across his chin could be scruff if he grew it out. He's always been ready to graduate and be on his own, but now he doesn't have a choice.

Mom and Dad have already talked to a social worker. Once Chris is released, they'll be coming home with us while Julie is transported to the funeral home.

'He needs his rest.' I squeeze Joey's shoulder. 'He'll wake up soon.'

Joey wipes his nose and sniffles. We both suffered from the minor symptoms of gas poisoning with a headache, some dizziness and sleepiness, but I expected him to be like Chris: laid out on a hospital bed in need of monitoring before being released, white skin pale. Instead, he's up and walking around.

I probably wouldn't have been able to get either of them out of the house if Chris hadn't gotten Joey so close to the door, if the door hadn't been left open to bring in enough oxygen to let me stay conscious.

'Aren't you tired?' I drape an extra blanket over Joey's lap. 'You can fall asleep.' I crashed for a couple hours early this morning. Not Joey, though. He's still in his pyjamas, but he hasn't left Chris's bedside.

I'm powerless to help either one. When I look at them, I see us sitting in the backyard, roasting marshmallows over the fire pit or splashing in the pool while Julie laughs. I see Chris fixing the web shooters on Joey's Halloween costume before Julie snaps a photo of the ultimate Spider-Man. I see Julie wiping butter from Joey's chin after he bites into an ear of corn on the Fourth of July or all of us in my living room last week, drinking peppermint hot cocoa by the tree while the cinnamon rolls baked in the oven.

If I had done more, we would have had another year together. And another. And another.

When I first heard my diagnosis, I thought I was going to die, that I might not be around for Thanksgiving, Christmas or New Year's at all. Dr Gupta quickly said it wasn't immediately life-threatening, but they'd have to do a biopsy right before Christmas to determine my prognosis. My hair hides the small incision on top of my skull, and even though we should have the results on the third, the weight of a death sentence hovers. Part of the reason I so badly wanted to celebrate with Sierra on that boat was because I've never been more aware that this New Year's could be my last.

But I'm still here and Julie's not.

'Your mom . . .' My voice breaks, and I almost can't get the words out. Joey's big eyes melt over me before I try again. 'Your mom used to tell me I was strong enough to get through the hard times, but if I didn't want to talk about it, we could play a game or watch a movie. And you know what?'

His mouth stays closed, but he lifts his chin and brows a fraction of an inch.

'She was right,' I whisper.

She was there for me when my mom couldn't be, when my dad was overwhelmed with two kids and needed his sister to move in. She was there when I told her about my diagnosis. She was always there for me.

And now that she's gone, I'm the one here for Joey.

He mumbles something.

'Sorry, I couldn't hear you.'

I lean closer. He twists his hands, takes a big breath, and says, 'Did I do it?'

I sit back and cock my head, taking in his hunched shoulders and wiry arms. 'Do what, buddy?'

'Did I hurt my mommy?'

His voices cracks and takes my heart along with it. He hasn't called Julie anything but 'Mom' since he began kindergarten in the fall.

'Oh, Joey.' I rest my hand on him, but he's so small under the blanket, I can hardly feel his knee. 'No, of course not.'

'But I couldn't wake her up.'

Somehow I steady my voice and squeeze him. 'I know. But you tried. It wasn't your fault. You love your mommy, and you wish she was here.'

Joey doesn't respond. He's locked on his brother, the only piece of his life that remains.

Question after question swirls inside my head – did Julie smell the gas when they walked in? Did Joey? Why did Chris return from his friend's house? – but none of them feel right to ask. Not here. Not now.

Chris's head rolls to the side. Joey's shoulders straighten. This time his attention's rewarded with a bleary blink. Chris's eyes swim, obviously having difficulty focusing. He finds my face and zeros in.

I have no right to do anything but cry, but seeing him there, blinking at me, alive and whole, I can't help but smile.

'Hey, you're awake,' I whisper.

'You were always the smart one in the family.' His voice is raspy despite the humour, but it must be a reflex because then reality sets in. The light behind his eyes dims. His shoulders curl. He presses his lips into a hard line and focuses on the lights above, tears gathering. He remembers he's in the hospital, and he knows why.

'It's okay. I've cried too,' I say.

In response, Chris only releases a slow breath, like he's extinguishing the candle of his grief but can't quite manage the task.

Eventually, he manages to choke out, 'I don't understand what happened.'

From the tremor in his voice, it's obvious he knows the facts that the nurse already told him last time he was conscious – his house had a gas leak that killed his mother and nearly killed him and his brother – but, like the rest of us, he can't fathom how or why.

'I called for help as soon as I smelled it and saw they were home,' he says.

'You must have passed out right after,' I say.

'It's my fault,' Joey says.

Chris shakes his head and swallows slowly, his Adam's apple bobbing with the effort. 'I came home just for a minute. A minute and then I saw them.'

They're both drowning in blame, and all I can do is struggle against the same current.

I've played it back over and over, what I could have done differently to grab Aunt Julie too. She was simply too far away from an exit. I've been repeating that over and over, hoping I'll believe it.

But if I'd been there sooner it could be me lying on this bed.

Or down in the morgue.

As much as I doubt it for myself, it's easy to tell Chris, 'You did all you could. Joey wouldn't be here if it wasn't for you getting him as far as you did.'

Chris's chin crumples.

'Joey . . . Joey . . . I'm sorry.'

Joey throws himself on top of Chris and wraps himself around his torso, but Chris can't stop covering his face in shame.

'Chris, no. If it's your fault for not saving her, then it's mine too.'

'No.' Chris shifts. Joey stands, sniffling. 'No,' Chris whispers, shaking his head.

I repeat the words his mom always told me. 'You're strong enough for this.'

'I should have . . .' His speech is slow, and trails off, the drugs or exhaustion or grief taking him back under. His head falls to the side, eyes closed, mouth slightly open.

At least when he's asleep, he gets to escape the pain of reality. Joey settles back into his chair, the blanket at his feet, and after a pause, he speaks with his focus still locked on his brother.

'I wish Mommy was here.'

As grateful as I am that they're both alive, I'm devastated that

Julie's gone. And twisted in those emotions is a gust of guilt – not only for being unable to save her, but because in this moment, sitting beside her two sons, I should be focused on how they'll go on living after their mother's death.

Instead, I can't help wondering if I'll be next.

4

January 1

Aunt Julie taught me to make lists of good things to help survive the bad. Today, while waiting in the police station to follow up on the initial questions from the hospital, they don't bring the comfort I need them to.

1. Joey is okay.
2. Chris is out of the hospital.
3. I'm alive.

But I still haven't slept. The facts keep replaying, and they still don't make sense. It's like studying for a test, knowing the information and still not recognising any of the multiple-choice options.

Aunt Julie is dead. Aunt Julie won't be coming home. I'll never see her at one of my dance recitals clapping too loudly or laugh at her attempts to play games that require too much strategy. Chris won't hear her cheering after they call his name at graduation in the spring and Joey won't get another birthday cake made by her hands.

Stop. I can't fall apart. Not here, not in front of everyone.

'What's taking so long?' I tap my fingers against my leg, waiting for the door to open so I can give the police my official report.

Waiting seems to have become a permanent staple in my life. Waiting for the next migraine to arrive, waiting for the next doctor's appointment. Waiting. Waiting. Waiting.

My biopsy results should be ready at my upcoming appointment, but I'm afraid Dr Gupta might be wrong and I don't have as much time as she expects.

I've already had to accept that there isn't any rhyme or reason behind why I have a tumour, but maybe there's a reason for Julie's tragedy and her death isn't senseless. Maybe there's some explanation that will fill the gaping hole that opened inside me when Dad said, 'Julie's dead.'

'I'm sure they'll be with us soon,' Mom answers.

I check my phone and find a string of messages from Sierra.

where are you?

studio opens in five

i know you're not making me start the new year with Madame Lift-Your-Leg-Higher all by myself

okay, i see you are. then you're going to miss it when i tell this woman i am not a dog at a fire hydrant if she comes at me with that nonsense again this week.

for real? you're not coming?

wait is it another migraine?

omg are you okay? my mom sent me a link to some nosy neighbours thing she's in on facebook and it's all about your aunt's house ella i'm so sorry. i hope everyone's okay. the article doesn't say. the comments have me worried

ella?

I fire off a quick reply letting her know I was there, I'm okay, and I'll check in later. Dad is down the hall at a vending machine with Joey pointing at a selection through the glass. An older couple waits at the counter for the officer behind a desk. Chris stands at the other end of the hall. The doctors said he's fine, but his hair is matted at the back from lying on the hospital bed all morning, his eyes dark.

Blake, Julie's boyfriend, stands opposite him. The few other times I've seen him, he had firmly styled hair and a clean-shaven face. Now his eyes are pouchy, white skin tinged green. If possible, he looks worse than the rest of us, and I have no doubt he's still recovering from being sick.

With a huff at another minute ticking by, I abandon Mom on the bench and walk towards them. They speak in hushed tones, but as I approach, pieces of their conversation drift to me.

'I know, but—'

'No.' Blake's voice is firm but not harsh. 'Don't think that way. All right? You remember what I said?'

'It's no one's fault. It was an accident.'

'That's right.' The man speaks like a coach talking up his star player after a bad play. His phone lights up and he swipes away a notification. 'Now you keep repeating that to yourself over and over until you believe it.'

Chris suddenly looks smaller here, dwarfed by the mural of

law enforcement behind him, or the weight of grief really has shrunk him, with his shoulders hunched, head hanging.

Blake takes a step back when I approach. The sleeves of his dress shirt fit too tight, his collar too high, like everything he had right in the world is now wrong. 'Ella. I'm glad to see you're all right.'

He means physically. None of us are all right otherwise.

'Julie said you were sick.' I keep my attention on Blake as Chris angles himself away and wipes at his face. 'Are you feeling better?'

Blake gently places a hand on his stomach. 'Something I ate. I spent the night on the bathroom floor.' He wipes a hand over his face, tugging on his cheeks, unable to clear the fatigue resting there.

'Are you . . .' It feels silly to finish that question with 'okay'. We're all hollow, filled with more questions than answers, ones I'm not willing to keep inside any longer.

He nods anyway.

'Do you have detectors in the house?' I ask Chris.

'Smoke detectors?'

'Carbon monoxide or gas leak detectors.' I pull out my phone and show him an article on Google. 'Like this.'

'Doesn't look familiar. Safety wasn't really Mom's top priority.'

Who needs to be safe when you can be fun? I can almost hear Julie saying it now.

'If they didn't come installed, we didn't have them,' he adds.

Blake swipes away another notification on his phone. 'It's a devastating tragedy, but nothing could have prevented it. The police already know that. This is all—' His phone lights up again. 'Sorry, work.'

'They should give you some time off under the circumstances,' I say.

Blake's mouth pops open like a fish, but he recovers quickly. He pockets his phone, the stress lining his face. 'Were you the one who asked Julie to meet at her house?'

'Me? No, she called me to babysit. She said she wanted to come check on you.'

'I had no idea. So if you hadn't agreed, she would have brought him with her and never gone home to begin with . . .' He trails off, and then regret registers on his face, like he's only now realised he said it out loud. 'But you can't think that way, Ella.'

The force of his words nearly knocks me off my feet. If I'd never agreed in the first place, if I was in the middle of Lake Michigan at the party with Sierra, if I'd never had a migraine to begin with . . . would Julie still be alive?

I – I can't make this about me right now. *Focus on making sense of what happened, finding a reason that isn't my fault.*

'We smelled the gas right away. Why couldn't she?'

'She had COVID not too long ago, right?' Blake chimes in. 'Yeah, she couldn't smell the flowers I bought her last week.'

'Blake Bartnicky?' An officer scans the hall and lobby, standing in a doorway of another room.

Blake gives Chris a pointed stare. 'You remember what I said?'

When Chris nods, he walks to the door, shakes the officer's hand, and they disappear inside.

I gesture in Blake's direction. 'He's right. It was an accident, and we should keep repeating that until it sinks in, like he said.'

I'm saying it as much for myself as I am for Chris. I'm glad he has more people like Blake to support him, considering all the time he's spent thinking of others. I remember when we celebrated Mom being done with physical therapy and Dad took us all to one of those restaurants with merchandise in the front. Aunt Julie found a bracelet she adored, but she'd, of course, forgotten her wallet at home. A few minutes later, Chris told her to check her purse again. She found cash in a pocket and asked Chris if he'd slipped his birthday money in there.

He had. I saw him do it, but he knew as well as I did that Aunt Julie wouldn't want him to spend his money on her, so with the straightest face, he said, 'No, I left my money at home.' That's Chris for you.

His head snaps up. 'You heard Blake say that?'

'You said most of the same when you were lying in the hospital.'

'I did?' He sounds confused. 'What else did I say?'

'That you felt like it was your fault. You were apologising to Joey.' He couldn't look at his younger brother, much less comfort him.

Chris's cheeks flush. 'I don't remember that.'

In different circumstances I would have made fun of him for

being loopy, told him he serenaded a nurse and asked for her number, but I can't. Not now. It feels like not ever.

'Well, Blake is right. It's not your fault.'

But if you never agreed to babysit . . . I shut the whisper out. Julie needed me. If I hadn't offered, Chris and Joey might be gone too.

Chris bites his lip, like he wants to believe the reassurances but doesn't know how to stop beating himself up; we're more alike than anyone else in the family.

'Yeah.' His face shifts back into the mask, but he doesn't sound nearly convincing enough. I recognise it as the same expression I throw at Mom when the first pricks of pain settle in my skull and she asks if I'm okay.

'Did anything else happen before you left?'

'No, nothing. I mean, Mom and I were mad at each other, kind of arguing. It's stupid now. But' – he laughs once, a broken sound through the grief – 'then Joey farted on the couch, just let a massive one rip. And Mom and I cracked up and we all piled on the couch.'

Sounds like a typical day at Julie's.

His smile falters. His voice returns to a rasp. 'Now he's never going to make her laugh again.'

Dad approaches with Joey trailing half a step behind, granting Chris a chance to clear his throat and pull himself together. 'They said you won't be able to get back in the house until some time tomorrow,' Dad says, 'so on the way home we can stop by a store for some essentials to last you the night.'

'I'll find somewhere to stay, and—'

'Nonsense,' Dad says. 'That's what family's for.' He claps a hand on Chris's shoulder, but Chris doesn't respond. Like mother, like son. Julie never liked accepting help either, but maybe Dad's thinking about his own relationship with Julie. Things have been tense ever since they got into it at Thanksgiving. I never did hear what it was about.

'We'll put you up in Sean's room,' Dad continues. 'He's trying to get a flight home. His professors seem to be understanding, but international travel might take some time to coordinate.' My brother's spent the year studying abroad.

Dad checks his phone, which lights up with a call. 'I better take this.'

He steps away while Joey plops down in a nearby chair, curled into a ball like he might fall asleep right here and now. I don't remember Chris's dad. I was only four when he left. Joey's dad was with Julie about a year before he was born, but didn't stay long after that. Both boys have lost so much.

'How was it in there?' I ask Chris, gesturing to the door where the police have been conducting their interviews. He's days away from turning eighteen, and even though he never asked for it, Mom sat in on his questioning too.

He shrugs. 'I told them everything I could. Mom and Joey left for the store before they were supposed to go to Blake's. I was the last to leave the house and didn't see or smell anything weird.'

'Why'd you come back?'

'Forgot my phone.' He grips it like a friend who betrayed him, as if he's forgotten I'm here. 'I – I had to choose. I walked in and saw Joey slumped on the stairs and I saw my mom, and I ran to her, but I had to choose and maybe I chose wrong.' He sucks in a shaky breath. 'I can't believe this is happening. It feels like someone else's life.' He balls his hands into fists. 'I can't sit here. I need to *do* something.'

'You can't fix it. You can only push through.'

Chris blinks, and for the whisper of a second, the familiar crook of his smile shadows his face. 'When did you get so wise?'

The answer is in the last few months. I thought Dr Mullins could fix my pain, but he didn't. And Dr Gupta's diagnosis doesn't relieve the symptoms. The tumour has to be monitored for growth before we decide on a treatment plan.

I could tell Chris the truth, but he doesn't need it now. Not yet.

I breathe out through my nose in a half laugh. 'Some of us are born this way.'

As the migraines keep coming, the doctor appointments pile up. The few people who know about my tumour treat me differently. Dad keeps researching the science behind it, trying to understand. Mom's nervous gaze hovers over me whenever she thinks I'm distracted. Teachers grant me extensions coated with pity. Sierra is gentle, like I can't handle her teasing the same way anymore. That's why I haven't told anyone else.

Aunt Julie is – was – the exception. When I told her, she squared her shoulders, lifted my chin, stared me in the eye, and treated me like the same girl who raced her around the block and won.

Waiting on a treatment plan feels like waiting for the police ruling. Once I have a direction, a plan, everything will make sense. It has to. The alternative is feeling this way forever.

'Our turn,' Mom says, coming over on her way to another door.

Leaving both boys in the uncomfortable chairs in the hall, I follow.

Detective Peterson sits across from me with a file and a laptop in front of him. His hair is cropped so close to his head it's obvious he's trying to hide how much hair he's losing. His head shines almost pink, a contrast to his white face.

'Do you know how it started?' My voice is raw, scratchy, or it sounds that way because the cold, empty room doesn't have anything warm or comfortable to absorb it. 'The gas leak, I mean.'

My brain only processes things in pieces today. Detective Peterson's eyebrows are bushy. So is his moustache, like a caterpillar under his nose.

'We'll get to that,' he says. 'What was your relationship with your aunt like?'

'We were close.' I'm painfully aware of Mom sitting next to me. It would hurt more if my own mother died, right? Never mind. I don't want to think about it. 'She was always full of energy and life. She saw me trying my best and said that was all anyone could ever ask of me.'

But my best wasn't good enough to save her.

'You said you were supposed to babysit your younger cousin?'

'Yeah. Last minute. She had a change of plans, and I offered to go over so my cousin Chris wouldn't have to cancel his plans.'

'Do you watch him often?'

'Maybe once a month, if that. Only when Chris isn't around.'

'I would have expected a teenager like yourself to have other plans on New Year's.'

'I did, but I had to cancel earlier in the day.'

He types on his computer.

'And why did you cancel?'

'I get headaches sometimes.'

'Migraines,' Mom clarifies. 'She has a brain tumour.'

'Mooom.' I hate how young I sound with that one word, the whine in my voice.

She raises her brows as if to say *He should know*. She probably thinks he'll lighten up, take it a little easier on me, pity me more because my aunt dying and my cousins being poisoned by natural gas aren't enough.

Apparently, he needs to know I have a brain tumour too.

The worst part is, the effect is almost immediate. First there's the surprise, quickly followed by the sympathy, the brows pulled together in a frown, trying to convey how sorry he is for the news when I know deep down a piece of him is thinking *Thank God it's not me, not my child. Someone else.*

He clears his throat. 'Sorry to hear that. And you were still going to babysit, even with the, uh . . .' He waves his hand in the air, afraid of the word.

'Tumour?' I resist rolling my eyes. 'Yeah. I have a tumour, but I'm still fully capable of living my life.'

Except when I'm not.

'So you cancelled your other plans but felt comfortable going to your aunt's house?'

I can't help but notice his voice is gentler than before. Part of me wants to kick him and find out if he'd toughen back up, or if he'd forgive me and dismiss the outburst because of the abnormal growth in my skull.

'My meds actually worked and the pain passed, so when she called me to come over, I was happy to help.'

'What time was that call?'

'Umm.' I pull out my own phone and swipe until I find the call history. 'A little after seven.'

'May I?' Peterson holds his hand out.

I don't know why, but I consult with Mom, my face asking, *Is this normal? Legal?*

She nods, and I pass him the phone. If it can help them figure out what went wrong at Aunt Julie's house, I'll do anything.

The next part of this conversation looms like a dark, suffocating cloud. Chronologically, what happened next was that I found the boys, but I don't want to have to replay it. I don't want to make myself see those images again.

'And what time did you arrive at the house?' he asks, returning my phone and typing on his computer again.

'A few minutes before eight; I wasn't there long before talking with 911.'

He asks what happened next, what I saw when I pulled up to the house, when I walked in. The questions are basic, factual. They should be easy to answer. I swallow around the thickness that constricts my throat.

Mom reaches over and squeezes my hand, and I'm ashamed I whined at her only a few minutes ago. The truth is, I'm lucky she's here. I'm lucky to be alive, that I still have my mom. I hate that I'm relieved, that I'm grateful I'm not in Chris's and Joey's shoes, just like Detective Peterson's glad he's not in mine.

'You already have her statement from last night, correct?' she asks.

'Yes, thank you. We want to make sure there's nothing else.'

I clear my throat. 'I thought I saw . . .'

'Yes?'

'A man.' He's standing at the edges of my memory. It might be nothing. 'He was in the road when the ambulances came.'

He makes a note. 'A neighbour was on site when paramedics arrived. We'll check into it, but everything else points to an accident, unfortunately not uncommon. I also have the notes from our medical examiner. It won't be a surprise that the cause of death is gas poisoning.'

He says it gently and he's right, it's not a surprise. Still, it doesn't make it any easier to hear him talking about her like this, like she's the caption of a photo in the news.

The interview ends soon after with no answers for how this could have happened. There's no explanation, no *reason* for this.

Only bad luck.

5

January 1

A migraine attacks on the drive home.

The pulsing behind my eyes begins like a distant drum. My vision goes blurry in patches. Dr Gupta calls it an aura. My body's warning before the onslaught. There's not much I can do to stop it.

I tell Mom I'm only tired, but she suspects more. I muster a reassuring smile for Joey next to me in the back seat.

By the time we arrive in our neighbourhood, I can barely keep my eyes open without wincing.

I don't eat.

I don't return Sierra's texts.

The pain chains me to my dark, cool room for the rest of the day.

The price I pay is insomnia at night.

If I'm really desperate for sleep, I can finish the Edgar Allan Poe analysis waiting for me on my laptop as the final piece of makeup work from my absences before winter break.

I grab my phone instead. It's still open to the messages with Sierra asking how I feel about my doctor's appointment tomorrow. I tell her *Fine. Did you get your costume altered for the recital?*

With any luck, she'll take the bait and fall into a long chain of texts about being worried for our performance next weekend and her senior solo.

I swipe the convo away and adjust my phone for a light, walking down the hall to use the bathroom.

That's when I hear it.

A soft whimpering, a quiet sob.

It's coming from Sean's room across the hall. I crack the door ajar.

A dark lump covers the top bunk with steady breathing, telling me Chris is asleep. But on the bottom bunk, a smaller lump stirs, and while I haven't adjusted enough to the light to make out the dark, watery eyes peeking from under the sheets, I know they're there.

'Joey?'

A sniffle answers.

I pick my way across the floor already strewn with Chris's clothes and sit on the edge of the bed.

'Are you having trouble sleeping?' I ask.

His little voice squeaks, 'She always used to sing to me before I went to bed.'

I don't have to ask who he's talking about. My throat constricts, but I won't break.

'I remember that. She used to sing "Twinkle Twinkle Little Star", right?'

'Yeah.'

My hug won't fix anything. I can't bring his mother back. I'm as powerless against this as I am against my own migraines.

But I squeeze him harder just the same, and he squeezes me back.

'Mr Brown is all alone,' he sniffles.

'What?'

'Mr Brown, my bear. I left him at the house.'

I've never known Joey to sleep without his bear. Chris gave it to him when he was only two or three, and even though Joey's getting to an age past stuffed animals, I'm not surprised he's clinging to any familiarity he can find.

Chris rolls over in his sleep. I bring my voice down to a quieter whisper.

'You know what? I bet your mom's up in those stars tonight, watching over you.'

'Chris said that too, but I didn't believe him.'

'He's right. She is.'

I haven't lost my mom, but I almost did. I was nine, only a few years older than Joey is now, when the driver fell asleep at the wheel and crashed into her car. I'd been at my first sleepover but got scared and begged for my parents to come get me. I fell asleep waiting for her to arrive.

'Tell you what? As soon as the police say it's okay, I'll go get Mr Brown from your house. Sound good?'

Joey sniffles again but nods, rolling to face the window, to the few shimmering dots in the sky poking through the clouds of the night. He yawns. 'I'm kind of sleepy.'

'Yeah? What are you going to dream about tonight?'

'Flying.'

'You still want to be a pilot, huh?' I brush his hair back from his forehead.

'So I can fly up high and see her.'

I kiss his forehead and before closing the door, I sing one quiet verse of 'Twinkle Twinkle Little Star'. He snuggles under the sheets.

Back in my own bed, my thoughts swirl around Joey, Chris and Aunt Julie. Around gas leaks and houses, not migraines and doctor appointments.

I believe Joey's mom really is gazing down on him. She's up there, somewhere, in the blackness of night. A luminous sparkle twinkling over us.

Julie never could have predicted this is how her life would end, but death came and took her as quietly and quickly as my migraines sometimes take me.

She'd want me to protect Joey, and that's exactly what I'm going to do.

6

January 2

The sun rises as I pull into Julie's driveway, but nothing feels familiar.

Chris was still asleep when the police called to inform us they released 'the scene' after determining that the gas leak originated from the old furnace. As soon as Dad said we could pick up clothes and essentials, I volunteered. Joey's desperate to get his bear. My parents were busy with notifying people and arranging a funeral, so when Joey said he wanted to come with me and he looked so bored sitting on the couch, I agreed.

After spending most of yesterday in bed, I'm glad to be out.

I turn off the ignition, trying to figure out how so much can feel different in so little time. I've always loved Julie's house, out in the middle of nowhere while ours is crammed in a neighbourhood with the same floor plan as two others on our street, modelled for cost and energy efficiency. Hers is a puzzle with every previous owner bringing a piece, extending the borders, adding walls and taking them down.

I remember being envious of the bright murals Aunt Julie

painted on the walls – wildflower landscapes with fairies hiding in the petals if you searched hard enough and mountains floating in the clouds like a dream. They're beautiful despite her never finishing one before beginning another. The too-steep stairs were fun to slide down in sleeping bags, and the front room my mother complained had no purpose made for an excellent hot lava obstacle course.

Now the house is lifeless, and I can feel the hollowness from the driveway. Will it be sold? Can my parents keep it in the family?

Somehow all those fun memories are drowned out by the one isolating fact ringing in my ears: this is where Aunt Julie died.

Joey's face reflects in the back seat windows, a mix of different emotions, and I can't name the dominant one. Grief? Comfort? Confusion?

What does he see when he looks at this house?

'On the way home we can get some ice cream,' I suggest.

'It's cold.'

'Then we'll get hot cocoa too,' I say, but the end of the sentence drifts out too slowly, my attention pulled elsewhere.

A tall figure lurks across the road. In the shadows. Unmoving.

'Who's that?' I ask.

'Where?' Joey asks, peeling his focus from his own house.

'Over there, next to—' But the figure is gone. I strain but don't see anyone. 'Never mind.' A chill goes down my arms remembering the person I saw across the road the other night. But it must be a neighbour, like Detective Peterson said.

'You don't have to come in,' I tell Joey, still scanning the tree line across the way. 'You can stay in the car as long as you want.'

His nod is almost indiscernible.

'I'll be right back,' I say, and climb out of the car, sucking in the bitterly cold wind that pushes against the door.

The driveway is uneven from years of settling and weeds clawing through the cracks. All the blinds are drawn. I should probably check the mailbox before I leave.

'You need something?'

A guy approaches from the only other visible house down the road. He's taller than me, but not as tall as Chris, and wearing a black baseball hat that looks new, especially compared to his worn leather jacket. I don't know how he's not freezing. I wish I'd brought gloves.

'I'm Ella.' I wave. 'My aunt and cousins live here. Lived here,' I correct, barely squeezing the words past the lump in my throat. I will not cry in front of a stranger.

'Oh.' His voice softens, losing the protective tone. He adjusts his cap, revealing a nasty purple bruise around his right eye, like someone punched him hard. 'Right. Sorry. I'm Dominic. Their neighbour.' He flicks a hand over his shoulder, and I bite the inside of my cheek, still pushing back the tears.

Focus on the house tucked behind a group of trees. Don't think of Julie. Squint at the black truck in his driveway. He might assume the red in my eyes is from the cold.

My acting skills must suck because he says, 'I'm really sorry about Julie. Can I help with anything?'

I will not let him see me cry. He's watching me like he can see directly into the crater that opened in my chest yesterday.

'Thanks, but I'm fine.'

He's still staring. *Why is he still staring?*

I am not broken. I *am* fine, and I'll prove it.

I laugh, hollow, brittle – not at all my real laugh, but he won't know that – and say, 'Dominic? Wait. I remember you. Chris's thirteenth birthday party.' It was five years ago, but he's memorable enough. 'You had a buzz cut. You ate my cupcake.'

'Wait, wait. Ella? You fixed your hair.'

'Pfft.' I'd argue more against the implication that there was something wrong with it, but something shifts, and he's looking at me like a person again, not something to be fixed. I'll keep it that way. Besides, eleven-year-old me did not know how to control frizz.

'The way I remember it,' he continues, 'that cupcake was set on the counter for anyone.'

'You were getting seconds before I had my first.'

'Yeah, well, I was thirteen and hungry and immature.' He flashes a grin. 'Forgive me?'

'Forgive you?' I say, locking my mask in place. No one is wounded here. No one is hurting. I will fake it until I become it. 'You haven't apologised yet. And if I remember correctly – and I definitely do – you also dominated in Mario Kart and cursed every time someone hit you with a lead shell. *And* you got green frosting in my hair.'

'Fair enough. I'm sorry.' Something about the self-satisfied smirk tells me he enjoys being remembered this way. When I don't respond, he adds, 'You like to hold grudges, huh?'

'No.' I don't *like* to. Dominic was irritating at the party but also unequivocally cute, charming. Except he knew it.

Last year we were looking through pictures and found one of the party. I asked Chris about Dominic, but he said he'd been suspended; Julie shook her head, muttering something about his mother. I can't remember the details, but I remember wondering what he could have done to be kicked out of school.

'Can't blame you,' he says, grinning the same way he had in that picture. 'Julie always makes the best cakes.'

Boom. Just like that the mask is knocked from my face. We both go still, her name hanging in the air. He doesn't correct his use of the present tense, and neither do I.

He clears his throat, and I step towards the front path. 'My cousin wanted me to drive by and get some things he couldn't get before.'

I never thought my aunt's house would be under investigation by the police, but at least they didn't find anything malicious. Only a poorly maintained furnace.

Gas is the quiet killer that doesn't leave a trace.

Joey watches me quietly from the car as I approach the front of the house.

'How is Chris?' Dominic shoves his hands in his pockets and scrunches his shoulders against the cold wind.

'Terrible.' But Chris probably wouldn't want anyone thinking of him that way. 'He's tough,' I add, trying the front door, finding it locked, and quietly cursing myself for forgetting the key at home. 'It's just hard right now.'

I move to the window, feeling along the edge, careful not to peel off any more paint.

'What, uh, exactly are you doing?' Dominic asks.

'Door's locked.' I try to get a grip on the edge of the window to pry it open. 'Forgot the key.'

'You could . . . ask for one.' The smirk on his face is exactly the same one he got every time he drove Toad across the finish line ahead of my Luigi.

I swallow my pride, but it doesn't go down easy. 'Do you have one?'

A dimple flashes in his right cheek. 'No grudge now, huh?'

'Does that mean you have one?'

'I used to feed their old cat. I'll see if we still have it. Hold on.'

He jogs down the road and is back in a minute. After he opens the door to the garage, he looks at me still waiting in the driveway.

'You coming?'

'It's . . . it's safe, right?'

'Yeah.'

I hesitate in the cold.

Dominic opens the door. 'The police and firefighters were in and out of here all day yesterday. It only takes a few hours for gas to clear in a house with airflow from windows and doors. Plus they brought in fans. I'm not sure whether the electricity's been turned back on, though . . .' He flicks the flashlight on his phone. 'Shouldn't be a problem once you open some blinds.'

If his explanation wasn't enough to pull me over the threshold, one more look at Joey is. Anything for him.

I step into the cool garage, pulling my phone out for its flashlight too, but I stumble on nothing.

'You okay?'

'Yeah.' But I'm not. It's been happening more often, losing my balance. Another side effect of the tumour.

Dominic steps aside and holds the door.

'Thanks.' I try to sound grateful. 'How do you know so much about clearing gas safely anyway?'

'My dad. He has his own heating and cooling business. Knowing gas and electrical safety was basically a requirement since I was five. I've been working with him for years. Not always officially.' He moves the light under his chin. 'Don't tell the IRS.'

'Noted.' I squeeze past him in the doorframe, taking new stock of his physique. With his broad shoulders and shadowed jaw, it's hard to believe this is the same kid who belted out 'Happy Birthday' so loudly I had to cover my ears.

The house feels frozen in time. A half-empty juice glass sits on the counter next to a stack of bills. Joey's Connect Four box rests on the table. The couch is still patched where Julie sewed a floral print to add 'character' instead of replacing the old furniture. On the purple wall behind the thick banister – the one that wobbles from us repeatedly sliding down it – hang pictures of Julie and the boys at various ages, moments of joy captured in the past now inspiring years of heartache.

'Do you know what you're looking for?'

'Uh, maybe?'

'Whew.' Dominic fans in front of his face. 'I'm going to empty the trash,' he says, moving to the can by the fridge. My New Year's sunglasses lie on the floor, the rose-coloured lenses cracked on one side. They must have fallen off when I pulled Joey out, and I never noticed. I add them to the bag before Dominic heads to the garage.

The door to Julie's room is open. I cross the empty spot where the police or firefighters or EMTs or whoever got her body. Before I realise I'm doing it, I'm inside, running a hand over her side of the bed, where her head dreamed her last dreams. Where she probably cried at least once or twice over her sons. Where she expected to fall asleep like every other night.

I pull up the covers, tucking the sheets in tight, inhaling the scent of vanilla that wafts up when I do, the half-empty bottle of lotion still on her nightstand. When I turn around, Joey's standing in the doorway.

'Jeez,' I gasp, barely stifling a full-out yelp and clutching my hand to my neck like an old woman. 'You scared me!'

Joey's focus locks on his mother's bed.

'Come on,' I say, ushering him out. 'Let's go find Mr Brown.'

He moves, but his focus stays on the bed for two more steps.

Joey's room is a mess. His blankets hang off the bed. Nerf bullets, cards and a handful of rubber ducks litter the floor.

'Do you know where you left him?'

Joey shifts some items in a box, throws one of his blankets up to look under the bed. 'No.'

I push open the closet door, moving a small pile of clothes aside to get there.

'My parents said they're going to come over later this week and box up all your stuff; they'll probably find him then. Are there any other toys you want?'

'I want Mr Brown.'

'I know, and we'll keep looking, but you'll probably want more than that, right?' What I don't say is we'll be lucky to find him in all the places he could be hiding, so it's better to have a backup.

'Your mom told me I could get my trucks.'

He helps me dig through a big box in his room filled with dozens of the same little metal cars, but he seems to know exactly which two he's looking for. I grab some clothes from his closet, including a nice outfit for the funeral.

'Anything else?'

'A tractor.'

We dig for a while before Joey speaks again.

'Mommy always looked pretty while she was sleeping.' His voice is flat, hollow. So are his eyes. Like something natural has left him, replaced by something I can't quite put my finger on. 'Was she still mad at me?'

'What? No, of course not. Your mom could never stay mad at you.'

'Ella?' Dominic calls from the kitchen. 'You say something?'

'No,' I call back. 'Hold on!' Joey still stands on the other side of the room, looking off at a blank wall. 'Pick out some clothes you want,' I whisper. 'I'll be right back.'

'Got everything?' Dominic asks, when I meet him in the kitchen.

I need to pack some clothes for Chris, but after what Joey said in the bedroom, he needs more reassurance about the accident than the police can give.

'Not yet. Before I grab more, did they say the gas leak came from the basement?'

'Yeah, they use a gas monitor to locate the specific leak. Pretty simple.'

'What do you mean?' I ask.

'Come on.' He opens the door to the basement. 'I'll show you.'

Joey's still searching for Mr Brown, I'm sure, so I follow Dominic.

Without electricity or big windows, our phone flashlights become crucial.

Only a few steps into the stairwell, the whole atmosphere changes. The air is cooler. The wood steps are dusty. I shiver. The basement isn't finished. The halo of light from my phone doesn't extend far, but it's enough to illuminate the spiderwebs and cobwebs hanging boldly in the corner and down from the ceiling. Cardboard boxes are stacked around the wall, but where one might normally find big black letters identifying them as 'Halloween costumes' and 'holiday dishes', Aunt Julie's replaced her messy handwriting with doodles and paintings to represent each box's contents.

'Loads of houses out here use gas for some of their appliances,' Dominic explains. 'Stoves, washers and dryers, the water heater. But the biggest one is the furnace. It's back here.'

In the corner, there's a section of the basement I recognise. Our own basement is finished with a storage room with all this stuff, but I never have a reason to go in there. I can identify the circuit breaker on the wall. There's a big cylinder near it with a large, yellow bag of salt next to it. Dominic leads me to the biggest appliance, a rectangular thing that goes from floor to ceiling with the silver vents leading out of it.

'They left the cover off,' Dominic says, moving the metal door aside. A screw drops, and he places it carefully through the hole again. 'Here.' He crouches beside the open panel, angling his light inside and pointing.

'The gas comes into the furnace here and gives energy to the heater. The fans push the air over the heat exchanger and to the rest of the house.'

'And it's powered by gas?'

'See back there? That blue tube?'

'The one with the black tape on it?'

'Yeah, that one. It looks like Julie had a small gas leak before, but whoever fixed it for her didn't have a clue what they were doing. That tape wouldn't be secure enough to stop the airflow for long. And up there, you can see the fire team flagged another leak they found, too.'

His patient instruction reminds me how much people grow between middle school and high school.

'I wonder why Julie didn't ask your dad to fix it . . .'

'Beats me. He told me he would have come over and looked at it for free if he'd known. I think he feels bad, like he could have prevented it.'

'So this whole house could really fill up with enough gas from those two tiny holes, huh?'

'Well,' Dominic says, standing and looking around the room. 'Over there is the front of the house, which means . . .' He spins, orienting himself. 'Yeah, her room was right above here. See that vent? It leads directly from here into her room. She would have gotten the heaviest dose and received it first. Maybe,' Dominic says, surveying the area, 'we can try the fuse box and flip the electricity back on.'

'Ella?' Joey's little voice comes from upstairs.

'We should head back up,' I say, leaving the furnace and vents behind.

'Wait,' Dominic calls, trailing me.

Joey isn't where I expect him, but a scratching comes from my right. A little crawl space hides in the back of the coat closet, almost invisible if you don't know it's there – something Chris found ridiculously funny after winning rounds and rounds of hide-and-seek before reluctantly revealing it to me and Sean. It leads to an old room where the three of us used to play before we got too big and Joey took over.

'Are you okay?' I call, heading for the hidden room, sure Joey is on the other side.

'I'm fine,' Dominic replies, but I'm not sure whether he's

trying to be funny or genuinely mistaking my concern for him. 'What're – where are you going?'

'Ella!' Joey calls for me again, as I crash into the room. 'Come here! Quick!'

SNAP!

Joey shrieks and I jump as Dominic appears next to me.

'What was that?' I ask.

'Sounded like a mouse trap,' Dominic says. 'What is this place?'

'Old laundry room before one of the many remodels.'

Joey, Mr Brown now clutched in his arm, points to where the sound came behind the rusted washer and dryer.

I hop onto the machine and the metal top clangs. The flashlight from my phone lights up the back.

'What're you doing?' Dominic asks.

'We can't leave it.' I don't like the idea of finding the trap, but the smell of dead mouse later will be worse.

'Is there something in there?' Joey asks. 'Is it dead?'

'I don't see anything . . . wait. There's a tube not connected.'

'What?' Dominic asks.

'Yeah,' I slide off the machine. 'Back there, go look.'

I jump down and Dominic leans over, shining his own light into the narrow canyon between the dryer and the wall. A wide metallic tube crowds most of the space, but a skinny, rusted one is underneath, bent at weird angles like it's stiff.

'Is that the gas line?' I ask. Joey moves behind me, his little hand finding mine.

'Yeah, yeah I think it is.'

'It's not connected to the wall. What does that mean?'

Dominic hops off the rusted machine and dusts off his pants. 'It means there was more than one appliance leaking gas in this house.'

Detective Peterson never mentioned that. Of course, he wouldn't know if they never found this room.

'Well, it could still be an accident, right? A . . . a coincidence?'

'An old line having a few holes, that's an accident. Someone thinking they could plug the problem with tape, that's negligence. But an entire hose being disconnected?'

Joey's head flicks from me to Dominic and back again. We came here looking for answers, but this wasn't what I imagined. I wanted to show Joey that it wasn't anyone's fault, only a horrible tragedy that no one could have seen coming.

Instead, there's another source of a gas leak, a bigger one, and the hose couldn't have been unscrewed by mistake.

I say what we're both thinking. 'It was intentional.'

7

January 2

Someone wanted to kill Julie.

I should understand what this means. Those words should make sense.

This wasn't a tragedy. It was purposeful. Intentional. Malicious. Murder.

Dominic is cognisant enough to call the police, and upon their direction, we vacate the house immediately, waiting for them on the front porch.

I call Dad, tell him in broken, barely coherent sentences. He's in the car by the time he hangs up.

'I can't . . .' I take a deep breath to steady my voice. 'I can't imagine anyone trying to hurt them.'

'I know,' Dominic says.

I blow on my cold fingers. I should go in my car with Joey, but my feet don't want to move. When Dominic was on the phone with the police, Joey told me he didn't understand what was happening. I wasn't sure how to answer, not yet, so I told him to wait in the car. It's still running with the heat on. He drives a little truck over the back of the seat while we sit out here in the cold. It feels appropriate, to be numb.

'Here,' Dominic offers me the gloves off his hands.

I stare at them, my brain still slow to process.

'Take 'em,' he says. 'I have pockets.'

'I have pockets too.'

His voice strains, jaw tight, but there's a softness in his eyes, one I don't remember from when I was eleven. 'I can't stand here watching you think about your aunt without doing something, and there's nothing I can do except—'

I take the gloves. They're warm.

A car pulls into the driveway, but it isn't Dad. How did Chris get here from my house so fast?

He gets out slowly and swings the door shut, appraising me and Dominic with mild curiosity. 'What're you doing here?'

The question could be for both of us, but he's facing Dominic, the bigger question mark.

'You don't know?' he asks. But it's clear from his confusion that Dad didn't have a chance to talk to him yet. He must have left before we called.

'You shouldn't be here,' Chris says, and for a second, I wonder if he registers my presence at all.

Dominic opens his mouth again, but I put a gloved hand on his arm and say, 'I came to get some of Joey's things and Mom told me to get an outfit for him for the funeral. I forgot the key and Dominic let me in.'

Chris squints at the two grocery bags at my feet. 'I could have gotten that. You didn't have to—'

'Chris, we found something.' I don't know how else to say it except directly. 'The gas leak wasn't an accident. The police are on their way.'

'What do you mean?' A tornado of disbelief, confusion and denial rips across his face. 'The police said – they said it was a hose attached to the furnace. That's what they said. We knew it was leaking – not serious. It was small. We thought it was fixed. I told the police that. They know that.'

'But the dryer hose – the old one in the secret playroom – it's completely unhooked.'

'What? No.' He steps towards the house, but Dominic puts a hand on his chest, gentle but firm. He waits for Chris to lock eyes with him before speaking softly.

'You shouldn't go in there. The police are on their way. They'll want to secure it as a crime scene.'

Chris shakes him off, his face reddening but not from the cold. He steps forward again, but Dominic moves his whole body to block his path.

'I have to,' Chris says. Dominic doesn't budge. 'Get out of my way. I'm going into my house.'

'No, you're not thinking straight.'

'That's my house. My mom . . . my – the dryer, and . . .' He keeps trying to nudge Dominic away, and the confusion quickly gives way to frustration. His chest puffs, his shoulders square, his jaw clenches. 'That's my house. Let me through.'

Dominic doesn't back down, and Chris's right hand forms a fist. I've never known Chris to hit anyone, but Dominic is seconds away from earning a matching bruise on the other side of his face.

'Chris! No!' I wedge myself between them. Chris doesn't break eye contact with Dominic, but Dominic's still relaxed, calm, never escalating through any of it, only protecting. I try to put myself in Chris's shoes, imagine learning someone murdered my mom, but I can't. It's too painful. Too much.

'Don't you get it?' I try to keep my voice calm like Dominic's, but it cracks and the tears well up before I can stop them. 'Don't you know what this means? It's going to be a crime scene because this wasn't an accident.'

'Yes, it was. It was an accident.' Chris retreats and repeats the words Blake told him at the station, like he's convincing himself again of what he doesn't want to believe. 'It was an accident.'

'No, it wasn't.'

He wipes at his nose, which is dripping, and not from the cold. 'The police declared it an accident. It was an accident! Why do you want it to be more than that?' He runs his hands through his hair, pacing across the lawn, over the same patch of grass where the EMTs strapped him and Joey to the gurneys. Now I understand why Dominic offered me the gloves, but there's nothing I can offer Chris.

Two police cars arrive, lights on but no sirens. Joey's face presses against the back window, watching his brother while the police enter the house. If Chris took it like this, how is Joey going to understand?

Even though Julie's the one who died, could someone have been trying to kill them too? Even me?

No. That doesn't make sense. No one even knew I was coming except Julie and my parents. All the plans changed at the last minute. None of this makes sense.

Dominic approaches the officers, Peterson among them, while I take Chris aside.

'We're going to figure this out.'

'None of us planned to be home that night. How could this have happened?'

Chris drops into a squat, hands on his knees, head towards the ground, drawing steady breaths. Another truck rolls up from the opposite direction. A man jumps out, jogging up to the house.

He has the same long nose and sharp jaw as Dominic. From their embrace, I'm guessing it must be his dad.

'What's happened? Another accident?' he asks.

'My dad was here on New Year's,' Dominic says.

'Yes. I saw the lights that night and came outside. Sorry for your loss.'

He's the neighbour Detective Peterson told me was on scene.

'Were you outside when we got here today?' I ask, hoping he's the figure I saw when we arrived, but even as I ask it, I know he's not tall enough to match.

He points to his truck. 'No, no. I just came home.'

Dominic explains everything to his dad, and Detective

Peterson barks, 'Track down whatever idiot cleared this house and get him in my office. Now!'

They must not have known about the hidden space.

Peterson marches towards me and Chris, his voice surprisingly steady after that outburst. 'When you came into the house, did you notice anything odd or out of place?'

'No,' I say, 'but I wasn't really looking for it.' What else might be in the house? What other information is waiting to be discovered? What other secrets do those walls keep?

'What about the dryer in particular?' the detective asks, typing out more notes on his phone. 'Did it look like it had been moved?'

'I'm not sure . . . do you think someone unhooked it?'

'We're going to rule out the possibility.'

'No one else has been inside,' I say. 'You declared the source of the leak to be the furnace this morning and released the house as safe hours ago.'

Besides, if someone was trying to steal the dryer and that's why it had been unhooked, surely they would have taken the newer appliance closer to an exit.

Peterson doesn't comment. He knows as well as I do that the hose was unhooked the night Julie died. He knows it killed her.

'Where did you go inside?'

'We were in Joey's room, picking out some of his favourite toys, and Dominic took me downstairs to see how the furnace worked.'

He pauses to evaluate me but then turns his attention to Chris. 'What about you? Did you enter the home?'

Chris doesn't respond, doesn't even look up.

'Son, where did you go inside the house?'

'He didn't. He got here after we called you,' I say, but without looking at Detective Peterson. Chris remains squatting on the ground, a gargoyle of grief.

'Chris?' I nudge his shoulder.

'I didn't go in. I – I – I need to call Blake. He has to know.'

'Maybe someone else should—' I glance at Detective Peterson. Surely he's more experienced with delivering this kind of news to a boyfriend or any loved one. It's hard enough to lose someone, but then to hear it wasn't an accident? Devastating.

'No, I'll do it.' Chris marches towards his car, his face dark but determined.

'Sorry,' I say to Peterson. 'He's upset.' And hates for people to see him that way.

'It's all right. We'll get a statement another time.'

'Does it prove someone tried to hurt them? If the furnace wasn't the only source of a gas leak?'

'We'll have to file an official report before changing the ruling from an accident.'

'You mean changing it to . . . homicide?'

Homicide. Murder. The word feels false, like it shouldn't exist outside of movies and TV shows, certainly not in connection with my aunt. My beautiful, kind-hearted aunt.

Detective Peterson looks reluctant to answer. Instead, he asks, 'Do you know anyone who would have wanted to hurt your aunt or your cousins?'

'I did see someone, over there, watching the house when we got here this morning.' It wasn't Dominic's dad. It's possible it was another neighbour, but it was definitely someone who didn't want to be seen.

Peterson strains his neck, scanning the area I'm pointing to, a spot between some trees lining the lots.

'What can you tell me about this person?'

'I . . . I don't know.' A pressure builds behind my eyes. 'It was hard to see.'

'Was it a man or a woman?'

'They were in the shadows. I just know I saw a figure.'

Peterson gives me the slightest quirk of his brow before squinting across the road again. It's small, but I see it. The doubt. The dismissal. It's the same expression Dr Mullins wore when I described my migraines to him.

'Someone was there,' I repeat more firmly, but just then an officer comes out of the house and calls Peterson inside. He excuses himself and leaves me standing on the sidewalk.

Chris is still talking in his car, visibly upset. I can hear him through the windows.

'Blake? Blake?' He brings the phone away from his ear, touches the screen a few times and returns it to the side of his face. A few seconds later, he stops, staring at it hopelessly.

When I knock on the window, he rolls it down.

'We got disconnected.'

His voice is too cold, too hollow. What did Blake say before the call ended?

Chris's phone vibrates, and I can almost see the spike in his heart until he looks at the unknown number scrolling across the screen and ignores the call. Not Blake.

'Do you want me to drive you home?' I offer. 'You shouldn't . . .'

'I'll . . . I'll stick around. See what the police say.'

'I should get Joey home.'

'Huh?' Chris barely registers me.

'Joey. I should—'

'Oh yeah. Bring his stuff.'

'I didn't get a chance to grab anything of yours before . . .'

But he doesn't hear me again, fixated on the house as officers enter and exit.

Dominic jogs over when I reach my car door.

'I'm really sorry, about everything.'

I don't know how to respond, so I pull at the fingers of one glove to return them to him.

He wraps his hand around mine and squeezes, the warmth seeping through. 'Keep them.' His hand stays on mine until I concede. He glances at my car where Joey sits silent in the back seat. 'Are you sure you're okay to drive?'

'Yeah, yeah,' I say. The truth is, a slight haze has settled in and it could signal an incoming migraine. If it is, I want to be home, near my medication, a soft bed and a dark room.

But it might not be a migraine coming at all. Sometimes I get so anxious about whether one is coming that I become hyperaware of my body and wonder if I'm really feeling what I'm feeling, or if I'm becoming paranoid and imagining it.

'I'll be fine,' I say to convince myself as much as to convince Dominic, 'but I'm not sure about Chris.'

'We'll make sure he gets to your house okay.'

When I climb into my car, Joey's no longer playing with his truck. 'It wasn't an accident, was it?'

No is such a little word, only one syllable, yet it fills my mouth like a bubble, unable to escape. Joey doesn't collapse like Chris. There's no shock. No surprise.

He's a statue, emotions locked tight behind his sculpted mask. Joey hasn't talked about that night. He's hardly talked at all except to me last night. But that silence won't help us get answers. Or justice.

'What were you and your mom doing on New Year's Eve? Did you smell the gas?'

He only answers with a shrug. The pamphlets the social worker left at the hospital included information on how difficult it can be for little kids to process trauma, how it's common for them not to want to talk about it, and then suddenly it might all pour out at once. Joey's hardly spoken to anyone else since the hospital, and that's probably what I need to wait for: the flood when he finally speaks.

I shut the car door and can't deny it. A migraine is coming.

As we reverse down the driveway, Dominic raises his hand – not with enough enthusiasm for a wave, but an acknowledgement of all that can't be said.

His dad keeps his hands at his side, staring. When I reach

the stop sign at the end of the road and turn, he lingers in the rearview mirror.

I'd only just convinced myself no one is to blame and now there's no denying the truth.

Someone walked into the house planning murder.

8

January 3

Doctor's offices always seem to have one interesting picture on the wall. Not two, not three. Only one per room. This one has a table of different plants and where they grow in America.

After everything that's happened the past week, you'd think we could cancel or reschedule this appointment, but that's not how specialists work. This appointment has been on our calendar for a month. The sooner the tumour's treated, the sooner it's gone from my life forever.

It's harder to ignore the questions about treatment plans now that we're minutes away from hearing them, but running over the facts of New Year's Eve helps.

The police aren't giving us any information now that they've declared it an 'open investigation'. Only once they're done taking new pictures and gathering their evidence will anyone be allowed inside the house again. Detective Peterson assures us this shouldn't take more than a day or two, but that doesn't bring us any closer to answers.

Meanwhile, I'm stuck in this office learning that the Venus flytrap only grows in the Carolinas.

Before meeting Dr Gupta, we tried everything. Using ice packs and hot water. Having a food tracker and sleep tracker. Monitoring caffeine and water intake. Dimming the lights.

None of that works when the diagnosis is a tumour. Even now, with a prescription for the pain, it doesn't make life easy. At first I tried over-the-counter stuff. Basic pain relief. It doesn't make a dent. At least with the prescription, I can sometimes recover after only a few hours.

When Dr Gupta first uttered the words *'brain tumour'*, it felt like time slowed. My brain froze. My heart might have stopped. It felt like it did.

When you get that piercing pain for no reason that spikes through your brain like a nail hammered in, who doesn't wonder if it's a tumour? When you search your symptoms online and WebMD says it could be an abnormal growth, who doesn't stop to think *what if?*

But then I thought, *It can't be a tumour. That's so rare. I'm being ridiculous. It's just a headache.*

But it wasn't just a headache. It was a series of them. Migraines. At all hours for varying lengths of time. And after months of trying different dietary restrictions and allergy tests, Dr Gupta ordered a scan to be on the safe side.

And ever since, I've been unable to avoid those words: *brain tumour*.

I did the research, read the printouts. I know there are over one hundred different types of brain tumours. I'm not as rare as I believed. Over one million Americans have one.

But only 6 per cent of them are kids and teens.

Mom told the school, asking them to be flexible with my schoolwork and deadlines. Some teachers were really understanding. Almost too understanding. I don't want to be treated any differently, and still one of them exempted me from Christmas exams. I almost prefer my math teacher's approach of requiring the exact same amount of work as always. At least then I can pretend I'm going to be fine.

'Chris has really been struggling,' Mom says, putting away her phone and pulling my attention from mine. 'We haven't really talked about how you're dealing with the loss.'

She has a knack for bringing up the tough topics out of the blue. She's observing me like a cracked bowl that's been glued back together and she's not sure it's going to hold, which is ironic considering that's how I thought of her for so long. I was afraid she wouldn't pull through after her accident, so for months I didn't fully trust that she would.

'It's not easy, but I'm not the one who lost my mom.'

'I know. And Joey too. It always seems harder with someone so young.'

It does. I know people feel sympathetic for Chris, but the idea of a six-year-old boy losing his mom seems to elicit more '*aww*'s.

'It's weird because usually when they're at our house, Joey is running and jumping around. But these last few days have been so . . . quiet.'

A sad smile crinkles Mom's eyes, like she's remembering him the way I do, not as the sad, quiet shell he's become.

The clock on the wall ticks and ticks and ticks. You'd think they wouldn't have those in here, make it like a casino where people don't know how much time they've wasted.

My phone buzzes with a message from Sierra. I gave her the latest updates about the house this morning.

are you okay?

The question shouldn't bother me. Sierra is my friend – my closest friend since my school friends ditched me and she moved here three months ago. It doesn't sound like a long time, but when she came to the studio in silver leggings and hair split in perfect puffs, we clicked instantly. She helped me on my chem homework before practice, and I read over her English papers after.

I will be if this doctor ever shows, I tell her.

i know your aunt was really important to you. im here if you want to talk.

Thanks. I'm doing okay.

you don't have to do this by yourself. you don't have to be okay. with me, you can be not okay.

Check out this article about gas leaks. I send her a screenshot, and she lets me change the subject.

> Like carbon monoxide, natural gas is odourless and colourless. As a result, dangerous amounts of this gas can build up undetected. To prevent death and serious injury, mercaptan, also known as methanethiol, is added to the gas. The foul odour is designed to be easier to notice, but the gas can still be deadly within minutes. If you suspect a gas leak in your home . . .

whoa deadly within minutes? so were they home when the leak started?

My fingers tap the screen. Who would have wanted to hurt Julie and her family, who would have had the means to do it?

Maybe. I hit send and think about how Dominic said the airflow went directly to Julie's room, the closest. Plus, the nearest grocery store is at least twenty minutes away, and Julie said they still had one more stop before they'd meet me at home.

No, they couldn't have been at the house for very long before I arrived. The hose must have been disconnected when the house was empty.

'Who are you talking to?' Mom asks in her typical I'm-not-nosy-I'm-only-interested-in-your-life tone.

'Huh?' I close the thread and process what she asked. 'Sierra.'

'Have you,' she begins, and I can feel the end of her question coming before it lands, 'told her about your migraines?'

'You mean my tumour?'

Mom's brows shoot up and I can almost see her trying to plan her next move of attack without setting off a bomb. She's right:

she needs to tread carefully because I can see exactly where she's going with this. Again.

The more I was absent from school – once a week for the last few months, and more when the doctor appointments began – the closer my 'friends' got without me. The more often I had to cancel plans, the easier it was not to invite me in the first place.

Yeah, if they knew about my diagnosis, they'd probably reach out, be caring and concerned. But I don't need them after the diagnosis. I needed them through the symptoms.

I didn't plan on telling Sierra, but I'd noticed my balance was off in the studio. At first I told myself I could improve with enough focus and practice, like Madame Leheller always barks. I even thought it was my imagination, that I wasn't really stumbling that much or bumping into walls.

The doubts and fears were pounding against my back like a river, the current growing stronger and stronger until Sierra gently noted my wobbling arabesque one day after dance. Her question cracked the dam, and I broke.

I told her about my tumour in wet, sticky sobs. I confessed how scared I was. She did everything a friend should: wrapped her arms around me, let me cry, listened without interrupting. Telling her solidified a bond between us that didn't exist before, a depth to our friendship I can't put into words. And I'm grateful for her kindness and the way she checks up on me, but I'm also embarrassed about how I cried so hard I couldn't even sit up straight, how I collapsed into her, how easily I fell apart.

I don't want anyone to see me like that again. I won't let the dam break.

No one else knows. I don't need to be looked at with the same pitying looks my teachers and even Detective Peterson gave me. I don't need anyone questioning if I'm capable when I know I am.

I can complete my schoolwork. I can perform in my dance recital. I can do everything I did before. My smile is a mask, happy and healthy. No one will want to pull it down and see the truth underneath.

'Madame Leheller should at least be informed—'

'So she can take it easy on me? Because you don't think I can handle it otherwise?'

'I didn't say that. I—'

The door clicks open. Mom's face conveys all her sadness and disappointment, so I'm sure the conversation isn't really over, but for now, she bites back any response and directs her attention to the doctor.

'Well, we have good news and bad news.' Dr Gupta slides her stool in front of us with the digital scans pulled up on the computer monitor. Mom's face is solid, a rock. But she must be putting all her attention into hiding her fears, because she's forgotten about her hands. They wring the fake leather of her purse like she's strangling a snake, white knuckles and all.

'The good news is the tumour's growth is marginal enough that it's not emergent. It's not cancer.'

Not cancer. The words pop a balloon in the air. Mom's shoulders drop some of their tension. Something like a laugh burbles from deep inside me.

'That means I'll be okay?'

'No cancer means no chemo.'

'That's still good news, right?' Mom asks.

'There's been surprisingly little research conducted on brain tumours over the last twenty years, and the slow growth leaves us with two options.' Dr Gupta spends the next several minutes explaining the difference between radiation to shrink the tumour and surgery to remove it. There are pros and cons to both, and while she's confident it can be removed through surgery, radiation would be a longer, less invasive treatment.

Each word drops its own artillery of mental images exploding in my brain: a giant machine. A scalpel. Hospital gowns. IVs.

'The decision is ultimately yours, but if left untreated, the tumour will likely grow, however slowly, and ultimately be fatal, but we're not going to let it get to that point.'

Mom asks questions and takes notes while Dr Gupta gives a whole list of other symptoms to watch for until treatment begins: seizures, short-term memory problems, hallucinations, drowsiness, personality changes . . .

I sound like the small print on a medical infomercial except my brain is selling a lifetime supply of pain and worry. Even if I'm not going to die in the next few months, this battle isn't over. It's still trying to dictate my life.

'Why can't we treat it now? Today. Take it out.'

Dr Gupta frowns. 'I wish it were that easy. Regardless of which option you choose, there are risks. It's not a decision to be taken lightly. Consider the information I've given you, sleep on it. Do you have any questions about the treatment options?'

I swallow and shake my head.

Another message from Sierra comes through.

Have you seen this? she says, including a link to a small newspaper I don't recognise.

'How have you been coping otherwise?' Dr Gupta asks, genuine concern in her voice.

'Hmm?' I look up, trying to appear attentive and save the article for later.

She pulls her stool closer. 'I know at the beginning you were worried there was something you could have done to prevent this, but sometimes there's no rhyme or reason to where these things strike.'

She must notice how tired I look. Not even Mom has the energy to tell her about Aunt Julie.

'I know.' I've had to force myself to believe it. I drove myself to the brink of breakdown trying to figure out *why me* when I first heard the news.

There is no reason why I have a brain tumour, no logical explanation why mine isn't a lethal form of cancer. There's no good answer for why the gas only killed Julie on New Year's. Nothing exists to explain why some people die and others don't.

But there is a reason I'm alive. There has to be. If I've been given this life, if I've escaped death when others haven't, then the least I can do is live for them.

As that resolution settles into my bones, another message from Sierra comes in, another article she found online.

The opening paragraph proves that nothing Dr Gupta says next could be as shocking as the words in front of me.

9

January 3

I spend the drive home reading and rereading the article Sierra sent, noting the similarities and differences to my aunt's house.

ONE DEAD IN SPRINGTOWN HOUSE FIRE

Firefighters responded to a fire on the north side of Springtown Thursday evening. While the house was initially thought empty, responders have declared that the 54-year-old homeowner was found in the debris. He was pronounced dead on site.

It took crews around three hours to extinguish the flames. The Springtown Fire Department says it is working closely with local and state authorities to investigate the fire. Residents near the home claim they smelled gas in the hours before the explosion, but the state fire marshal's office has no record of any reports being filed.

The article ends with a word from the fire chief to call in any suspicion of gas leaks.

Sierra's follow-up message says it all: *coincidence?*

My mind buzzes with possibilities, ones that are almost enough to let me ignore Mom's tense glances. Almost.

She waits until we pull into the garage before landing her bomb, the one waiting in her arsenal since sitting in Dr Gupta's office.

'What do you think about what Dr Gupta said?'

'I don't really want to think about it at all, to be honest.'

'You're going to have more and more doctor appointments.'

'I know.'

'It's going to get harder to hide your condition.'

'I'm not hiding it.'

'You're not telling people either.'

'You're right, I'm not.'

I pop the door open and climb out before she can retort. When I enter the kitchen, Hank barks once and bounds over, large paws scrabbling against the planks on the floor and shedding strands of golden fur when I pet his backside. I'm pouring a glass of orange juice when Mom enters.

She heaves a sigh, obviously trying to control the tone of her voice before she begins round two. Or is it three now?

'Choosing a treatment plan is a big decision. We'll have to talk about it.'

'It doesn't mean we have to talk right now.'

'You can join a support group—'

'No way.'

'You're going to miss more dance before your recital. What are you going to tell Madame Leheller when you're gone? You can't keep pretending this isn't happening.'

'I'm not.'

She gives me a pointed stare. 'You're not as good at hiding things as you think you are. This is clearly affecting you. I just don't understand why you don't—'

'What am I even supposed to say?' My voice goes deeper, mocking. 'Hey, what's up? Oh me, yeah, I found out I have a brain tumour last month. No big deal. Cheers!' I raise my glass and take a swig.

'It is a big deal, though.' She battles my annoyance and sarcasm with calm, gentle tones.

'Trust me, I know.' I swirl the contents of my cup, doing whatever I can to avoid her.

She takes the opportunity to step closer, wrap her arms around me and whisper into my hair. 'You don't have to go through this on your own.'

I inhale whatever scent has become uniquely Mom's. I remember wanting so badly to hug her like this – to have her hug me – when I was scared at that sleepover the night of her car accident. I wanted to hug her again during those months of recovery. Instead, Sean and I were always warned to be gentle, be careful, not too hard, let her rest. I couldn't lean on her, so I began leaning on Julie instead.

'Your dad and I will always be here for you. You know that.'

But Aunt Julie told me that too and she's gone. I clutch Mom tighter. There's no guarantee of tomorrow, and the people you lean on can disappear, leaving you to fall even harder.

It's easier if I take this on my own. I don't just need to prove to Mom and Dad that this tumour won't affect my life. I have to prove it to myself too.

Mom pulls back as Chris walks into the room, carrying an empty cereal bowl to the sink. How much did he hear? Does he know? His face is steady, relaxed. It gives away nothing.

He's washing out his dish when Mom says, 'Don't worry about that. I'll do it later.'

'Huh?' Chris removes his earbud. He didn't hear anything, and I relax when Mom repeats herself. 'I don't mind,' Chris says. 'I'm used to it.'

Mom looks ready to argue or crack a joke about teaching me a thing or two, but she retrieves her phone from her back pocket instead. 'It's the funeral home.' She's at the foot of the stairs when she says, 'Hello?'

'Where have you guys been?' Chris asks, as I follow him back into the living room and we fold ourselves onto separate couches.

This is the perfect opportunity to tell him the truth, to take Mom's advice and confess.

'Nowhere special. Was that breakfast or lunch?'

'Second breakfast.' The words are hollow.

He doesn't press me, and that's reassurance enough that he has too much occupying his thoughts right now to worry about my health. It's nice to see him out of the dark room upstairs, a good sign, at least.

Hank settles next to him, head lying on his lap. Chris scratches him behind his ears before a call comes through on his phone and he swipes it away.

'Work?' I ask, remembering how many hours Chris usually puts in, taking advantage of a programme for seniors, so he only has to be at school half days and can earn more. 'I hope they're giving you more time off than Blake's job.'

'Wha—? No, I, uh, actually don't have a job right now. They laid me off.'

'Because you can't come in? That's ridiculous! I bet you could sue. You should—'

'No, no, nothing like that. They let me go right before Christmas. My boss didn't want to do it, but he couldn't justify the cost' – Chris uses air quotes around the last three words – 'and wanted to give me time to find something else.'

'Oh.' I relax into my seat again. 'I bet my parents will help with money as much as they can. They said you can stay here as long as you need to.'

'I'd rather do it on my own.'

Typical Chris. Just after Joey was born, he spent the night over here with Sean and they thought I was asleep. Chris told Sean about the night Joey's dad left. He was fighting with Julie so loud, neither of them heard Joey crying, so Chris went in, got him from his crib and rocked him to sleep. When he woke up in the morning, Joey's dad was gone and Julie was making waffles with whipped cream, sprinkles and ice cream for breakfast, saying how great it was going to be, just the three of them, on their own.

'At least you don't have to worry about calling off work, then.' I try to channel Julie's positive thinking, but the words taste sour, wrong.

'Yeah.' His resigned tone definitely suggests he'd rather have something to do than sit on a couch.

He's as restless as I am. I hate knowing I could be productive instead of lying around like I do when a migraine strikes. Will I have to sit around even more during treatment? For how long?

No, think about anything else.

'Have the police called with any updates?'

'They've officially ruled it a homicide.'

I've been thinking of it that way since Dominic and I found the disconnected dryer hose, but hearing it declared by the authorities is like hearing my diagnosis for the first time: the only logical explanation and yet unfathomable.

Sierra's article is still in my DMs when I unlock my phone. The similarities to Julie's story unnerve me: homeowner found dead in house filled with gas. Except this one ended more gruesomely with a spark igniting and causing an explosion.

'You left right after your mom and Joey did, right? At what time?'

He pops his earbuds into their case. 'Six-thirty? Ish?'

'But you didn't smell anything in the house then? Or see anyone nearby?'

'No. Nothing. I already told the police that.' His words hang in the air as limply as his hands hang at his side. 'Later, I walked in, smelled the gas, saw my phone on the table, saw . . . them—' It's hard for him to say, like he's flashing back to the images of Julie on the floor and Joey on the stairs before he passed out. 'Then I called 911. I already told the police all of this.'

'I feel like there's something missing. Do you know when the dryer was last used?'

'The police asked me that too,' he huffs. 'Like no one believes me when I say I don't know anything.'

'What? No—'

Chris's phone buzzes again, and this time he holds it up while '*County Police Department*' scrolls across the screen. 'And they keep calling with more questions and asking me to come in. I keep saying the same thing!'

'Chris, I—'

'I don't know anything else!' His voice sounds like it's clawing through a straw to escape. 'Don't you think I want to know why my mom died? Don't the police know I would help if I could? I helped her do the dishes after every meal.' He points to his chest. 'I brought the mail in for her every day since I was four just so she had one less thing to worry about. They never saw the way I still hugged her good night before I went to bed even though I'm nearly eighteen. They never saw the cards I wrote to her on her birthday that made her cry. Why don't they get that I have nothing else to give them? I would die for my family! I almost did.'

His shoulders heave like he just finished a round in a boxing ring, and his statement hits like an uppercut to my jaw.

'I know. You always put your family first. I believe you.'

'Then why doesn't Detective Peterson?'

'Because he's a constipated nutcracker.'

And just like that, the fight drains out of him and he barks out a laugh, the first one I've heard in days.

'How does that even work? Does that mean he can't, like' – he swipes at his nose and then mimes using a nutcracker – 'crush walnuts, or after he eats them, he can't—'

I throw a pillow at him. 'The point is, I'm not an idiot like he is, but I do want to figure out what happened.' I pass Chris my phone. 'My friend Sierra sent me this article.'

'I think I heard about that fire, yeah.' Chris scrolls through the rest before passing it back.

'I hadn't considered the house could have been destroyed,' I say.

'Trust me, I wish it had.'

If it was between his mom and the house, of course he'd rather lose everything else. I clear my throat, not sure how to respond other than to plough forward. 'It got me thinking. I mean, Springtown is less than an hour from here. It's not that far.'

'What are you getting at?'

'They could be connected. There could be more.'

'Like a serial killer? It says the guy who died in the explosion is the one who filled the house with gas. Whether he did it on purpose or not, I don't think he's responsible here.'

'Yeah, but maybe the police got it wrong. Maybe that's what this serial killer does – tries to make it look like an accident and you ruined his plans by coming home, or I did by showing up.'

'Or the police got it wrong *this time*. It could all be an accident. You don't believe someone could really want us dead, do you?'

'That's my point. It could be someone who didn't know her at all, some psycho who's been going undetected. There could be more victims out there.'

'I don't know.'

'Why not? It's a possibility, right? More believable than someone who knows her wanting her dead.'

He picks up his phone and Hank removes his head from his lap. 'I'm supposed to report to the station to answer more questions. I'll toss out the theory and see what Detective Peterson says.'

He doesn't sound convinced.

Chris has barely left the room when Joey walks in. He and Chris were both asleep when we left for my appointment this morning. I note that Joey is still wearing his pyjamas, but if Mom doesn't care enough to make him change, I'm not about to. I think I wore the same sweatshirt for three months in sixth grade.

'Have you seen my dad?' I ask instead.

Joey plops onto the couch next to Hank and pets him, though the dog doesn't even reward his efforts with a tail wag. 'He said he had to go grocery shopping.'

'Oh yeah, I remember him saying that last night. Hey, let's do something fun!' I jump to my feet on the couch. 'Sledding? Dance party?'

Joey blinks at me.

'Or . . . we have some paper plates. We can make animal masks and pretend we're in the jungle.'

'Maybe later.'

I fall back on the couch with a soft *fwump*. Aunt Julie always made the whole cheering-up-a-sad-kid thing seem easy.

'Where's Chris?' Joey asks.

'He's helping the police figure out what happened to your mom.'

As soon as I mention the police, Joey's full attention goes to scratching Hank's ears.

'That one policeman yelled a lot at the house. I don't like yelling.'

'Who? Detective Peterson?' He was pretty mad that someone made a mistake in clearing the house without flagging the dryer, but I don't know if I would call it a lot . . .

'Marshal used to yell.'

'Who's Marshal?'

'Mom's other boyfriend.'

'Other boyfriend? Not Blake?'

'Before Blake.'

'Oh,' I exhale, glad to hear Julie wasn't cheating. I thought I knew her better than that, and I'm glad I'm right.

'Who did he yell at?'

'At stuff. Like the door if it didn't shut right, or the TV if his team made him mad.'

'Did he ever yell at you or Chris?'

'Only Mom, but then we didn't see him anymore.'

'What do you mean?'

'He and Mom yelled a lot one day and then he left. Mom said he wasn't coming back anymore.'

Hmm, maybe a serial killer is statistically improbable like Chris said. An ex-boyfriend after a messy breakup, on the other hand . . .

'Do you remember anything else about him, his last name?'

'He played hockey.'

The police keep bugging Chris, and they don't see how much it's tearing him apart – he keeps that hidden from anyone he doesn't trust. But like him, I can't sit here and do nothing while someone in my family is hurting.

'Could you tell the police about that fight? About what you remember?'

Joey freezes. 'I don't want to,' he says, and his chin wobbles.

'It's okay, it's okay.' I pat his knee.

I run a search on my phone for Marshal, our county and hockey, and get a name from the local paper in an article about a team winning sectionals last year and the coach's name: Marshal Voight.

He has no social media, so he's either out of touch, anti-screens or very private.

I put his name back in Google and click images. The third row forces me to hold in a gasp.

'Is that him?' I show Joey the picture.

'Yeah.'

It could be nothing. A coincidence. But something about the

black hoodie he's wearing in the picture – the way he holds his hands in the pocket, elbows out – reminds me of the figure I saw across the road from Julie's yesterday.

Detective Peterson was already sceptical when I mentioned the figure to him. I doubt a bad temper and a weird feeling because of a picture is enough to convince him.

Voight's team has a practice schedule posted online, and they'll be starting in twenty minutes.

I could make it there before practice is over.

Except I can't leave Joey here by himself.

I toss a pillow at Joey, his floppy hair falling across his forehead. 'Want to go ice skating?'

He shrugs, but it's not a no.

'Come on, we'll have fun,' I say, pulling him up with me.

And maybe I can give the police a name that will be more productive than pestering Chris.

10

January 3

'We have to wait for practice to be over before we can get on the ice,' I tell Joey. I haven't been inside this building in years, but it feels the same: thick layers of paint on the walls, a vending machine that looks old enough to be from the nineties, championship banners that haven't seen a victory in just as long.

'Do you think the police will find out who hurt my mom?' he asks.

'They're trying their best.'

Phase one of Operation Distraction is a fail.

Time to initiate Diversion Plan B. 'Have you ever played Skee-Ball?'

Joey lights up, and I feed a ten into the machine before it spits out a gaming card charged with tokens. The Skee-Ball is by the counter but still in view of the rink with the doors propped open.

'Swipe away. I'll be right over here.' I walk to the ice, listening to the steady *kshhhh, thud thud* of the ball rolling up the ramp and into the rings at the end. With Joey busy out here, he won't have to see Marshal and can avoid any bad memories of him too.

Players scrimmage, skating around in chaotic directions, which I'm sure are practised plays.

'KEEP UP! KEEP UP!' The scream comes from my right where a tall Asian man stands by the bench next to a couple players. Judging by the clipboard in his hand and the whistle around his neck, I've found Coach Marshal Voight.

Honestly, the idea of approaching him is terrifying, but if I can survive a brain tumour, if I can pull my cousins from a gas leak, I can do this, for Julie and for Chris.

'Excuse me,' I say, leaning over the edge of the players' box. He's even taller up close, especially elevated by skates.

Marshal ignores me or doesn't hear, too busy tracking his players on the ice. I repeat myself, louder.

He gives me a half glance and a distracted 'Huh?' before one of his players gets slammed into the plexiglass wall. 'Come on, Miller!' He slaps his clipboard against the railing. 'Don't let him get by you like that.' And number eight launches himself after the puck.

'Do you know Julie Forrester?' I blurt.

Now his neck jerks in my direction, and he evaluates me like competition in a game. 'Yeah, what about her?'

I haven't had to tell anyone else. Not like this. I square my shoulders. 'Did you know she died in her house three nights ago?'

He whispers a curse and shakes his head. 'I had no idea.'

Marshal's either really good at acting, or telling the truth; without social media, I can believe this is the first time he's hearing the news.

'How did she . . . what happened?' he asks.

'Gas leak.'

Another curse, this time louder. His players on the bench aren't interested in the scrimmage anymore.

'Do you know when the last time you saw her was?'

'What?'

'Were you near her house yesterday or on New Year's Eve?' I press.

He raises both hands defensively. 'Whoa, I don't know who you are, or who you *think* you are, but you're sniffing around the wrong tree.' His voice booms, every inch of his height shrinking me with its force. 'We only dated a few weeks, and I haven't seen her in months.'

'But you were at her house yesterday.' I'm sure of it now. He's wearing the same black hoodie and his height—

He leans in close. 'I run two and a half miles every day and run that route past her house three times a week, and if the real police ask me, I'll tell them the same thing, but right now, I've got a game to prepare for.'

He blows the whistle and circles his finger in the air, signalling the team to wrap it up. They funnel into the players' box. Outside the rink, Joey throws another ball up the ramp. *Ksshhhhh, thud thud*.

Voight's tone leaves me trembling. He's not scared to talk to the police, but that doesn't necessarily mean he's innocent.

It doesn't mean he's guilty either.

'Ella?'

Number eight steps aside from the stream flowing into the locker room and pulls off his helmet. With sweaty hair, a flushed face and skates raising him a few inches higher than usual, Dominic says, 'What are you doing here?'

'Talking to your coach, apparently. What're you—' But obviously he's practising hockey. I refocus. 'Did you know Voight dated Julie?'

The news pushes Dominic's head back on his shoulders. 'Really? When?'

'Some time between the Fourth of July and when school started.' That is, if what Joey said on the way over is accurate.

'So wait, why were you talking to him?'

'Well, he clearly has a temper and they had a bad breakup, and I thought . . .'

'You thought he had something to do with it?'

The shock in his voice makes me blush. 'It sounds stupid, I know.' What a waste of time.

Kshhhh, thud thud. At least Joey's having fun.

'Miller, let's go!' Marshal calls from down the hall, waving Dominic in.

'No, it doesn't,' Dominic says, whispering to me, 'It's always the boyfriend, right? Isn't that what they say?'

'Yeah, that's what I—'

'*Miller*, get in here now or you get ten laps.'

Dominic walks backwards towards his coach, marching awkwardly on his skates. 'You might be on to something. I'll be out after I clean up. Wait for me.'

Before I can respond, he's in the locker room and Voight's shutting the door behind him.

'Let me know if you need help putting those on.' I hand Joey a set of skates while we sit on the bleachers, trying to hide how much I'm buzzing wondering what Dominic will tell me. Running past Julie's house doesn't prove anything, but if Dominic knows something about his coach, he can bring it to the police and Joey won't have to talk to them at all.

Chris hasn't sent an update from his follow-up questions at the station, but he might be home by now.

How was it? I text him.

Glad it's over.

I suppose that means he's okay.

Did they know about the house in Springtown?

Silence.

Or he's not okay after all.

Dominic might have a lead for us, I say.

Dominic Miller? The guy who got kicked out of school? He was probably out partying all night on New Year's. What would he know about it?

Now I'm the one who doesn't respond, because I don't have an answer.

A few girls practise spins and a dad waddles along with his two young kids. One of the spinning girls with a long blonde ponytail stops and locks in on our position.

Kayla.

My closest friend before Sierra. She doesn't approach the bleachers, doesn't even wave. She tilts her chin higher and spins towards her friend.

She's obviously still mad I couldn't go to a concert for her birthday because a migraine crashed through my skull. When I called to cancel she accused me of faking it to get out of going. I can still hear her crying as she said, 'You could take an Advil if you really wanted to.' She iced me out after that, making sure I never had the chance to disappoint her again.

I could call her over and make her sink through the ice in shame in a single sentence: *I have a brain tumour and my aunt died because I couldn't save her.*

But if she knew I was walking around with a tumour, she'd probably assume I shouldn't be on the ice, think I was too fragile to keep living a normal life. I shouldn't have to explain that Dr Gupta hasn't put any limitations on my physical activity so long as my migraines don't interfere. It's another reason to keep the news on a need-to-know basis.

Instead, I tighten my laces and grab my phone, like she hasn't hurt me too.

'How 'bout a race?' I step onto the ice. 'First one to the far side of the rink wins?'

'No,' Joey says, but half a second later, he's dashing ahead of me.

'Hey! You cheater,' I call, pushing to catch up, but also not pushing my hardest, only enough to make him chuckle in light of his victory. Kayla's across the rink with her other friend, and

I pretend they're not looking at me. By the time I reach our designated finish line, Joey is racing across the ice with a belly laugh.

'It's like I'm flying for real,' he calls, arms spread wide.

It's the perfect sound, angelic, over the slice of metal blades on the ice, even if I did have to get a stitch in my side to hear it. I prop my hands on my knees.

'Winded already?' Dominic glides lazily to my side.

'It's been a while since I last did this.' Kayla and her friend have disappeared, but the sour taste in my mouth lingers.

Dominic's wearing the same hat he wore yesterday and a hoodie with the logo of a team I don't recognise but probably should.

'So you think I might be on to something with your coach?'

We begin a steady pace around the rink. Joey hugs the side of the wall across the way and waves. It's best he's not within earshot.

'I can't stick around long,' he says, checking the time on his phone, 'but I know Voight didn't do it.'

'What? How?'

'The team had a party that night, at his house. That's where I was.'

An alibi. A solid one with roughly twenty-five witnesses.

And I was ready to call police based on a hunch.

I feel like such an idiot.

Not that Dominic needs to know. I gesture to the bruise on his face. 'Is that from the party?'

'This? Overtime. Dude was mad I checked him earlier in the game.'

'So if your coach wasn't involved, what did you mean when you said I was on to someth—' My foot slides out from under me and my butt lands on the ice. Hard.

I try to push myself up but fall back again. 'Is that why you asked me to stay? To laugh at me?' I grumble.

'I'm not laughing.' While technically that's true, the smirk on his face is worse and it only highlights his dimple.

'You're not helping either.'

He crosses his arms. 'I've already learned you don't like asking for help.'

Knowing I'll only fall again if I don't, I grind my teeth and extend my hand. He clasps it and lifts me so easily, I nearly lose my balance again until I grab his forearm with my other hand. The result is both of us standing extremely close, our faces only a few inches apart, close enough I can smell the spring rain soap he must have showered with in the locker room.

'Thanks,' I say, stepping back and hoping the blush spreading up my neck is sufficiently covered by my scarf. 'You were going to tell me why you asked me to stick around.'

'You might be right that someone she knows is involved.'

'Really?' I lean with my elbows against the half wall around the rink, hoping to hide the fact that I'm catching my breath and my balance. 'Are you just being a good neighbour to help?'

He loops back around to my other side. 'The police had a few too many questions for my dad.'

'Your dad?'

'He works with gas lines, remember? So the police stopped by this morning and seemed a little too interested in him being home by himself that night.'

So Chris isn't the only one they're questioning.

'But there's no way he would hurt Julie or anybody,' Dominic adds quickly. 'He spent the night watching reruns of *The Office*. But after what happened with my mom, I'm not taking any chances.'

Before I can ask for details, my toe catches on the ice and I nearly tumble to the ground again. Dominic catches my elbow and gently stabilises me.

We're close again. Too close.

Under the guise of tightening my ponytail, I pull my arm away and glide farther from his side, asking, 'So if not your dad or Julie's ex, who are you thinking?'

'Her current boyfriend.'

'Blake?'

'I don't know his name, but I saw him parked in Julie's driveway at least once a week.'

Joey's thankfully still out of earshot. I type out a message to Chris: *Do you know where Blake was before he got 'sick' on New Year's Eve?*

Is Dominic suggesting him? Based on what evidence?

Before I can respond, he sends another. *Blake hasn't been around long, but he's looked out for us more than anyone else.*

He's not exactly willing to jump on this line of questioning, and I hear the undertone. Chris has never had a dad around, but the way Blake was comforting him at the police station the other day, maybe Chris wants to look at him like one.

'So, what do you think?' Dominic asks, checking the time again.

'I think we need some more information.' Voight's withering glare and the public audience of his team is not a level of humiliation I want to experience again.

'Then let's get some.' He's skating away backwards when he says, 'I have to help my dad at work for a bit, but I can meet up later tonight.'

'Do you want to call me or—'

'I already have your number,' he says.

'How?'

But he's either too far away to hear me or pretends he doesn't. 'I'll pick you up,' he calls.

I could skate after him, or leave now and . . . do what I'm not sure exactly, but as I watch Joey up ahead, arms outstretched, probably imagining himself as a pilot flying through the clouds, I plant my skates in the ice.

This is where I need to be right now.

I take another lap. For Joey.

11

January 3

Dominic drives us down the road, sun setting in the distance, when Sierra sends a text: *just checking in.*

I fight the impulse to read it as *I can't think of you without thinking of your messy life.* She's being a good friend, concerned, because of Julie and everything else with my health.

I only wish there wasn't an 'everything else' to filter through.

I snap a picture of Dominic behind the wheel, capturing his defining features nicely: his strong jaw and dark hair, skin a warm olive.

I send the image to Sierra with a quick explanation of the evening's plans. Mission Redirect the Conversation, engaged.

yessss. She immediately responds. *wait, did you say stake out or make out?*

Direct hit. It feels good to smile after the last few days.

'Is that Chris?' Dominic asks.

'No, just a friend being ridiculous. Hey, how come you and Chris don't hang out anymore?' After Chris went on high alert when he saw Dominic with me at the house, and his reaction to me mentioning him with the Blake theory, I thought it best not to tell him my evening plans.

'When we were thirteen, Chris and I were on the wrestling team together.' He swallows, deciding something. 'Until I got kicked off the team for stealing money from the coach's office.'

'Oh.'

'Don't I look like the thieving type?' The way he says it, he expects me to say yes, like other people have told him that before, like I'm supposed to be unsurprised because he stole my cupcake at the party.

'No. Is that why you were kicked out of school?'

'Uh, nope. That . . . that's a different story. So you successfully convinced me to drive you out here. Are you going to explain what you expect to find?'

'It was your idea to drive by Blake's house.'

'Okay, yes, but it was *your* idea that you let me think was *my* idea.'

I turn away, like his dimple has no effect on me. Definitely no effect. 'It's fine. Accepting was a cheap excuse for a ride.'

'Oh,' he smirks. 'Okay, sure.'

'It's part of paying off your debt for that cupcake.'

'Would it help if I said the cupcake wasn't for me?' His tone grows serious. 'Joey wasn't even two and he dropped his on the floor. I got him another one so he wouldn't cry.'

'Wow, giver of rides and rescuer of toddlers.' Except I can't quite manage the sarcasm I'm aiming for. He may have broken some rules and been suspended, but he's not a mess like Chris says.

Considering how much of my life *is* a mess, I'd say I'm a reliable judge.

'There, I think that's it.' We approach a faded yellow duplex with an eagle painted on the mailbox and an American flag flapping next to the garage.

'75663,' I read off from the second page of Google search results. It's legitimately terrifying how easy it is to find someone's address online.

'Yup, that's it.' He points to the numbers on the mailbox.

'Is he home?'

'I can't tell.'

'Well, should we stop and wait to see if he's there or if he leaves?'

'I thought you were a regular Nancy Drew. You can't park right in front of the house you're staking out.'

'So we circle the block and park a few houses down?'

'Better. We park right . . .' Dominic twists in his seat for a better view out the back window. 'Abooooout here.'

He shifts the car into park, satisfied.

I rotate to look over my shoulder at the yellow house three doors down.

'How are we going to see him? Isn't it going to look even more suspicious if we're looking out our back window?'

'It *would* look suspicious, if that was the plan.' He pushes some buttons on the car door, and something catches the light.

The side-view mirror moves, and when it stops, the yellow house is framed directly in my line of vision.

'Okay, Columbo.'

'Do you even know who that is?' he asks.

'No, but the mystery reference fits, right? Doesn't it?'

'I don't know,' he laughs. I'm rewarded with another flash of his dimple. Ugh, why does that feel like such a victory?

'So how did you get my number? Did Chris give it to you?'

'The real mystery isn't how I got it, but when.' He hangs his head in shame. 'Your number's been in my phone for almost five years.'

'You're lying,' I say, but it comes out as a laugh.

'I don't lie anymore.' He raises one hand in a scout's honour, but he's holding up the wrong number of fingers. 'I asked Chris for it after the party, but I was too chicken to ever use it.'

Too-cool-for-me Dominic wanted my number even with my frizzy hair and my losing streak in Mario Kart.

I clear my throat and stare seriously ahead. 'It's a good thing you waited. I was still mad at you for stealing my cupcake.'

'Does that mean I'm forgiven?'

'Maybe.'

I scope out the modest homes nearby. 'How do we even know if he's home?' The neighbourhood looks nice enough. Quiet.

'That's part of a stakeout. Blake might take out the trash or destroy evidence or throw a suitcase in the car and try to drive off into the sunset. We have to wait and see.'

'I've never been very good with waiting. Here.' I pull out my phone. 'I did a search for him on Google, and nothing came up besides his work website, the obituary for his mother and his LinkedIn.'

'I don't understand LinkedIn. Why do old people need another social media?'

'It's all work-related. But that's beside the point. Since it's public and has his work history, we know he began working for Edwin Haines last year.'

'The finance place?'

'They specialise in investments, yeah. My math teacher's husband works for them and he came in at the end of last year to talk about math in his job. He said it's pretty hard to get started, but knowing teachers get paid crap and judging from the vacation pictures Mrs Rice showed us, once you're established like her husband, these guys can make bank.'

'So Blake is on his path to financial security. How does that help us?'

'It doesn't, except he's not listed on their website.'

'Does that mean he lied on his LinkedIn?'

'I don't think so. Because he is listed on this archived newsletter from September, but then in October, he's only listed as a junior agent.'

'He got demoted?'

'I don't know. He could have lost a big client or messed up an important account or something.'

He picks at a piece of skin around his nail. 'What does Chris think about all this?'

'Still in shock, I think. You guys used to be really close, huh?'

'We both only had one parent around.'

'Wait, please tell me you planned a parent trap to get your single parents together. Please.'

He scrunches his face at the ceiling. 'I'm not *not* saying it.'

I squeal. 'How old were you?'

'I dunno. Ten? Old enough to realise that a plot involving some anonymous flowers and homemade brownies wasn't going to cut it. Especially when we didn't know how to bake.'

'Stop it. You were going to deliver brownies like Julie made them for your dad?'

His nose scrunches up in a clear confession. Somehow this feels like a more intimate secret than his problems at school.

'That's adorable.'

'Well, after getting in trouble for making a mess in his kitchen, we pretended the whole idea never happened. I haven't spoken about it in years, and *you*,' he says, pointing at me, 'better not bring it up again.'

I grab his finger and twist it out of my face. 'I would never!'

'Pinky promise?' he asks. I maintain direct eye contact when I wrap my little finger around his. The sun has sunk below the horizon, leaving us surrounded by darkness.

'Pinky promise.'

His eyes are a light shade of brown, and with the streetlights flicking on, they glow like honey. In the confines of the car, the rest of the world does not exist. I want to bottle this feeling and save it, take a dose whenever I need it as easily as I take my pain prescription.

'My mom left a few years before that birthday party,' Dominic says, dropping my finger.

Chris has been struggling with his own loss, and obviously his experience isn't the same as Dominic's, but I don't know what to say to either one of them.

'I'm sorry' is all that comes out. It's not enough.

'Don't be. My mom is responsible for her own choices. Or at least, that's what I learned at Alateen.'

'What's that?'

'Alateen? It's a younger version of Al-Anon.' He must read my confusion. 'A support group for family members of alcoholics.'

'Oh, wow. Did it help?'

'I didn't go at first. Not until after I punched a guy for saying she probably didn't "leave", and my dad was just hiding the body.' He raises his finger in the air. '*That's* why I got kicked out of school. And why I want to make sure no one starts rumours about my dad again.'

'Jeez, why would someone joke about that?'

'No one else knew my mom was an alcoholic. She kept up appearances until one day she was gone. I guess it was easier for people to believe my dad had something to do with it.'

Dominic talks like he has no secrets, no fear of judgement for my reaction. How does someone get to be that way?

Headlights flood the car, and we both jump.

'Someone's coming – no, don't turn around.' Dominic has

already slipped down in his seat when he grabs my arm. I spin forward and slink down next to him, peeking into the side mirror as a four-door Nissan pulls into Blake's driveway.

A woman checks her appearance in her mirror, floofs her hair and walks out. She's wearing kitten heels and a tight pencil skirt. A silky green shirt flashes from under her coat before she draws a hood over her head against the cold.

'Who is that?' I whisper.

By the time she reaches the door, Blake opens it, stepping aside for her to enter.

'He was expecting her,' Dominic says.

'A friend?' As much as I try to squeeze a note of hope into my voice, I can't quite manage it. This does not look promising.

Dominic tries to raise one brow and fails horribly, but the sentiment is clear: he's as sceptical as I am.

Blake wraps his arms around her before they step inside, and my jaw drops.

What kind of jerk gets over his dead girlfriend in less than a week? I know they hadn't been together that long, but come on. He can at least pretend to be upset for appearances.

'Now what?' Dominic asks.

'Her car lights didn't flash when she got out.'

'So?'

'So her car's not locked. Hold on.'

'What are you doing?' Dominic sits straighter in his seat and mumbles a curse just as I shut the door behind me.

I almost crouch low before deciding that it would look more

suspicious to any nosy neighbours who might be spying out their windows. I should have double-checked because someone jogs down the street with her dog.

Who jogs in the middle of winter? Isn't that what treadmills are for? Given that she's out here, you'd think she'd be committed enough to stay focused and keep moving. Maybe because she doesn't recognise the car or because I'm now standing in the middle of the road, she slows and says, 'Do you need something? Are you lost?'

'Oh, um, I'm selling wrapping paper for um—' What extracurricular is always raising money? 'The band. Would you like to buy any?'

Her eyes glaze over at the word '*selling*', and her 'No, thank you' comes while checking her watch. She's already moving along. I flash Dominic a thumbs-up while he gives a panicked wave, calling me back to the car. I slow my pace until the jogger has rounded the corner, confirm there's no movement at Blake's front door, and swing around the passenger side of the mystery woman's car.

The front handle pops open with ease.

12

January 3

I never knew there could be such a rush from breaking into someone's car. Except I'm not *breaking* exactly. More like *sneaking*. I'm sneaking into her car for one piece of information. That's all I need.

Though there's still a small twinge of nausea at the possibility of being caught.

Blake's house remains quiet. That woman could stay inside for hours.

Or minutes.

Focus.

I need a name.

The car is a mess. The black leather is barely visible through the scattered papers and discarded plastic bottles.. Using my knuckle, I press the release for the glove compartment. A white registration card sits on top.

Perfect.

Phone ready, I snap a picture and shut the door behind me, careful not to slam it.

Every muscle in Dominic's body is coiled tightly when I slip back into his car.

'Someone could have seen you!' His head whips around to all the windows, but the street is empty.

I can't ignore the excitement, the thrill.

'Why are you whispering? I didn't take anything. Except this picture.'

Curiosity wins, because instead of arguing his point, Dominic squints at the zoomed-in image of the car's registration. 'I don't recognise that name, do you?'

'Nicki Davis.' I swipe to my internet browser and type it in. 'Her LinkedIn says she's been with Statewide Mutual for the last five years.'

'Wait, the guys with the commercial? The one with the jingle?'

'No, the one with the gimmicky spokesperson.'

'But an insurance agent?'

I scroll. 'Auto, home, life . . . looks like they have it all.'

'Does her LinkedIn have a list of clients? She could be Blake's agent.'

I click around a few places. 'I don't see it. It's probably some kind of legal liability with confidentiality or against company policy or something.'

'It's still a possibility. She could be his insurance agent.'

'It's 8 p.m.'

'They could be going over his policy.'

'Is that what the youths are calling it these days?'

His face contorts in disgust. 'Better not be.'

'We might be able to find her on Facebook.'

'Ah, Facebook. The original old-people social media.' He clicks away on his phone. 'Wait, this looks like her . . . never mind. Her account's set to private.'

'Do a search for her name and Statewide Mutual.'

It's only another second before he says, 'Wait, this is something. Posted by a . . . Sarah Troyer.'

'Am I supposed to know who that is?'

He hands me his phone.

Sarah Troyer does not have her account set to private at all. In fact, it looks like every single post is set to public, from Christmas cartoons to retail rants. 'She's quite a firecracker. Looks like she's the sister of – whoa. Okay, her brother-in-law died when his house exploded from a gas leak.'

'No way that's a coincidence.'

'Sarah Troyer's post is all about how Statewide Mutual has been so difficult to deal with and telling anyone who has that insurance to drop them and find coverage somewhere else.'

'Of course she did. Did the post get any traction?'

'Four likes and three comments, and two of those are from her.'

Dominic makes an ouch face.

'She seems to have a complaint every other day.' I scroll up and down. 'Everything from customer service workers to a bad landscape job. But the majority of this particular rant focuses on her brother-in-law's assets being locked up because he had paperwork saying he had more insurance on the house than the company had record of.'

'Sketchy.'

'Very sketchy. And she names Nicki Davis as the insurance agent on the paperwork.' I hand him back his phone and type the guy's name into mine. 'Wait. This is the guy in Sierra's article, the explosion in Springtown last month.'

'So you're telling me Nicki Davis was the insurance agent for a house that blew up from a gas leak about a month ago in a town almost an hour away, and now she's in the house of the guy who was dating your aunt, whose house also filled with gas four days ago.'

'This is what I'm telling you, yes.'

'Wow.'

'I know, right? Two deadly leaks in the same month? It's way too convenient to not be connected. Detective Peterson said minor gas leaks can happen without anyone suspecting, but these weren't minor.'

'Except,' Dominic adds, 'one was ultimately a fire, so there's that big difference.'

'Unless the first one wasn't meant to explode and that part was an accident?'

Dominic looks sceptical but seems reluctant to voice it.

A porch light behind us flicks on and we jump like bottle rockets on the Fourth of July. Blake's front door opens again. Nicki leans in for a hug and gives him a swift kiss on the cheek.

'Did you see that?' Dominic asks, as if my eyebrows raised up to my hairline don't answer his question. What if Blake didn't get over Julie that fast? What if he was with her before?

A throbbing spikes through my head.

I snatch my phone and type to Chris, *Do you think Blake was cheating on your mom?* but delete it before I hit send. That's not a text. That's a whole conversation. Instead, I ask, *Does the name Nicki Davis mean anything to you?*

His response is almost immediate. *No.*

'Chris hasn't heard of Nicki Dav—' but another text comes through.

Wait. Your dad's been on the phone with her twice today. That's my mom's insurance agent.

'She's Julie's insurance agent,' I say.

'So is Blake another client?'

'Do insurance agents usually kiss their clients?'

Dominic doesn't need to answer.

As much as I hate it, I'm going to have to tell Chris about this. Not via text, though.

The edges of a migraine creep in. It's coming on fast and hard. I fight to ignore it. This is too important.

Chris sends another text. *Where are you?*

I'll tell you later, I fire off, squeezing the bridge of my nose and praying for relief.

'Are you okay?' Dominic asks.

'I'll be fine.' I rub my temples, talking through the pain. 'Migraine. I get them sometimes. It's worse when I haven't been sleeping well and—'

Knock knock knock

Dominic jumps so high, his head nearly bumps the ceiling of

the car, and I audibly gasp. We were both so focused on Chris's messages that we didn't notice a man approaching Dominic's door, a man now gesturing for him to roll down the window. Dominic complies.

The man bends, leaning his elbow on the car. His hair is dark and curly but gelled back so it looks permanently wet. His cheeks are round and tinted pink, but there's no mistaking that baby face with his dark eyes.

Blake Bartnicky, hair styled as precisely as it is in his LinkedIn profile, stands on the street next to us, three doors down from his house.

'Looks like your tire's a little flat there,' he says, gesturing to the rear tire on Dominic's side.

'Oh, is it? I'll get that checked out,' Dominic replies. Behind us, Nicki Davis opens and shuts her passenger door. It must not have latched when I took the picture.

Does she know someone was in it? Does she know it was someone in this car? Me? My heart pounds against my ribs, and I nearly gasp again when my phone buzzes and buzzes and buzzes. Chris is calling. I flip the screen over, hiding the name.

Blake leans closer and squints at me. 'Ella? What are you doing here?'

'I, uh—'

Blake's eyes flick between me and Dominic and narrow. Only then does a smile slide up his face, stiff and cold and haunting.

'Checking in on me?' He chuckles, and it's warm enough to

make me doubt my perceptions. 'That's very kind of you, but I told you at the station I'm feeling much better.'

I have to know if he's genuine.

'Good, good. Glad your stomach's better. How're you dealing with the loss of Julie?'

Dominic's head whips towards me so fast I'm surprised his wide eyes don't pop out. He's screaming at me to back off, but I have to know.

Blake's silent, our gazes unbreaking. What's he thinking behind that poker face?

'I'm sure I'm doing about as well as you: wishing I could go back and do that night differently. Guess it's just a lesson for the rest of us.' He pauses, runs his tongue over his teeth. 'To be extra careful.'

Is that a threat?

And then he steps back, his shoulders relaxed, intensity gone so quickly I have to question if I saw it at all. 'That's why you better get the tire checked out.' He pats the hood of the car as he walks backwards.

'Y-yes, sir,' Dominic says. 'Thanks for letting me know.' Dominic rolls up the window and puts the car in drive as he says, 'Have a nice night.' The window closes as Dominic drives away.

Blake stands in the middle of the street, glaring after us.

13

January 3

'You sure you're okay?' Dominic asks on the drive home.

'Yeah. I'm fine.' The words aren't at all convincing. Between the oncoming migraine and the possibility that Blake really is behind Julie's death, nothing could be further from the truth.

I climb out of the car anyway with a wave.

For an hour – in his car, pinky locked in his, excitement thrumming – I'd forgotten. Escaped.

Until the migraine locked me back in reality, my tumour jangling the keys.

After taking a dose of medication, I go straight to my room. Sierra sends some messages hinting at her stress for the SAT coming in March. I should be inviting her to unload instead of crawling into bed.

I toss and turn.

I need to figure out how to tell the police what we discovered about Nicki Davis without admitting to breaking into her car.

How to tell Chris about Blake cheating on his mom without devastating him.

How to be the friend Sierra deserves.

But I can't focus on any of it until I escape the pain.

January 4

I wake up to a text from Dominic asking to hang out later and one from Mom, which I respond to first. She asks, *Want me to bring lunch home for you?*

Always. Where are you? Mom and Dad have both taken a bereavement week, so they're not at work.

Her reply comes when I'm halfway down the stairs. *Dad's checking in at the office. I'm running errands. The suit you brought home for Joey is too small. I need something else for the viewing on Saturday.*

Joey must be with her. Poor kid, trying on clothes for his mom's funeral in three days.

Let him wear something comfortable . . . more him.

That's a good thought.

A throbbing begins between my temples. It's small, only spiking when I move my eyeballs, and it's hard to tell if the aura's left over from last night, or if it means a new one will pounce today. I can't suffer through another one, not when I've already missed so many dance practices and the recital is a little over a week away.

The kitchen cabinet holds my meds, and I cradle the little bottle beneath my chin. I don't want to take them unless this really is a migraine. I could wait it out. If it's anxiety, sometimes clutching the bottle delivers a placebo effect: the pills are here, within reach, so there's no need to turn into a full-fledged migraine.

I clutch the bottle tighter.

Social media usually offers a good distraction, but when I see a new message request and open it, my hands go slack.

I know what you're doing. Stop, before you hurt yourself. Or before I have to make you.

What the—?

The pill bottle falls to the counter with a clatter. My head snaps to the kitchen window, half expecting to see someone standing along the property line, watching me.

Cold sweat breaks across my forehead while I read the message again. The words don't fully make sense, no matter how many times I read them.

Three sentences have never felt more sinister.

The account doesn't have a profile picture, and the username is Kevin with a string of numbers after it, so it may not even be a real name. They aren't following anyone and have no followers. I almost delete the message, pretend it didn't happen and doesn't exist, but the account was created with one purpose: to send me this private DM.

And I'm pretty sure I know who sent it.

I screenshot the message to the only person who knows Blake saw me last night.

Dominic's replies come through immediately.

Wait

What?

Who sent this?

When did you get it?

Chris walks into the kitchen and opens the fridge, pulling out a gallon of milk.

'El? Can you grab me a bowl?'

'Huh? I, oh . . .'

I hand him a plate from the cabinet, which he accepts with a funny look.

'What's the matter? What's wrong?'

'I—' Words fail. I flip over my phone so he can read the message himself. His face runs through a storm of warring emotions: confusion in his brow to surprise in his eyes, disgust on his lips.

'What is this? A joke? What kind of sicko sends this?'

'I – I don't think it's a joke.' As much as I'd like to believe this is some rando trying to troll me, the timing is too specific to be coincidence.

'What does it mean, *I know what you're doing*? What do they want you to stop?'

'There's only one thing I can think of, and it involves the gas leak and Blake Bartnicky.'

Chris blinks in stunned silence before saying, 'What did you do?'

'Dominic and I went to Blake's house last night to stake him out.'

'What? Why? He was my mom's boyfriend. He wouldn't do anything to hurt her. He . . . You have no idea what he's done, or been willing to do.'

'So you don't think he sent this?' I raise my phone.

'No. Even if you were creeping on him, why would Blake be contacting you? Threatening you?'

'He might if he thought I was getting too close to something.'

'He – he's been nice, always helping us.'

'Helping how?'

'I don't know – doing chores, putting up Christmas lights, patching the leaky roof, fixing the—'

Chris stops, but it's too late.

'Was Blake the one who tried to fix the furnace?'

He doesn't answer directly, but his response is confession enough. 'That wasn't the major source of the gas leak,' he says. 'The police determined the dryer was.'

'But what if the furnace was a decoy?'

'What do you mean?'

I pace, the pieces locking into place.

'What if Blake knew about those minor leaks and knew they'd look accidental, that there was proof your mom knew about them and didn't fix them properly? What if he banked on police stopping their search for a gas leak once they saw the furnace leak – which they did – so he could disconnect the dryer hose and actually deliver a lethal amount?'

'No way. Blake wouldn't do that.'

'I know he's been nice to have around and he seemed

supportive at the police station, but who else would? Who else had access to your house?'

'Dominic.' The name slaps me into silence. 'You said he still had a key to my house, and he knows about gas lines. I told you he got kicked out of school—'

'Yeah, and he told me it was for fighting, but—'

'Did he tell you he got caught stealing? I was there when he got caught and I almost took the blame.'

'I—'

'Did he tell you he hit a hockey puck through the back window of my car and refused to pay the damages?'

'No, but, Chris, he's different now. He—'

'This was last month, Ella.'

Last month? Dominic suggested their problems were from junior high. Why would he hide something like that?

'Even so,' I say, pushing down my surprise. 'Those things don't mean he's capable of *murder*.'

'What about his dad? His mom disappeared a few years ago, and no one ever heard from her again.'

'That's not fair,' I growl. Dominic might have played it off like it doesn't bother him anymore, but he wouldn't have punched anyone if his mom's choice to leave didn't gut him, and I won't let Chris use a vicious rumour against him. 'What would his motive be?'

'I don't know, but it wasn't Blake. Why would he?'

I hesitate. Admitting Blake might have cheated on her would mean Julie's happiness wasn't real. Chris obviously looks up to and trusts this guy, and if I tell him, I'm the one tearing it down.

'I don't think you want to know.'

'Know what? El?' When I turn away, he grabs my arm, gently but firmly. 'Know what? Tell me.'

This could be the piece that convinces him. This could destroy any last hope he has of Blake being the upstanding guy he believes him to be. After a deep breath, I tell him what we saw: Nicki pulling up in a car, walking to the front door, leaving with a kiss.

'You're wrong.'

'Chris, I'm so sorry. I didn't want to tell you.'

'You're wrong.'

His words express doubt, but there's no mistaking the fury radiating off his body.

'I'm so sorry,' I repeat. 'She deserved better.'

He rakes his hands through his hair. 'You can't know anything for certain.'

I sigh. 'You're right, I can't. But the police can, and I'm calling to let them know.'

'Why?'

'Because—'

'He couldn't do this. You're wrong about him. You don't know him like I do.'

'What did he do that could make you ignore this?'

'He was there for us! He was responsible, and he helped Mom get organised so I didn't always have to.'

'So that means he can do no wrong? Look at the facts, Chris!' How can he still be defending him? My voice rises, desperate for the truth to sink in, to destroy this stupid wall of denial he's built up. 'What don't you get? He cancelled plans with your mom to make sure she was home! The woman he was with last night? Nicki Davis? She's connected to the other gas leak, and that can't be a coincidence.'

'It has to be. It has to be a coincidence because—'

'Because why?' I shout. 'Explain it to me.'

He yells back, 'Because the alternative is that Blake was trying to kill my mom!'

His mouth presses into a hard line, nostrils flared, chin crumpling. He turns his back on me and sucks in a deep breath, before shakily releasing it, and I know if he was facing me, I'd see the budding tears.

'But,' I whisper, 'someone *was* trying to kill your mom, Chris. Why not Bl—'

He spins around, whatever grief he was feeling wiped out. His voice is firm, clear. 'We don't know what happened that night, okay? The police are investigating.'

'They are,' I say gently, 'so we should make sure they have all the facts. Getting a message like this the day after he catches me outside his house doesn't make him look innocent.'

'There's still no motive. He and my mom weren't having any problems. They'd only been dating a few months. Everything was great! He was the first nice guy she'd met in a long time.'

'I know, I know. But the truth is no one can really know

what a relationship is like except for the two people who are in it.'

I take him through the journey on LinkedIn and Facebook, tracing the lines that connect Blake to Nicki to the house that exploded in Springtown.

'The police should know.'

'They probably already do.'

'Then there's no harm in me calling them.' I take out my phone to look up the number for Peterson's station.

'Ella, you can't. Please.' Chris is on his feet, hands wrapped around mine, begging.

'Don't you want to find out who killed your mom?'

'Of course I do, but I . . . I can't lose you too.' At the desperation in his voice, my tears well, and Chris looks away, like he can't bear the sight of me crying over him but also can't stop. 'If that threat really is from Blake like you say it is, then if he finds out you're talking to police, there's no telling what he'll do. I care about you, Ella. I don't have a lot of family left, and I don't want to see you get hurt.'

'Chris, I—'

The doorbell rings and Hank barks while racing to the front door, cutting me off from a decision. Hank skids to a halt in the foyer.

'Are you expecting a package?' Chris asks.

I tuck my hair behind my ear and wipe my cheeks. 'I don't think so.'

Three loud knocks come next, the last two almost entirely drowned out by Hank's barks.

'Hank,' I scold, restraining him by his collar. 'It's okay.'

I crack the door.

As if summoned by our argument, two officers stand side by side.

14

January 4

I gape, confused. What are the police doing here if I didn't call them? Perhaps they put together the same suspicions I already had about Blake and want to let Chris know in person. But on closer inspection, only Peterson is a cop. The other man's in a suit, not a uniform. He's tall, maybe six and a half feet, and bald.

'Detective Peterson, I—'

Chris is at my side instantly. He ignores my dumbfounded expression, my silent plea for him to understand I didn't summon them. Instead, he opens the door wider, revealing the duo. Hank goes wild, tail beating against my leg and panting to reach the visitors.

'Chris Dempsey?' the stranger asks.

'That's me.'

'May we come in?' Detective Peterson says. 'We have a few questions for you.'

His words set me on edge. Questions? 'My parents aren't home right now.'

'Oh, that's fine.' Peterson offers congenially, pretending not to notice my stiff spine. 'We're not here to speak to them, and Chris, you've just turned eighteen, right?'

It's . . . it's the fourth. I completely forgot Chris's birthday.

'Sorry to have to take up your time on your special day.' He steps forward, out of the January winds, but I'm frozen, mouth hanging in horror at my lapse.

Chris waves me off, like he's reading my mind. He steps aside for both men to enter.

'Who are you?' he asks of the tall man, taking his business card in return and shaking his hand, like he's practising to accept his diploma at graduation.

'Scott Langdon.' Hank sniffs at the men, who pet him and scratch behind his ears, putting me at ease. 'I'm with Statewide Mutual,' Scott continues. 'I'm here to talk to you about Julie Forrester's life insurance benefits.'

Statewide Mutual. That's where Nicki Davis works. Do they know about her connections to Blake?

Chris frowns at the card. 'Insurance investigator?'

'Scott's an old friend of mine,' Peterson explains, while I shut the door behind them. 'A retired detective from the force. When he said he was having trouble reaching you, I thought we'd swing by.'

'I've been trying to call you this last week,' Langdon adds.

'Oh. That was you.' Chris examines the card, like he's trying to figure out where this conversation could go. 'Sorry, I don't pick up unknown numbers.'

The calls Chris has ignored on his phone while trying to call Blake, while on the couch – it was this guy. Persistent.

'I have some questions for you, sir, before we finalise the paperwork.' Langdon lifts his briefcase higher, away from Hank's curious nose. 'Is there somewhere we can sit?'

'Oh, sure,' Chris says.

'Come on, Hank. Come,' I say, leading us through the foyer to the kitchen table, desperate to hear what these men know. If they have enough pieces, I might not have to confess going into Nicki's car at all.

The man takes a seat and rubs his tongue over his teeth. 'As I said, I'm Scott Langdon, and you are?' he addresses me.

'Ella. Julie was my aunt. Um, Detective Peterson, did you—' Chris shoots me a look. The message is clear in the tightness of his jaw. He's scared for me, of what that threat might mean if I don't keep my nose clean.

'Did you want some pretzels,' I finish, dumping a bag into a bowl and bringing it to the table. 'Something to drink?' Hank settles in a pile at the base of my chair with a soft *fwump*, but Chris doesn't relax.

When Peterson declines, I make the same offer to Langdon.

'No, thank you.' He clears his throat. 'My job is to look into new claims, verifying information and getting everything organised.'

'Isn't Nicki Davis Julie's agent?' I ask, avoiding Chris's eye.

'Yes,' Langdon says, 'but her role focuses more on coverage and customer service.'

'She covers the whole region, right? Even Springtown?'

Even fixating on Peterson's moustache, I can feel Chris's eyes burning into the side of my face. The two men on the other side of the table exchange a coded glance.

'Yes, she does,' Langdon says.

'I only wondered if you knew about her, um, connection to Blake Bartnicky.'

'Ella,' Chris warns.

Peterson squints, and I can't tell if he's judging me or I'm confusing him. 'We're aware, yes.' He leans forward, hands folded on the table, and suddenly it feels like I'm in the principal's office. 'And you're aware that we won't be sharing details of an open investigation?'

'Yeah, of – of course.' If someone took a photograph of the room right now, I'm pretty sure I'd appear two inches tall.

Langdon continues as if there's been no interruption. 'My role is slightly different than Davis's. I only come in on certain claims.' Before either of us can ask what kind of claims those might be, he adds, 'Your mom had quite a few policies with us: home, life, car. Our records show she was in good health at the time of her death. I'm here because one of the things my company pays me to do is investigate insurance fraud. Do you know what that is?'

Chris's jaw clenches, but he doesn't answer.

'Fraud? You think Julie somehow cheated your company to get money?' But I don't say it like a genuine question. I say it like I'm asking, *You know she died, so what are you, stupid?*

Langdon doesn't take the bait. He doesn't even lean in or sit up straight. The guy is a rock.

Chris, on the other hand, says to me, 'You should go upstairs for a while.'

'I—'

'Please.'

And in that one word I know this has less to do with me and more to do with what he's afraid he's about to hear. The other gentlemen wait patiently, but I can't see what's on the horizon like Chris.

'Sure.' I excuse myself, taking the pretzels and Hank with me out of the kitchen and up the stairs.

But I don't climb the entire flight.

Langdon's voice drifts up, meeting me at my perch on the stairs. Hank's panting muffles bits of conversation until I scratch his ears.

'Most people with life insurance will take out a policy with us to cover their annual income for their family members in the case of death. They pay us monthly, and then we pay their families, or more specifically, their beneficiaries, when the time comes.'

I tap the word '*beneficiary*' into my phone, skipping the AI answer and scrolling for a credible source.

The person first in line to receive money from an insurance policy.

Langdon's still talking. 'Most times this is pretty cut-and-dried, and we're able to release funds to the beneficiaries promptly to help these families.' He pauses, maybe bracing himself for a reaction. Or maybe trying to gauge it. 'However, sometimes there are . . . discrepancies that require further investigation or confirmation.'

Again, he pauses. Again, Chris gives him nothing in return.

'In your mother's case, we were surprised to note that she recently increased her life insurance policy.' There's some rustling of papers, but I don't dare peek around the railing to see if he's passing anything to Chris. 'Were you aware of this?'

'No.'

I'm squinting like it will help me hear better. Is he saying that since Julie increased her life insurance policy, her beneficiary will get more money now that she's gone?

Peterson's voice cuts in. 'Only a month ago, your mom almost tripled her coverage for her life insurance.'

Tripled? I can't stop my jaw dropping. I may not understand much about insurance, but I understand math, and in money terms, triple is a lot.

Chris must be as surprised as I am because instead of responding, Langdon speaks next.

'Usually, we might see that sort of increase if someone recently took a major promotion or switched jobs, since life insurance is meant to cover the deceased's lost income. However, according to our records, your mom has been at the same job with the same company for nearly twelve years. Is that right?'

'Yeah.'

Langdon's tone lightens, like a doctor working on his bedside manner. It's unnatural, calculating, like he knows this is part of an evaluation or a checklist, but not something he really believes in. 'Chris, was your mom acting peculiar in the weeks before her death? Sleeping more, or missing work?'

'No.'

'Was she . . . showing any signs of strong emotions? Crying unexpectedly or without cause, perhaps?'

Chris's voice grows firm. 'No.'

'Did she give you any gifts in the days before she died? A special token she wanted you to have, or did you notice her giving away any other items from your home?'

I stifle a gasp of surprise, and Chris spits out the question my brain has only just registered. 'You think she killed herself?'

Hank whines, which is when I realise I've stopped petting him. 'Shhh,' I whisper in his ear.

One of my electives at school about interpersonal relationships did a lesson on the signs of being suicidal, and giving away special items without cause is one of them.

Langdon's tone doesn't falter. 'My job is to investigate the claims of anyone who falls under certain criteria. Your mother increasing her life insurance benefits in the same month of her death without a clear reason certainly fits that description.'

That little—

Peterson's not keeping Blake's relationship with Nicki Davis or Springtown close to the chest out of professionalism. He and his buddy don't think they had anything to do with it. They believe Julie increased her plan so she could kill herself and leave her family with more money.

'She wasn't depressed,' Chris says.

Depression can look different for different people, but Chris is right: Julie didn't show any of the textbook signs. She was active, involved. She never stayed in bed. I never saw her cry.

Peterson's tone is gentler but firm. 'Sometimes people who are depressed hide their suffering from those they love the most. I'm not here to pass any moral judgement on her, Chris.'

A clatter – a chair hitting the floor. Chris's voice booms, and I imagine him on his feet as I jump to mine. 'My mother didn't kill herself.'

I'm at the foot of the stairs when Langdon shuffles his papers, as if we should be impressed with his work experience. 'She also took out life insurance policies on you and your brother. Were you aware of that?'

'What are you saying?' He doesn't stop glaring at Langdon when I enter the kitchen, but he doesn't leap over the table either. Peterson's studying Langdon too, looking uneasy.

'Only the facts. You weren't supposed to come home that night, is that correct?'

'None of us were supposed to be home,' Chris says.

Langdon clucks his tongue. 'Well, son,' he says, quickly discarding the 'sir' he addressed Chris with at the start of the meeting, 'it's my job to finish this investigation, and unfortunately . . .' He closes his briefcase and stands as if preparing to leave. 'If my findings show she took her own life, her policy becomes null and void, meaning no one receives anything.'

'Screw you, man.' Chris's hand slams on the table at the same time Peterson says, 'Come on, Scott, you don't believe the kid is hiding something to still get the money, do you?'

'I think it's time for you to leave,' I say over the commotion. Only Peterson acknowledges me in the doorway, Hank placing himself between me and Langdon. Chris and the retired cop are locked in a glaring contest.

'I'm only examining every angle,' Langdon says.

'Scott,' Peterson says again.

'What is this?' Chris spits. 'Good cop, bad cop? Get out of here, man.' He waves them both off.

Peterson lifts Langdon's briefcase for him. 'There's nothing else for us here, come on.' He addresses Chris. 'We'll be in touch.' When he passes, he slows, mouth opening as if he's about to apologise for the interruption to our day, but he doesn't.

They walk to the door, Chris and I both ushering them along with Hank at our side, like we're daring them to step back into our hospitality.

Before Langdon crosses the threshold, he adds, 'I'll get my answers, Chris, with or without your cooperation.'

Peterson closes the door before he can see Chris flip him off.

Chris pounds the door once, breathing heavily.

I wait before finally saying, 'I'm sorry, Chris. They were way off base.' Even if Peterson didn't seem convinced that Chris was hiding anything to keep the insurance money, he was definitely on board with questioning Julie's mental health.

If Julie was suffering, she wouldn't want to hurt her boys, but the chemicals in her brain might have convinced her she was protecting them by leaving – but no.

Not with Joey home. I know Julie. She wouldn't.

None of this makes sense, but I can't deny that the changes in the insurance policy feel significant . . . too convenient, like that home in Springtown also having a gas leak. There must be something here we aren't seeing.

'My mom wouldn't do what he's saying.' He paces and Hank whines. 'She cared about us. She loved us. She wouldn't . . . leave us. That guy knows nothing about her. Nothing.'

Julie was the epitome of fun and laughter. She always put her kids first and filled the room with joy. My cousins had everything they needed and more.

'I know. I know. He's . . . just a constipated nutcracker with an elf sidekick suffering from diarrhoea of the mouth.'

But Chris doesn't laugh like last time, doesn't break stride. 'Talking to me like I'm some kind of idiot. Like I don't know how insurance works and implying I'm only after her money. I wouldn't take that insurance money if they cut me a check right now.'

I skim the folder Langdon left on the table.

'Wait. Look at this.'

15

January 4

This is big. This could change everything.

'What?' Chris scowls at me reading Langdon's papers. 'I don't want to look at anything from him. Throw it in the trash.'

'No, come look at this.' Something electric sparks across my skin, sending my hair on end.

Langdon's accusation isn't right. Aunt Julie made s'mores with us every summer and had silly string fights in the living room. She would never risk hurting Chris and Joey. And these papers, the ones right here in my hands, could prove it.

Reluctantly, he skims the documents. 'What's this supposed to mean?'

It's pretty steeped in legalese, and it's easy to get lost in the long sentences and technical terms, but some pieces are clear as day. 'Nicki Davis is your mom's insurance agent, but she only switched to her a few months ago.'

'Does that matter?'

'It confirms what Langdon said, about your mom increasing her life insurance and taking out life insurance on you and

Joey. These are dated last month.' I point at the bottom line of the page.

'It doesn't make any sense.' He gestures wildly. 'Most people don't insure their kids because life insurance is meant to replace the money someone's job gave their family.'

'So what would be her reason?'

'Let me see it.' His fury with Langdon melts, replaced with curiosity and an edge of fear when he takes the papers in his own hands. 'That's not my mom's signature.'

I study it, not really knowing what I'm looking for. I know Julie's handwriting, but I'm not an expert on her signature the same way her son would be. Then it hits me.

'Wait, see how it's exactly the same on every page? I bet it's a digital signature, one of those where you just click and it enters it for you.'

'So, in theory, anyone could have signed these documents pretending to be her?'

'I mean, I don't think it would be easy. I'm sure there's some kind of verification involved, whether it's a login and password to their system, or a driver's licence – or one of those two-step verification things sent to her phone?'

'So anyone who might have access to her wallet or phone?'

'Look who she has listed as beneficiaries.'

He takes the papers back while I point to the bottom of a page.

'Me and Joey,' he says. There's no note of suspicion or surprise in his voice, as there shouldn't be. Most parents would name their children as a beneficiary so they can inherit their money.

'If something happened to your mom, this insurance says that you and Joey get to collect on this insurance policy. But look who's listed after that.'

I point and Chris's jaw drops.

'Blake Bartnicky.'

'Yes, if all three of you died, he would collect life insurance for everyone.'

'Are you serious? That's—'

'A six-figure motive. And, if she died before you turned eighteen, he might have control of the assets until then.' His mom's death days before his birthday is not only tragic. It's strategic. 'Blake wins either way.'

His hands crush the paper in his shaking fists, chest heaving. 'That little piece of – ARGH!' He cries out, screams from the bottom of some pit that has cracked open inside him. 'I TRUSTED HIM!'

Thirty minutes ago, all I wanted was for Chris to see the truth about Blake, but now that he has, I'd give anything to take it back. I've never seen Chris with his shoulders hulked and neck veins throbbing. Maybe ignorance really is bliss if the alternative is having your reality blown apart.

He looks fully capable of dismemberment. But I know him. I know he would never hurt his family, me included, and the screams pouring out of him right now are not simply rage.

They're betrayal.

'I trusted him! How could he?'

He doesn't want an answer. It would be easy to call Blake

names or reassure Chris that it's not his fault – that Blake's goal was obviously to make everyone in the family trust him. That's what he's good at, the manipulative, scheming, son of—

Chris doesn't need to hear any of that right now. He needs to feel it, go through it. I can't take it from him.

So when he thunders out of the room and crashes around upstairs, I don't chase after him. When the front door slams and his car pulls out of the driveway a few minutes later, I don't call him back.

In my panic to hear why Peterson and Langdon were at the door, I nearly forgot the message threatening me to stop, but as soon as I unlock my phone, it's waiting for me.

I know what you're doing. Stop, before you hurt yourself. Or before I have to make you.

Combined with everything Langdon said, I'm more convinced than ever this isn't from Dominic, but knowing *who* sent it doesn't make it any less frightening.

Not until Blake's behind bars.

January 5

The next morning, I take off my dance shoes in the corner of the studio next to Sierra, avoiding the glares from the other girls in the class. Usually, the music pumps through my limbs and the strain of my muscles cancels out any worries or doubts bouncing around in my head. Not today.

My steps were half a beat off, my chin wasn't lifted high enough and my limbs were too stiff to be fluid.

When my parents came home last night, I showed them the documents the insurance investigator left behind, but I conveniently left out telling Mom and Dad about the threatening message. Showing them – or the police – would mean explaining why Blake would target me and how I ended up at his house.

Once he's locked up, he won't be able to do anything to me anyway. Needless to say, my focus has been on Blake, and I'm not the only one annoyed by my poor performance.

Madame Leheller approaches. 'Ella, when you've missed as many lessons as you have, I expect your studio time to make up for it.'

'Yes, ma'am.'

'If you keep performing like you did today, there won't be a spot for you in the recital, much less a solo.'

'I understand.'

She hovers imperiously, drawing breath through her pinched nose, before walking away with more stomp in her gait than the floating movements she's expecting from me.

Sierra leans in, unzipping her practice bag. 'You could just tell her. I bet she'd ease up on you if she knew about your aunt and cousins, not to mention your—'

'I don't need her to take it easy on me,' I say, cutting her off before she can mention the tumour. The studio's small, and sound echoes off the mirrors and wooden floor.

I have no aura, no worry of a migraine. I was looking forward to getting on the dance floor when I woke up – not having it taken away from me. If I lose dance, I might lose Sierra too.

I should be performing better. Everyone knows it. A group of younger girls whisper and stare from the other side of the room.

Sierra clocks them too and gradually increases her volume until she's impossible to ignore. 'If everyone was minding their own business, they wouldn't have to be relieved Madame didn't call out their sloppy arabesque.' She flashes them a wicked grin, her Southern accent offering a flawless façade of charm for her insult. 'We all know it was there.'

The girls don't stop staring, but the whispers cease immediately. Fighting a smirk, I pull on my sweats over my tights.

Sierra lowers her voice. 'Did your doctor tell you any more about treatment options?'

'I don't have time to think about that right now. Wouldn't that Nicki chick have to notice Blake being listed on those docs?'

'What do the police think?' she asks.

'Dad called Detective Peterson immediately to make sure they didn't overlook Blake's name on the life insurance policy. But since it's an "ongoing investigation"' – I hold up air quotes – 'Peterson couldn't comment on it.'

'So are Blake and Nicki in on it together?'

'Maybe Nicki gives Blake a list of clients who seem vulnerable, easy targets, and Blake befriends them, gets close to them and uses the info Nicki gives him to hack their accounts and list himself as beneficiary. Then when the opportunity presents itself, they die, and he gets the payout, splits it with her and no one knows.'

'You think?'

'What other explanation is there?' I hand her my phone. 'The police ruled that Springtown explosion to be at the hand of the homeowner.'

'So that means . . .'

'Scott Langdon's theory – that Julie somehow released the hose herself – could be the key. The evidence definitely suggests someone could be framing both homeowners to look like they were taking their own lives, deliberately or from negligence, when in reality, that's Blake's ploy to keep police from searching for him.'

'That's definitely a possibility . . . but if it looks like suicide, the companies don't pay, so Blake wouldn't get the money.'

'Maybe plan A is the money, but if the police start looking, then framing for suicide is already in place for plan B?'

'Maybe you should back off the whole investigator thing. We have the recital coming up and you have a lot going on . . .'

I wave off her concern. 'Hey, I was going to ask, do you think your mom can show my cousin around the airport some time? He's really into planes, and I thought it might cheer him up.'

Sierra shoulders her bag, always able to keep up with my quick change in topic. 'She doesn't get back from a trip until tomorrow, but I'm sure she would.' Sierra's mom's pilot schedule with the airline means she isn't always home, but the job comes with perks. 'If you're not going to be too busy with Dominic to make plans, that is.'

'Oh, subtle.'

'What?' She feigns innocence. 'He came up in conversation. It was right there.'

I exhale a laugh and shove my shoes in my bag. 'Right.'

'So, come on, what's the deal with you and him?'

'I don't know. He's funny, nice. He doesn't care what people think and is completely himself . . .'

'But . . .' she pushes, leading the way to the exit.

'But I'm not sure what to think. By the time Peterson and Langdon left and Chris stormed out, he'd blown up my phone with texts, a missed FaceTime and even a voicemail.'

'Voicemail?'

'Yeah.'

Sierra whistles. 'That boy's worried about you.' She passes me when I hold the door open for her and we both brace ourselves against the brutal cold.

'Yeah, well, I sent him a quick message to let him know I'm fine, I'm not worried. I mean, Blake will be arrested soon and this will all be behind us, but the details are too much to explain in person—'

'Yeah,' Sierra says, 'I'm going to be honest, I didn't follow all that insurance stuff.'

'Right. Way too much to text, so I invited him over tonight.'

'Perfect. By the way, I did a deep dive on his mom. She's not totally off the grid. An active social media account has her in Arizona.'

'Wait, what?'

'I have to look out for my friend, right? But his dad's in the clear too, so what's the problem?' She halts by my car instead of proceeding to hers.

While I'm both impressed with her social media digging and wondering if Dominic knows about his mom or even wants to know about his mom, I consider her question and fiddle with my keys.

'On the drive here, I remembered what Chris said about Dominic breaking his car window and refusing to pay for it. Even if they haven't been friends for a long time, Dominic should know that Chris and Julie wouldn't have money to fix that. Part of me wants to ask him about it, but part of me . . .'

'Is what?'

I know the rest of that sentence. I chew my lip, trying to make myself say it out loud. *Part of me is afraid he's not the guy I hope he is.*

I offer another truth instead. 'Honestly, I don't want to think about it at all.'

Sierra snorts. 'Of course you don't.'

'What's that supposed to mean?'

'That means this is standard Ella avoidance strategies 101. You always try to avoid thinking about the unpleasant things in your life by distracting yourself with something shiny or changing the topic of conversation.'

'That's not true.' I cross my arms.

'Oh really?' She manages to push her hands onto her hips

despite the cumbersome bag and puffy winter coat. 'Tell me again about how you nearly failed geometry last semester.'

'Hey, that is a hard class.' I pop the trunk and toss my bag inside. 'We can't all be brainiacs like you.'

'Whatever. We have different strengths, but I am not smarter than you.'

'Your PSAT score begs to differ.' The trunk slams shut, punctuating the fact.

'Anyway, my point is that you could have studied for that one quiz, but did you?'

'I was working on my English short story instead.'

'Exactly. So you turned in an assignment that was three times as long as it needed to be in a subject you're already good at, and what happened to geometry? Avoidance.'

Sierra crosses her arms again, as if resting her case. If biology doesn't work out for her, I have a feeling she'd do well in court as a lawyer.

'Whatever.' I head for the driver's side. 'This situation is totally different.'

A devilish grin lights up her face. 'Yeah, yeah, you're right. Have you finished that Edgar Allan Poe analysis, by the way?'

I slide into the front seat. 'It will get done.'

She doesn't have to say 'Mm-hmm' for her face to communicate it.

'I'm not avoiding it,' I say.

She raises her hands in surrender. 'Okay. Who am I to argue? That well-honed quality of yours might just save your life.'

'Because if I don't ignore everything else, Madame Leheller will kill me?'

'No, because if that Blake guy catches you sniffing around again, he might.'

16

January 5

When I get home, Chris's car is in the garage, so I park in the driveway. I haven't seen him since he left last night. Hopefully the space was good for him to process, but if not, I'll be here for him. Before I climb out of the car, I scroll my phone looking for updates about the case on the local newspaper's website. It's unlikely they'll report Blake's arrest so quickly, but that doesn't stop me from hoping.

Nothing yet.

Inside, I pour myself a glass of water, wondering if I can get on that Nosy Neighbours group Sierra's mom is part of, when I turn around and nearly jump out of my skin.

'Jeez, Joey,' I say, with a sharp intake of breath. 'I didn't see you there when I walked in.' I grab a towel for the water that is now covering half the counter and dripping onto the floor. Hank sniffs, but he's not tempted enough to help me clean.

Joey still looks small. I haven't been paying attention to how much he's been eating. Probably not enough. His voice is quiet, like it might be the first time he's spoken all morning. It feels like the only one he speaks to is me.

'Your parents were talking last night. About Blake. About calling the police because his name was somewhere it wasn't supposed to be. Is it true? Is he going to jail?'

'Well . . .' I delay, wanting to protect him. But hiding the truth might not be the best way to do that. 'I think so, yeah.'

Joey's chin crumples. I'm at his side in half a heartbeat, gathering his little frame in my arms. He sucks in a deep, shuddering breath and slowly lets it out.

'Ella, if I . . .'

I wait, but when he doesn't continue, I pull away to study his face. 'If you what, bud?'

'If I know someone . . .'

Mom's voice interrupts from upstairs. 'Ella, is that you?'

'Yeah,' I call back, still focused on Joey.

'People are starting to come in to town for the funeral this weekend, so we're picking up your dad's cousin Adam from the airport tonight. You'll be on your own for dinner.'

"kay,' I shout, before returning to a gentler tone. 'Know something like what, bud? About Blake?'

Joey stares at his knees.

'It's okay. The police are going to take him, and when you're ready, you can say what you need to. All right?'

He swallows and nods.

I hate Blake. Obviously, I hate him for what he did to Julie, but also for what he's still doing to Joey. He gives me one more hug before sliding off the stool and disappearing into the living room just as Chris's thunderous steps announce his descent on the stairs.

I wipe up the last of the water, hoping Sierra's mom can arrange that cockpit visit for Joey, when Chris enters the kitchen.

His appearance is nearly as startling as Joey's was, but for an entirely different reason. Dark circles frame his eyes. His hair is as matted as it was the day he was discharged from the hospital, like the thought of brushing it or glancing in a mirror hasn't occurred to him. When he rakes a hand down his face, I notice a scratch, probably from doing that same motion countless times since he realised Blake's betrayal.

His pain is etched in every feature.

'Hey, I was about to make some grilled cheese for lunch.' I put the pan on the stove to get warm. 'Want some?'

'Nah, I'm heading out.'

'Hold on, my car's blocking you in. How long will you be gone?'

'Depends.'

'Dominic might be here when you get back.'

'He's coming here? Tonight? Why?'

Admitting I want to hear Dominic's side of the car story feels like stabbing Chris in the back, and I haven't decided if it will be the right time to bring up his mom possibly being in Arizona like Sierra thinks. Instead, I say, 'To hang out.'

'The guy's trouble, El.'

'Come on, we know he didn't send the threat.'

'Do we?'

'Yes. I thought we agreed. Besides, since Dad called the police about Blake being named beneficiary, he's probably already down at the station. I was hoping they'd print it in the news, but I haven't seen anything.' I check my phone again to be sure.

'That's because they haven't arrested Blake.'

'The insurance information is right there in front of them. How long does it take to file a warrant or whatever.' I suddenly realise I have no idea how arrests work outside of police dramas.

'It's obvious to us, but think about it. The police probably had all that information from the beginning, before Langdon ever brought it to us.'

'I thought for sure he would be arrested this morning.'

'Blake must have a rock-solid alibi, someone lying for him. You heard Peterson and Langdon last night. They're obviously convinced it's my mom's fault, that she did this. Your dad told me this morning how Peterson basically brushed him off on the phone last night.'

'So you don't think he'll be arrested?' As much as I want to be shocked, part of me knows he's right. The insurance might prove fraud but not murder. If they don't have anything to connect him to the scene of the crime, any lawyer could argue that Julie's death is still an accident or suicide.

'If he hasn't already?' Chris huffs. 'No.'

'Maybe I should tell them about the threat. Maybe then—'

'Threatening someone in one, single anonymous message is

hardly going to sway a judge. It's not proof. They probably don't have anything to make the charges stick. Not yet anyway.'

Something about those last three words plucks my attention. 'Do you know something?'

'Like what?' He glances left and right, as if searching for what that thing might be. 'I know I have to get going, so can you move that car?'

'Where are you going?'

'Drugstore.'

'To pick up what?'

'Pre-workout. Sean must have taken his with him. You guys don't have any.'

The lie is solid and flows easily from his tongue. He grabs his jacket from the hall closet and awkwardly puts it around his back and shoulder. That's when I see it.

I'm quick. I lunge for his back and grab the plastic bag from his waistband. I fumble it, though, and the gallon-sized bag with a packet of papers falls to the floor. We both go for it, but I recover it first and step away.

'What is it?' I ask, flattening the bag to read through the plastic.

'Give it.' He snatches for it, but I clutch it to my chest and turn my back, protecting my prize while I read.

'It's a manual.' Or a copy of one printed from the internet. I spin to confront him. 'For a dryer.' The picture on the front looks exactly like the disconnected appliance in the hidden playroom at Joey and Chris's house. 'What are you doing with it?'

Chris grinds his jaw but doesn't answer.

'You said not *yet*. When you were talking about the police arresting Blake, you said they probably didn't have enough evidence *yet*. Where are you going to put it? That's your plan, right? To plant this somewhere for the cops to find and build a stronger case against Blake?'

'Shh, keep your voice down.' He puts his finger to his lips, and I remember Joey in the living room and Mom upstairs.

I lower my volume but don't back off. 'Where? His house? How are you going to make sure he's not there?'

Chris exhales through his nose, resigned. 'I haven't thought that part through yet.'

'You can't just hope he isn't home. Not with something like this.'

'I know. I'll figure it out.'

'Call him. Pretend to be a new client and ask him to meet you.' I'm not usually one to plot illegal activities – and I'm pretty sure planting evidence is illegal – but I'm not about to let Chris go down for poor planning. Julie deserves justice, and I'll do whatever it takes to get it for her.

'I thought of that, but he knows my voice,' Chris argues.

'He might not know *mah-n*.' I put on a Southern accent that matches Sierra's. 'And *ah* just moved here and need some help with my finances.'

Aunt Julie deserves to have the man who killed her be found guilty. If I could, I'd bring her back from the dead, but I can't. What I can do is cement the fate of the guy who took her away.

'I don't want to get you involved.'

'Why?' I stand to my full height. 'Don't think I'm up to it?'

He takes advantage of my distraction and grabs the bag back. 'It's . . . I don't want to see you in trouble if something goes wrong.'

'Sounds like a decision I should make for myself.' Before going into Nicki Davis's car, the worst thing I'd ever done was cheat on a capitals and states test in fifth grade, but with so many bad things happening out of my control, I have to take advantage of preventing worse.

He sighs, clearly unconvinced.

'Come on. If Blake is sneaky enough to have pulled this game in Springtown and here – not to mention who knows how many other places – what's to say he won't keep getting away with it? He obviously knows what he's doing, and the police are content with naming it a suicide. That's easiest for them. Open and shut. Forget whether it's true or not. And the insurance company? You heard Langdon. If it's ruled that way, he saves his company tons of money for not having to pay out, and—'

'I know all this,' Chris growls. 'That's why I'm doing something about it.'

'Good. Then let's do it well. Let me help you.'

Chris still grinds his teeth, but he's not looking at me. He's bending. I can see it.

'We can be each other's alibi if we're ever questioned. That drugstore thing isn't going to work if they check security cameras. We'll say we went to a park, to get out of the house and talk.'

Chris's stubborn streak is blazing. He cracks his knuckles and moves on to his neck, like he has to physically loosen his tendons to get himself to change his mind.

I've almost got him.

'Listen,' I say, 'I hate accepting help as much as you do. If it's not genetic, then we learned it from your mom. She wanted to do everything on her own, but I'm not offering to help because I don't think you can do this. I'm offering because I want to see that twisted murderer behind bars. Don't you?'

'Yes!' The word rips from him and explodes before us. He pants, trying to bring his rage back under control.

'Good.' I grab my coat. 'Then let's put him there.'

17

January 5

'He has to believe I'm a potential client to lure him out of his house. You're sure he won't be able to trace the number?' I confirm with Chris, Blake's number already entered in my phone and prepared to send.

'Yeah, the Google number is tied to an anonymous email.'

'I didn't even know you could do that.'

'Just be sure you don't touch the dryer manual when you dump it out of the bag.'

'No fingerprints. Got it.' Finding the dryer manual inside his house will be suspicious, but combined with the other evidence stacked against him, it has to be enough to topple the tower. *Has to be.*

Chris passes me the bag. 'Once you dump it, bring the bag with you—'

'Duh.'

'—and we'll call the police with an anonymous tip. Once they find it in his house, Blake will be their prime suspect.'

Except Blake never picks up his phone.

I call twice before giving up.

'As long as he's not home, we can get in and plant the evidence.' Chris drives down another street that brings us closer to Blake's neighbourhood.

I fight to keep my leg from trembling. 'What if he comes home while I'm inside?'

Chris strangles the steering wheel. 'He won't.'

'But what if he does?'

'If you're worried, I can go inside alone and you can stay in the car. Once you drop me off,' he says, turning onto Blake's road, 'circle back to the end of the street and be ready to call me if you see—'

The words die in his throat.

Four police cars are parked in Blake's driveway and on the street outside. The front door sits open. Chris drives at a crawling pace past the house. Two officers cross paths going in and out. One stands next to his car, on the phone.

'Are they arresting him?' There's no reason all those police cars would be there unless they found something. I crane my neck, looking for any sign of Blake handcuffed in the back seat of a car, but he's not there. 'I can't see him, but either way, this is good for us, right?'

Chris pushes on the gas once we've cleared the corner, out of sight from the cops. 'Not if they don't find anything incriminating in his house. He could be cut from the suspect list.'

'No way. Blake's the guy.' But I know it's only my stubborn hope speaking. 'They might have already found something to prove it.'

'You said it yourself: you didn't see him in handcuffs or in the back of the cop car. We thought the insurance paperwork would be enough to have him arrested, and it wasn't. You really want to take another chance and hope Blake was sloppy enough to leave something incriminating in his house?'

'So now what?'

'We have to be sure there's enough physical evidence to prove it.' Chris wipes his hand down his face again. 'If they're investigating him on the grounds of insurance fraud, they might be checking his office too. We have to guarantee they find something on him. We can make it there before it closes.'

'Seriously?' My skin twitches. I don't even register the landscape flashing by. The police swarming Blake's house made everything more real than talking about it in my kitchen. Am I really ready to tamper with evidence? Isn't that a major crime? But it's to make sure someone guilty gets caught, not to protect him . . .

'You backing out on me?' Chris coasts through a yellow light, checking the time ticking by on the dash. 'I've been to his office with my mom before. His secretary will recognise me. It has to be you this time.'

Julie was always there for me growing up, and her life ended too soon. She was taken from her boys, the boys who have both asked me for help.

How can I go home and comfort Joey knowing I had the chance to help and refused? Knowing that the man who tried to kill him is still out there, and he might not be done with us yet?

They need me. There's a problem we can actually fix without an expert having to step up and do it for us. No sitting in waiting rooms for answers or options. Chris believes I can do this.

'I'll take care of it,' I say.

He grins, a smile like the one he used to have when we spotted a toad in the window well, a smile I haven't seen enough of since Blake murdered his mom.

Chris pulls off the highway and parks the car, pointing to a tiny building attached to an optical centre with only twelve parking spots. Blake's office.

I climb out of the car, tuck the bag under the back of my shirt in the waistband of my jeans, and don't look back.

A bell over the door tinkles when I walk in. The woman sitting at the desk looks older than Blake, with short curls and too much makeup.

'Oh, we're closed.' She doesn't smile. This might not be as easy as we thought.

'I'm here to meet with Mr Bartnicky about some investment options.' I think I can pass for a Southern college kid looking to invest early.

'Did you have an appointment?' She checks something on her computer, a calendar, I assume. Her voice is tight. I'm clearly an inconvenience in an already busy day. 'I thought I got everyone. I've been busy all day cancelling appointments. Mr Bartnicky isn't in today.'

'Is he sick?'

A funny look comes over her face. 'Why don't I take down

your name and number so someone from the corporate office can call to set something up next week.'

'Oh, um, sure. Actually, do you have a restroom I can use first? It was a long drive from class.'

'Of course.' She gets up to direct me down the hall, but the phone rings and she excuses herself back to her desk. 'It's right through that door and down the hall on the left.'

I follow her directions, past a little kitchenette and bathroom. Opposite those is a room with a big desk, a window behind it and plaques on the wall.

Blake's office.

It's pristine. The desk is completely clear except for a phone and a pen holder with a singular pen in it. Books with titles in gold ink line the shelves. They feel like they're for show, interspersed with some knickknacks from Target. It might not be expensive, but the effect is still polished and professional.

No one would ever suspect him from the outside.

I pull the plastic bag out from my back waistband and tug my sleeves over my hands. The first two drawers of Blake's desk are locked. Same with all the filing cabinets. I don't think it will look convincing to drop them in the top, skinny drawer full of pens organised by colour. Blake was clearly a man who put things where they belong, and an appliance manual next to his paper clips and a calculator will look suspicious.

I can use that to my advantage. If he has a place for everything, something out of place will grab attention.

Is this what it feels like to be high? This ecstasy of power and control is unlike anything I've ever experienced. An X-ray of my brain would surely be lit up with thrill and excitement. No dark, mysterious masses of concern here.

'Okay, no problem, buh-bye.' His secretary's voice floats back from the lobby. I dash to the bookshelf and empty the bag's contents behind the books, careful not to touch them myself. When I step back, the top is just visible, hopefully enough for a police officer to notice, but they definitely appear hidden.

When I step away and shove the bag into my pocket, his secretary is standing in the doorway.

'What're you doing?' she asks.

'Oh, I—' I clear my throat and coat my voice in the Southern accent again. 'I finished in the restroom and caught a glimpse of the books. I'm a big, *big* book lover. I can't help myself checking what books people have on their shelves.' I'm rambling now but can't stop. 'Whenever someone posts a picture, I zoom in, trying to read the titles.' I mime pinching and expanding my fingers while squinting. 'Do you ever do that? Zoom, and . . . and read?'

'No.'

'Well, thank you for the restroom.' I squeeze past her out the doorway and walk towards the lobby, very aware that I never got the chance to fake flush. 'I really appreciate it.'

She scurries down the hall after me. 'What's your name? I need to make the appointment for you.'

'Oh, I don't have my calendar on me. I'll . . .' I don't stop and beeline for the door. 'I'll have to call back.'

The bell tinkles again when I leave and once more when the secretary opens it. 'Excuse me!' she calls.

I speed-walk without looking back. 'Go, go!' I shout when I reach the car.

'What happened?' Chris throws us in reverse as soon as I'm inside.

'Just go!' I yell, and he whips around the corner of the parking lot.

Two police cars turn into the strip mall as we pull out.

18

January 5

'Did you do it?' Chris asks.

I watch the cop cars through the back window as they park outside Blake's office. 'I did it.'

The noise that escapes Chris is a mix of a laugh and a whoop. His palm hits the steering wheel in celebration.

My hands vibrate from the adrenaline. Every second in that office was laser-focused. No distractions, no diagnosis, no worried parents, no concerned friends.

Only one goal and the thrill of accomplishing it.

'She got busy with a call,' I say, clicking the seat belt, 'and that helped.'

'You're welcome.' He waves his phone at me.

Blake Bartnicky is going to be arrested for Aunt Julie's murder. We did it. We actually did it! A tablespoon of sand has been filling my chest every minute since seeing Blake's name on the beneficiary line, and it drains through my feet as we turn onto an empty street.

I'm still grinning like a fool when Dominic's text comes through.

We still on for hanging out tonight?

Yeah, see you in an hour.

'Is that Dominic?' Chris asks. 'Look, El,' he says, his expression as serious as his tone. 'I can't stop you from hanging out with the guy, and I know you went all Nancy Drew with him or whatever, but he can't know about this. No one can. If anyone finds out what we did, it will only give Blake's lawyers fuel to have the evidence thrown out and he might get off the hook altogether. This has to be stay between you and me, all right?'

The weight of our actions should have occurred to me before, but somehow, hearing Chris, it feels more real. I just committed a crime.

But we did it for Julie. For Chris's mom. We're only helping to expose Blake for who he is and what he's done.

'El?' Chris asks again.

'Yeah, yeah. Just you and me. For sure.'

The rest of the drive home is a weird blend of accomplishment and disbelief. No matter what the world throws at us, we can make it right. The police will find the manual. They'll look back at the beneficiary paperwork. With those pieces in place, Blake's guilt will be too obvious to deny.

The only thing left to do is to sit back and wait for the news of his arrest.

January 5

When we arrive home, Mom and Dad are trying to leave to pick up his cousin. Mom's searching for her black gloves while Dad waits by the door. Joey sits on the stool at the counter. Chris heads up to his room almost immediately. Hank, as expected, can hardly handle himself with all the excitement of coming and going.

'We have to be at the airport in thirty minutes,' Dad calls up the stairs to Mom.

'I know, I know,' she shouts back.

Dad shakes his head before addressing me. 'We'll probably have a bite to eat. Are you and Chris planning to stay in for the evening?'

'Yup.' I wink at Joey, whose shoulders push up to his ears with a bashful smile. The high of accomplishing our goal still hasn't worn off. 'And Dominic might stop by for a movie later.'

Dad checks his watch. 'Your mom put some food in the oven for everyone.'

'Anything good?'

Dad's response, whatever it may have been, is cut off by Mom's call as she hurries down the stairs.

'I'm almost ready. Oh,' she calls from the other room. 'I saw we're supposed to get some snow in the next few days and I was going to have you get the salt out of the shed.'

'Now?' Dad checks his watch again.

'I'll get it in a little bit.' I jump in. 'No worries.'

'Thanks, hon,' Dad says, giving me a squeeze. 'We can always count on you.'

Mom grabs her purse but then plants both feet and swivels to confront me. Again, I feel it coming. 'Are you sure—'

'I'm fine. We talked about this, Mom.'

Dad smiles sympathetically, but I can't tell if he feels bad for me enduring Mom's worry, or bad for Mom because I'm so ungrateful for it.

I give them both a hug. 'You're already late. Go have fun with your cousin.'

'You guys have fun here too.' Dad opens the door, ushering her out.

'Call if you need anything,' she says over her shoulder.

'We'll be back in a few hours.' Dad closes the door to the garage behind him. The room relaxes into a quiet hush.

'Adults.' I press my lips into a disappointed line.

'They're so boring,' Joey says.

'Oh yeah?' I go in for some tickling, and he darts away with a laugh. Hank barks, trying to get in on the fun.

'Oh, hush,' I tell him while checking my phone to see a message from Dominic, confirming he has the liquorice for our movie night. My abdomen flutters at his name. I wonder if he's reread some of our messages like I have.

I've hardly thought of my diagnosis at all today. No weighing whether I want to give Dr Gupta permission to have someone cut into my skull to remove the tumour surgically in one shot or be strapped to a table nearly every day for half an hour while high levels of radiation target it for two to six weeks. A miracle in itself.

'I'm going out to the shed to get the salt. Have you picked out the movie yet? We'll need the remote.'

Joey hops off the couch to search. He's still looking when I slip on my coat and shoes. Even with the back light on, the path to the shed is pretty dark. It's tucked in the far corner of our property, and I have to use my cell light to avoid Hank's land mines.

Chris is right that I can't tell Dominic about what we did this afternoon, but maybe if we talk some more, maybe if he *is* the guy I hope he is, maybe I can share my diagnosis. Or a piece of it. Enough to test the waters.

I'll have to decide in the moment, just like bringing up his mom again.

Our shed has always given me the creeps at night. I've seen too many mice scurry out from under it. And a snake once too. In the summer, it's suffocatingly hot with no ventilation and the sun baking down on the black roof. In the winter, it's freezing with no insulation and wind howling against the siding, like nature is screaming at me to get back inside. I have to rely on the light of my phone.

I nuzzle my nose down into the collar of my coat.

Wait.

I whip around. Was that a noise behind me?

The halo of light from my phone doesn't reach far. Hank watches from the back door. No one else is outside. Right?

The bushes along the back of the house tremble in the wind. That must have been it. I'm just paranoid because it's dark.

It's dark, and I'm alone, but there's no reason to be scared.

I feel safer once I reach the doors, enclosed in the small shed where my light stretches to all four corners, verifying I'm alone.

Dad always says he's going to clean out this place, but instead, it gets put off and Mom's gardening gloves and trowels pile up next to the old hose, extension cords and even some seed packets that never got used.

The door creaks. The noise might keep the mice away.

The bag of driveway salt is heavier than I expect, but with a mighty heave, I pull it from the back corner shelf.

I'll get Dominic's side of the story tonight, and by then—

SLAM!

The door closes with such ferocity, it shakes the shed. My phone falls, casting me into near total darkness, and a pot slips from a shelf with a thundering crash.

I grab for my phone, trying to catch my breath and almost laughing at myself for being so scared of the wind.

With my phone in one hand and the heavy bag of salt in the other, I push on the door. Only it doesn't open. I push again, shoving my shoulder against the raw wood. It gives slightly, but not enough to open.

'Hello!' I call, pounding on the door, but I know it's no use. Mom and Dad are gone, Chris is upstairs and Joey's probably sucked into a cartoon by now.

I shove on the door again. Harder. And harder.

My phone buzzes in my hand with a text from Dominic, but I barely register his message.

How far away are you? I ask before shoving on the stubborn door once more.

Almost there.

Dominic will be here soon and he can come to the shed and unlock—

SSSSSSSSSSSSSSSSSSSsssssssssssssssssssssssssssssss

When the hissing starts, my first thought is a snake and I jump, but it's winter and the sound doesn't stop. It's one long, continual hiss.

It's not a snake.

That thought is accompanied by my stomach turning from the rotten-egg stench flooding the shed.

Ssssssssssssssssssssssssssssssssssssssssssssssssssss

Gas leak.

19

January 5

I can't see. There's no light in the shed aside from my phone, but it's not enough to tell where the gas is coming in.

Ssssssssssssssssssssssssssssss

'HELP!' I scream.

I pound on the door, but no one can hear me. The neighbours' houses are too far away. The streets were empty when I walked out of the house. Joey and Chris are inside.

Stay calm.

Chris. I call his phone, the ring agonisingly slow against the hiss of gas.

No answer.

I call again, but I can't wait. No time.

Dominic.

He won't pick up if he's driving, but he might check the flash of a notification.

Hurry, I text him while I still can. *I'm locked in the shed. Behind the house.*

My stomach rolls.

Nausea.

It's an early sign of gas poisoning. Short, shallow breaths limit my air intake.

Dominic, I text again . . . call Chris again . . . he doesn't pick up.

No answer. How much time do I have left? How much time has already passed?

My fists hammer the splintered wood on the other side of the doors. I shove my shoulder against it, trying to barrel through by sheer force, but it doesn't budge.

I can't breathe.

The shed is locked. It's dark. There's no escape. No one can hear me. I could call Mom and Dad, but they can't do anything. I dial 911, my breaths coming faster and faster.

'This is 911. What's your emergency?'

'I'm locked in my shed. There's a gas leak. I can't breathe.'

'Where are you located?'

I tell her my address and throw my shoulder against the door. My phone slips from my hand and clatters on the wood, but I can't see it. I can't hear the dispatcher. I can't open this door!

I'll be dead like Aunt Julie by the time they arrive.

I can't breathe.

'Someone help me!' I scream.

I pound the door, drop to the ground where a sliver of air comes through from outside, take a deep breath from the crack, beg there to be enough oxygen to supply my brain.

A headache settles in.

I'm going to be sick.

I don't want to die. I'm not ready. I don't want to suffocate.

The door jiggles.

'Ella?' Dominic calls from outside. The handle turns. I'm on my feet when the door flies open, falling into his arms, coughing, spluttering. The smell of gas recedes as I breathe in cold, fresh oxygen.

'Ella, what's wrong?' He holds me away from him, like he expects to see blood or visible injury.

'I came out here for . . . for the salt.' I cough, the cold air meeting my hot breath and creating clouds.

'Take a deep breath.' He lowers me to my knees on the ground, and I hang my head between them.

'Someone shut the door on me. I couldn't get out and then the gas started pumping in and—'

'What?' Dominic's face flashes from concern to alarm.

'I could hear the gas pouring into the shed, but I didn't know where it was coming from and I couldn't get out.' Tears run down my cheeks, quickly turning them colder. The instinct to survive has passed and the adrenaline drains from my body, leaving me shaking.

I really thought I was going to die, in a way that was immediate and present, and not at all like the hypothetical prospect of having a medical condition that could be life-threatening.

It was staring me in the face, literally suffocating me, and there was nothing I could do to stop it.

It brings death too close. From lack of oxygen or a tumour, I don't want to die. I have too much life left to live. I'm not ready.

My hands tremble while I suck great gulping breaths of air trying to calm down. I'm shivering – not from the cold.

I'm not going to die. I'm not going to die.

My fist pounds the side of my head where I imagine the tumour to be.

You hear me? I yell in my head. *You're not going to kill me.*

Dominic returns to my side, and it's only then I realise he's walked around the entire shed with his phone flashlight while I cried. He pulls my hands away and tucks me into his side, cradling my head against his shoulder, providing warmth, protecting me from the brutal wind.

'It's okay. You're okay.' He runs his fingers through my hair, pushing it off my forehead. My shoulders shudder against his chest, but it's strong and firm. My tears leave dark stains on his sweatshirt beneath his unzipped coat.

I wipe my cheeks with my hand and take deep, stabilising breaths.

'Better?' he asks.

He's pulled me so close, I'm a whisper away from his lips, and in this tornado of wanting to live and the relief of being rescued, and gratitude for his calm presence, I lift my chin to him. I want something real to anchor me to the here and now. I want to show him how much his support means to me. I want to pretend the last five minutes never happened.

But when I close my eyes and lean in, I don't meet his lips.

'How do you know there was gas?' he asks instead.

My eyes fly open. Dominic's face is solid, serious, with a slight scrunch on his forehead that I could smudge out with my thumb.

'I heard it, like air releasing from a tire, and smelled it. I almost threw up because of it.'

Dominic shoves his hands into his pockets and squints at the shed again.

'What? What is it?' I ask, sniffling again while trying to control my breathing.

'There's no gas, Ella.'

'What?'

'I walked around the entire shed. There's no container, no hose, nothing that would indicate a gas leak.'

I jump to my feet and pull my phone off the ground, flipping on the flashlight. 'No, it was there.' I'm telling myself as much as telling him. I pace around the left side of the shed first, moving the light slowly across the ground, running it up the corners, along the top of the roof, repeating my movements on the back. By the time I reach the right side, I'm shaking again. My light zips from one end of the small structure and back, the light as frantic as my thoughts. 'No, it doesn't make sense. I heard it. I smelled it. I couldn't breathe.'

'But there's nothing here.'

I direct my flashlight into the shed, hovering in the doorway, too afraid to step in.

'Dominic, I swear. The stench was overwhelming.'

He walks past, into the darkness of the shed, and splashes his light in every corner.

'I don't smell anything,' he says, inhaling deeply through his nose. 'And I don't see anything in here that uses gas.'

'That doesn't make any sense. How is that possible?'

'Maybe . . .' Dominic's head is down, shoulders relaxed. His voice is soft and gentle. 'You said you haven't been sleeping well, so maybe you're just tired and—'

'No.' I stomp my foot, but the effect is lost on the soft ground. 'There's no way I imagined it. I felt it! It was real! It wasn't a dream. I know what I heard.'

It was too real. Too distinct. That hissing.

I can't hear it now. That almost proves I heard it before, right?

And the smell, where's the smell?

The wind's blowing. It would have been ripped right out of the shed with the way the door flung open.

Sirens scream in the distance, growing closer. 'The police are coming,' I tell him. The call with the dispatcher ended when I dropped the phone.

'You called the police?' His voice nearly cracks with incredulity.

'Someone locked me in a shed, Dominic. It was filling with gas!'

'Ella—'

'Whoever closed the door on me ran away when you drove up and they took whatever released the gas with them.'

Dominic directs his flashlight outward, to the expanse of grass in every direction. 'I don't . . . see anyone.'

'They ran away! I already told you.'

'But look.' He points the flashlight down, moving it up and down the path directly in front of the shed. 'The grass is almost frozen and pushed down where we've been walking. You can see some of our footprints.'

'So?'

The sirens shut off, but the lights shoot down our street. They're almost here. They'll see what Dominic can't.

'So there aren't any other footprints around, and if someone was standing outside the shed, holding a hose in a crevice – a crevice we can't see – then there should have been some grass bent down there too. But there wasn't.'

'I'm not making it up. I know what I felt, what I heard.'

'I didn't say you're making it up,' he says, more calmly still. He reaches to put a hand on my shoulder, but I scrunch away. 'I'm only saying maybe in your panic, your brain was playing tricks on you.'

My brain. My traitorous brain. The organ that let a tumour grow and might kill me. Now Dominic thinks it's playing tricks on me.

'No.' I spin away from him and then back. 'NO!' I shout. 'Someone locked me in that shed and filled it with gas! Someone tried to kill me!' My voice is shrill. I can hear how frantic I sound, but I can't stop it. 'It was Blake! It must have been Blake!'

'Ella, I was going to tell you when I got here—'

The cop car pulls into our driveway and the headlights nearly blind me. Two officers emerge, flashlights blazing.

'Here, over here,' I call, waving an arm and leaving Dominic behind.

A young officer approaches, frowning with... curiosity? Concern?

A second officer, a woman, joins the young guy. 'We received a call from this residence—'

'Yes, that was me. I was in the shed and the door locked – someone locked me in there.'

The officers glance at each other before looking back at me. I am obviously *not* locked in the shed; everything is fine. They've decided already, and I instantly know how much harder it will be to convince them otherwise.

But I know what I heard. I know what I smelled.

It was real.

It happened.

Blake was making good on his threat.

Hank whines inside, interrupting himself with an occasional bark. His nails scratch at the back door, desperate to get out and greet our visitors.

'Is anyone hurt?' the young officer asks. His jacket says *Varden*.

'No, no, I'm fine. I—'

Chris comes out of the house, jogging. 'What's happening? What's going on?' He didn't even put on a coat.

'I'm fine. Just—' Shaken? Is that the word I'm looking for?

I have nothing. No proof. No evidence. Only my words against logic and reason.

Maybe you're just tired . . .

What if Dominic's right? What if there's nothing to be afraid of and it was only the wind knocking the door shut?

Officer Varden steps away to use his radio and tells whoever is on the other end that there's no need to send an ambulance.

'I tried calling you.'

Chris pats his back pocket. 'I must have left it upstairs. What happened?' he asks again.

The female officer crosses her arms, shifting so the air is at her back.

'I – I was in the shed looking for the salt because it's supposed to snow tomorrow, and I went to get it like my mom asked, and so I was in there, and it was dark, and the door – it slammed shut. I couldn't get out. The door. The door was locked.'

'Locked?'

Chris approaches the open shed door with his phone light on, stepping around the back side and pushing it shut. 'There's no key in the handle.'

No key. Did I have the key? Or was it unlocked when I got out here?

'Dominic, did you take the key?'

'No, I – I don't remember if it was there. I just remember turning the handle.'

I had a key, didn't I? I took the key and I put it in the handle? But I don't actually remember doing it. Like when you're driving on the road and can't remember the last five minutes of landscape.

I must have had the key, right? I must have put it in the lock . . . but then where is it?

'The call said there was a gas leak?' Varden says.

'Yes, I heard hissing, like gas—' But then I see them. Really see them. The officers, Dominic, Chris. They're all looking at me with a touch of fear, but they aren't afraid for my life, that someone was on the property and locked me in a shed and tried to gas me out like they gassed out Chris's house.

No, they're afraid for me because I sound insane. I'm not making sense. I'm rambling and shivering and I sound hysterical. I know I do. And all the evidence says I'm wrong. I'm wrong. I'm wrong.

Am I wrong?

'I thought I heard gas being released,' I clarify with more confusion than certainty. I'm vaguely aware of Dominic wrapping an arm around my shoulder as my voice rises until it cracks. 'It must have been Blake, Blake Bartnicky. He was here and he locked me in the shed, and he tried to kill me just like he killed my aunt!'

'Ella—' Chris says at the same time the officers snap to attention.

'This is the Forrester residence, right?' Varden asks. 'Rick and Meredith?'

'Yeah. Those are my parents.'

'This is the family connected to that gas leak over on the west side of the county,' he says to his partner.

Chris stiffens while the officers share a knowing look. Something has clicked into place for them.

'Miss, whatever may have happened here tonight, it wasn't Blake Bartnicky.'

'How – how can you know? Was he arrested? Is he in custody?'

'Blake Bartnicky is dead.'

20

January 5

Blake is . . . dead?

'We were planning to talk to your folks tomorrow,' the other officer says.

The possibilities swirl in the frigid air, but I can't form any words. How did he die? Who's at fault? When did this happen? I'm leaning against Dominic, but I don't remember moving here.

'I take it you weren't aware of his death?' The officers scrutinise us, watching for reactions.

'Of course not,' Chris says.

Blake wasn't old. Not heart-attack old. He was probably in his forties like Julie and appeared in decent shape. It can't be a coincidence that in the middle of all this he winds up dead, can it?

'I was going to show you this.' Dominic reveals his phone with a two-sentence local news article.

A Fulton County man was discovered dead in his home early this morning. Police are investigating.

There's a comment on the article: *This is in my neighbourhood.*

Hamilton Place. The police have been coming in and out of the house all morning.

Hamilton Place. Blake's neighbourhood. The police cars we saw in his driveway earlier today weren't searching for evidence. They were dealing with a body. Blake's body.

Blake couldn't have been here tonight. But if he wasn't, who was?

'How did Blake die?' Dominic asks.

'We're still conducting our investigation. Incidentally, can you give an account of your whereabouts for the last twenty-four hours?'

'You think we might have done it?' My voice is high, tight.

'No one is jumping to conclusions. It's our job to be thorough.'

'But it means he didn't die of natural causes, right? Otherwise you wouldn't be asking us this.'

The officer releases a heavy breath through his nose. 'I am not at liberty to discuss an active investigation.'

'This is bull,' Chris says. 'You can't tell us anything, but you want us to tell you where we were?'

'It's only procedure.'

If my fingers weren't numb from the cold already, they would be now. Dominic's arm tightens around my shoulder and it feels like the only sturdy thing keeping me upright while sand shifts beneath my feet.

Will they know we planted the evidence in Blake's office? My throat's dry. If they find out, could we be fined? Go to prison? Be real suspects in his death?

'We were home last night,' Chris answers firmly. 'With Detective Peterson. Ask him yourself if you don't believe us.'

'And today?' the officer asks.

'We drove to the park.' Chris's lie is smooth, confident, but if they talk to Blake's secretary, she might mention something to them, something to make them look at security footage and recognise me and question why I was there.

But she probably knew about Blake's death before I came to the office. She gave me that look when I asked if he was sick and was cancelling all his appointments, so there'd be no reason for her to think the jumpy girl who visited after his death had anything to do with it. Right?

'And your parents?' the officer asks me.

'She's under eighteen,' Chris says, stepping in front of me like a shield while Dominic stands next to me. I should be able to defend myself, to let my words be as clear and confident as Chris's so they'll believe me as easily as they believe him. 'You can't ask her questions about an investigation without her parents present.'

The idea that either of my parents would be involved in a murder investigation is laughable, but the young officer cocks her head and rephrases the question, directed at over-eighteen Chris. 'Where were your aunt and uncle earlier today?'

'Stopping by their work and running errands.' They may be over two decades older than him, but Chris will protect them just the same.

The officers exchange another glance.

'Anything else?' Chris asks.

'We're going to have to call your aunt and uncle,' the officer says calmly. 'To let them know we responded to a call at their residence.' She leans around Chris to address me. 'Do you want to file a report?'

I blink, squinting at the grass, bent and trampled from everyone inspecting the shed. But there was nothing to find. And if Blake is dead, who else could have – would have – tried to kill me?

Do I want to file a claim? Go on record?

Everyone's waiting for an answer. The door was locked, and someone released gas. I'm right. I know I am.

But we thought we were right about Blake too, and now he's dead and nothing makes sense anymore and I—

'Ella?' Dominic rubs my elbow, jostling me from my thoughts. Joey's hand presses against the window upstairs. What do I tell him? Neighbours have come out of their houses, arms crossed against the cold at the edge of the street. Their necks crane, straining for a better look. Will this end up on a Nosy Neighbour site too?

'No. I – I panicked,' I finish. Dominic rubs my arm reassuringly, but I step away. 'I'm sorry. I . . . panicked. I'm sorry if I caused you any trouble."

'It's understandable,' the woman says, 'that with everything your family's been through the last few days, you feel a bit jumpy.'

'Yeah, yeah.' Do I really believe this? It happened. I could smell it. The gas. I heard it.

Didn't I?

And the door shutting? It could have been the wind, because if Blake is dead, no one else would be after me . . .

'Let – let me call my parents first. I don't want them to worry.'

An officer called them while I was on the way to the hospital on New Year's Eve, and I don't want to put them through that again. No matter if it was real or not, I never want to see that look on my dad's face again or hear my mom cry.

I press call on my phone and wait. Joey's face fills the back window. He must be scared, the police coming to the house like this.

The officers hover until someone answers. As best as I can, I explain to my parents what happened. The police confirm that everything is fine, but Mom and Dad ignore my pleas to keep their dinner plans and commit to driving home.

Varden hangs up and says, 'They'll be coming into the station tomorrow for more questions. And your house' – he addresses Chris – 'will be released to you tomorrow morning.'

Despite his anger with the officer only minutes ago, Chris can't hide the relief that washes over him.

'What time?'

'We'll call you,' Varden answers before climbing into the patrol car and driving away. His words sound like a promise, but the bite in his tone feels like a threat.

'Ella?' Dominic's gentle voice contrasts with the officer's. 'You sure you're okay?'

His sweatshirt is still splotched with my tears. He doesn't understand, not really. He thinks – like everyone else – I overreacted to a jammed door. And I just said as much.

Did I have a key to unlock the shed, or did I forget it inside and it was already unlocked?

Did I really hear someone behind me when I walked out?

Did I hear the gas? Smell it?

I was definitely nauseated.

I definitely struggled to breathe.

'Ella?' Dominic asks again.

'I – Chris?' I step away from Dominic's arms to Chris. His breaths are faint, his eyes distant. I place a hand on his shoulder, and he jumps. 'Are you okay?'

'I – I wanted him dead, but now that he is . . .'

I didn't know Blake nearly as well as Chris did, but I'm still surprised Chris would feel any grief over his death. And how do we tell Joey?

When Chris speaks again, it's almost a whisper, like he's forgotten I'm here.

'The people around me keep dying . . .'

'We should go inside,' I say.

Chris's eyes clear and his head snaps from me to Dominic. He sucks a deep breath through his nose and clears his throat. 'When did you get here?' He steps towards Dominic, the shield becoming a sword.

'Right before the police did,' I answer, seeing the storm brewing in Chris's shoulders but not knowing how to stop it.

'It's a little convenient that you're locked in and no one's around except him.'

Dominic scoffs, his breath rising in a white cloud. 'What are you talking about? I'm the one who let her out.'

Chris keeps advancing, ready to go toe-to-toe. 'Always trying to play the hero.'

I pull back on his shoulder, enough to make him stop but not step away. 'Chris, that's not fair. I texted him.'

Dominic hands me a bag of liquorice from his car. 'I think I better head home.'

'No, you don't have to—'

'Notice he isn't denying it,' Chris adds.

'Stop,' I warn. 'Just tell him, Dominic. Tell him I was already in the shed when you got here and you can come inside and we can talk and watch the movie and—'

'He can believe whatever he wants.' Dominic pulls open his door. 'Maybe we can do the movie another night.'

'But I have so much to tell you, and—' I hate the desperation in my voice. I'm not supposed to be the weak little girl who cries in a boy's arms when something goes wrong, but after this, now I want to lean on someone. I don't want it to be only me fighting.

Dominic slides into the driver's seat.

'Let him go, Ella,' Chris says, his voice as hard as it was when the police were here. 'You don't need him.'

Dominic clenches the steering wheel but doesn't disagree, doesn't defend himself.

'Wait.' I step forward.

Dominic stares straight ahead when he says, 'You get some rest, all right?'

His words slap me in the night, and I'm cemented to the ground as he starts the car and drives away. It feels like I'm floating in dark waters and Dominic's rowing away with the only light in the sea.

Get some rest.

He thinks I'm too tired and imagined it all. He's leaving because he doesn't believe me.

He's not the one who locked me in. I'm certain . . . but he still doesn't believe me?

I stomp across the yard into the house.

I refuse to drown.

21

January 6

Blake's death should have brought reassurance: he can't hurt us anymore. Instead, it's brought more unknowns. Who killed him? Why? Did the same person lock me in the shed?

And a quieter whisper: *Was I locked in the shed at all?*

After Mom and Dad got home, she called and left a message at Dr Gupta's office, who called back first thing this morning and said they had an opening if we could get here within an hour, which gave us fifteen minutes to leave. Now we're in a small exam room, this one with a picture of apples.

Julie wouldn't have dragged me to the doctor. One time Chris fell off the swing – with some help from an overzealous eight-year-old me – and cut his leg open. My mom would have rushed him to the ER and pounded on the desk until someone stitched him up. Julie knew he could handle it with a few bandages.

On the way over, Dominic sent me a message: *Hey. How are you?*

Once we reached the office and an appropriate amount of time being left on 'read' passed, I tapped out *Fine*. I went to bed confused about everything but woke up with bitterness stitched into the edges of my memory. When I got out of the shed, Dominic was too calm, too collected, like he wasn't taking me seriously.

But it's true. I'm fine. That's what Dr Gupta is going to sit down and tell Mom. I'm fine. There's no reason for me not to be fine.

His message is only part of the reason my smile is too tight as Dr Gupta enters the room. I didn't want to come. It wasn't enough that I told Mom I had a brief episode of panic. I can't imagine what she would have done if I'd told her someone was out to get me because I've been digging into how Aunt Julie died.

That's the theory that kept me up all night. If Blake didn't die of natural causes, then someone killed him. And if it wasn't us, then someone else is out there, and they must know what I've been up to. It's someone other than Blake. They want the whole thing to die with him.

But I know it sounds ridiculous.

Someone is trying to kill me? It's not a rational thought. It's unlikely. Improbable. Statistically unrealistic.

That's why I haven't said it to anyone else.

But having a brain tumour is all those things too.

'Thank you so much for squeezing us in,' Mom tells Dr Gupta as she takes a seat.

'We got the results of your bloodwork from your last appointment,' Dr Gupta says, 'and it's consistent with what we saw in your last report, so there's no reason to suspect anything is going on physiologically.'

I hear the underlying suggestion. If not physiologically, then psychologically.

I can't give them more reason to suspect that might be true. I can't let anyone know my theory until I have the proof to back it up. I've been down that road before. If I broke my arm, no doctors or teachers would have doubted me, but they can't see a migraine. I need proof that someone else might be out there, pulling the strings on everything.

My word should be enough, but if the cause of the pain is invisible, they're quick to assume it's exaggerated.

'Sometimes migraines can be affected by barometric pressure. With that big storm coming in, it wouldn't be out of the realm of possibility to attribute any new headaches to that.'

'Yes, but this wasn't so much a headache as a . . . well, perhaps a panic attack?' Mom edges around the words like she's afraid I'll bite her for them, but yeah. That's exactly what it was. I panicked. Who wouldn't? It was a normal reaction given the circumstances.

'Hmm. Is there anything that may have been causing you additional stress?' Dr Gupta asks, head cocked, concern wedged into the crease in her brows.

Mom's gaze weighs on me too.

Anything causing me stress? What? Beyond my aunt dying? Pulling my cousins from a gas-filled house where they almost died too? The migraines still confining me to bed at least twice a week? Discovering that my aunt's boyfriend was cheating on her and plotted murder for money? Hearing that he's dead and being left to wonder if someone else went after him to cover up something bigger, someone who might now want to come after me and silence me the same way even if it means locking me in a shed and trying to gas me out?

'No,' I say. 'Nothing I can't handle.'

I'm sorry about last night. Dominic's messages come through. *I should have stayed. You needed me, and I should have been there for you.*

It's the last bit that makes my nostrils flare. *Needed* him?

I'm not weak. I'm not sick. I have a tumour, and it will be removed. I don't need Dominic. I don't need help. I'm not a little kid.

'It wouldn't be unusual for the anticipation of treatment alone to cause an increase in stress. How have you been sleeping?'

'Fine.' I hardly slept at all.

'It's common for people to experience anxiety or depression after receiving a major diagnosis.'

I nod while she speaks, because if I tell them my real suspicions . . . I'll sound certifiable.

A pilot facing the brunt of a storm doesn't let the passengers worry. I'm in control of the plane and tired of circling the runway. No turbulence here. I have everything under control.

'You only have a few more days before school's in session again, so I want you to get plenty of rest. Take advantage of the time off.'

'Yes, definitely.' I exhale. 'I'm feeling better already. And I've decided to go with radiation instead of surgery.'

Dr Gupta scoots back in surprise. 'Oh. All right, then.'

'When did you decide?' Mom asks.

I shrug. 'When can we do it?' One less obstacle in my way.

'They can schedule that for you at the desk, but it might take a week or so.'

'The sooner the better.'

January 6

Ten minutes later, Mom's quiet as we walk down the hall of the doctor's office, but she doesn't try very hard to hide the nervous glances she throws my way. She's probably plotting to lecture me about staying home and getting more sleep. Like I need the speech. Crawling into bed has been bumped to the top of my to-do list.

First, I text Sierra, telling her about Blake's death.

no way that's an accident, she says.

I know. Sometimes Sierra feels like the other half of my brain that comes out to affirm my thinking when I need it most.

good thing the police are investigating it, she adds.

That's true. If there's something bigger happening, they'll find it. The cops last night said the house is released from being a crime scene today. Surely that means that anything worth finding would have been discovered.

Unless . . .

The police are missing something. They missed the disconnected dryer hose at first. Without Dominic and me, they might never have discovered that. And if they did know Blake was listed to inherit all Julie's money and didn't tell us, they still didn't arrest Blake, and now he's dead, and they're too busy looking at my family, and . . . what if they are missing something and we're all still in danger?

When we get outside, Chris's car is waiting with Hank in the back seat, both paws on the door, fogging up the window with his hot breath.

'Chris is going to drive you home while I meet your dad at the police station,' Mom says, smoothing down some hair on top of my head. 'We'll answer some questions, and everything will be fine. I want you to go home and rest.'

'I know,' I say, bristling at the words echoing Dominic's last night. Rest isn't going to fix this. 'Blake's death is suspicious, though, isn't it?'

She gives me a hug goodbye. 'Let's not let our imaginations run away from us before we have all the facts.'

As she walks away, I can't help but wonder about her reaction if I voiced my theory . . . if I even hinted that someone was still out there, after us. Would she believe me?

Who would? *Let's not let our imaginations run away from us . . .*

I've been burned too many times before to expect that kind of faith. People need proof.

Doctors need tests and scans. Police need evidence and facts. Everyone needs to see something to believe it.

Chris unlocks the door just as I reach the handle. When he came inside last night, we talked about what it could mean now that Blake's dead. I said a judge can't convict a dead man. Chris didn't say much except a dead man can't defend himself.

I suck in a deep breath through my nose, the frigid air chilling my lungs before I settle into the front passenger seat. Hank's face is next to mine before I can reach for the buckle.

'Yes, hi, I see you,' I say, scratching behind his ears and being welcomed with a puff of hot, stinky dog breath. Joey's in the back seat too, but he's sleeping, chin tilted up, mouth open. Guess I'm not the only one still tired from last night.

Chris is the reason Dominic left, but honestly, he only let me see Dominic's true colours sooner rather than later. I haven't responded to his apology. I don't need it. Once I have proof, he'll have to believe me too.

'He wanted to come for a drive,' Chris says as we pull out of the parking lot, and I assume he means Hank because I'm sure Joey would rather have been playing with his toys at my house but he's too young to stay alone.

'Aren't you going to ask what my appointment was for?' I change the radio like the answer won't bother me.

He scrunches his forehead. 'None of my business.'

Something about his response almost makes me want to tell him. Almost.

'Well, thanks for picking me up.'

'I needed something to do.'

He's lost weight this week. Not much, but enough. His skin's paler. He yawns and blinks, refocusing on the road.

'Tired too, huh?'

'Hard to sleep.'

'Yeah, I keep thinking about Blake.'

'He's gone. He can't do anything to us anymore.' His voice is firm, like he wants it to be true, but there's a sliver of doubt. We were both so sure Blake would be taken out of his house in handcuffs, not a body bag.

Chris must be able to tell I'm still unsettled because he adds, 'I'm telling you, it's done. Blake probably fell over drunk in his house or something. The police will say the same thing.'

'You're not worried? You don't think the same person who killed Blake could have killed your mom?'

Chris shifts in his seat. 'No. No one's even said someone killed Blake yet. Everything's going to be fine. You'll see.'

'You don't have to do that, you know.'

'Do what?'

'Act like you're okay if you're not.'

He lifts his shoulder. 'I'm fine.'

'I know. You're talking to the queen of fine. We're also practically the same person. You're not the only one Julie taught to shove down worries. You work, focus on getting things done instead of dealing.'

'I do it to make life better, not to pretend things aren't bad.'

'You can't always make life better, though.'

'I don't believe that. There's always something you can do, some action to take, instead of just sitting there or pretending the problem doesn't exist. You have to face it head-on.'

I want to ask what exactly he would do if he had a tumour in his brain that couldn't be removed until the doctors schedule the treatment. There's not a lot to do when you're told to sit and wait. Instead, I ask, 'So what's your plan now? To deal with . . . this?'

'Leave.' The word pops out firmly. A fact. Non-negotiable.

'Move away?'

'I can't stick around forever.'

'I know, but so soon. We haven't even had the funeral yet.'

'I'm not going today, but I can't sit around and do nothing.'

'How far will you go?'

'Far enough to forget about everything here.'

'Even us?'

Chris looks over, like he heard the words out of his mouth for the first time. 'It's not – you don't get it.'

'Then help me get it. We're the only ones you have left. How can you leave us behind?'

'Because – because what happens when you're gone too?'

The air's sucked out of the car as his words sink in.

Like his mom. Like Blake. Like Joey's dad and every other person he's ever leaned on.

I want to promise him I won't leave. I'm different.

But death doesn't always give us a choice.

'I'm here now,' I say softly.

'Yeah,' Chris laughs, recovering himself and changing the station. 'With your terrible taste in music.'

'Shut up.'

Chris thinks he's replaced his mask, but the cracks are visible. Those shadows aren't under his eyes for nothing.

He might want to believe everything will wrap up with Blake's death, but it has to be connected to his mom's. Even though the police have searched the house, there might be something they missed, something strangers wouldn't catch, something I'll be able to see, or Joey will notice.

Something to prove another person is involved.

Something that will make them all listen to me.

Something undeniably clear.

And I'm going to be the one to find it.

22

January 6

Traffic slows to a crawl, red brake lights flashing off and on like Christmas lights. It's starting to – not snow, exactly – more of a rain and ice mix.

Chris is right: we can't sit by and wait for the police to take action. I sat outside the house believing that the EMTs could save Julie, and she died. I won't make that mistake again.

If Nicki and Blake conspired against Julie, maybe there's some paperwork buried somewhere, an old file . . . something to show why her plan changed, or maybe a diary to show that Julie never would have listed Blake in the first place.

I need to search the house myself.

Chris glances at his phone and hands it to me. 'What's that traffic alert say?'

'There's an accident on the highway.'

Chris drums his fingers on the steering wheel. 'This could take forever.'

'Especially with that storm moving in,' I say, a plan forming.

'They always overestimate winter storms. It will be done in an hour.'

It's hard to argue his logic when eight out of ten times that is absolutely true. Though the odds never stop people from stocking up on bread and milk.

'All the main roads are going to be backed up like this.'

'People need to learn how to drive,' he says, craning his neck and moving to the shoulder to take the nearest exit.

'Should we pull over until the ploughs come through with the salt trucks?'

'And sit on the side of the road all afternoon?'

'It would be better than trying to make it back home . . .' I trail off, leaving the seeds planted. Just when I've given up hope on them sprouting, Chris flips his blinker and drives down another street.

'Where are you going?' I ask, even though I recognise the scenery.

'Back roads to my house. It's closer and I have to pick up my stuff anyway.'

'Good idea.' I beat back a grin. 'Glad you thought of it.'

Chris white-knuckles the steering wheel as the back end of the car slides around the corner.

'We shouldn't be driving in this,' I say. Then again, with this snow and ice covering the roads, there's no other option than to keep moving forward.

Joey's awake, but especially quiet in the back seat, like he can feel the tension and knows any extra noise in the car could cause Chris to drive off the road. Hank pants, head hanging in the gap between our seats like he's seconds away from climbing through the narrow gap and into my lap.

'Better than being stuck on the highway,' Chris says.

That much is true, but without traffic on these country roads, the sleet turns to ice ridiculously fast, and in some places we've been positively skating despite Chris driving at half the speed limit.

'Your bald tires don't seem to care about the difference.'

'Here.' Chris grabs his phone, swipes and taps. I suck in a breath and try to hide that I'm gripping the edge of the seat, but Chris keeps us straight and smooth, and a second later 'Ice, Ice Baby' pumps through the speakers. 'We're fine,' he says, adjusting that mask, but his knuckles remain white around the steering wheel.

Even Joey – who woke up when we slid around a particularly slippery corner – cracks a smile. Hank climbs over his lap to look out the window.

My phone buzzes. 'It's my mom.'

When I answer, she says, 'I wanted to make sure you got home okay.'

'Well, we're not exactly home yet.' She worries about me enough as a teenager, much less one with a brain tumour, but out in a storm like this? If ever there was a time to convince her I can take care of myself, it's now.

'Where are you?' A sharp bite pierces through her words.

'Still on the road.' I wince and can almost hear her taking a breath to suck in patience.

'Where?'

'Near Sierra's.' The lie pops out before I've even decided it's the only option. She won't want us on the road, but she also won't want us in Chris's house alone. 'We're almost there.' To our destination – not a lie. 'And Sierra's parents will totally be okay with all of us spending the night.' Also not a lie . . . or it wouldn't be if we were on our way to Sierra's house and needed to be safely out of the storm.

'You tell me when you get there,' she says, making it clear she's not happy but still exerting the little maternal control over the situation she can.

'Yeah, of course. It will only be . . .' I face Chris as we cross over a small bridge.

'Three minutes,' he supplies.

'Three minutes,' I repeat for Mom.

'Give yourself plenty of time to drive home tomorrow so you can get ready for the viewing. We're supposed to be at the funeral home at noon.'

Julie deserves to be laid to rest with answers. I will find them tonight.

'Detective Peterson wants to speak with you about Blake's death.'

'Why?' Did the secretary mention me after all? Did they watch security camera footage?

'I'm sure it's all routine. Dad and I were out of there pretty quickly this afternoon.'

She reminds me to wipe off Hank's feet before entering Sierra's house and to get as much rest as I can. I tell her I love her and hang up.

'The police want to talk to you again?' Chris asks.

'I guess.'

'They called me again this morning. I didn't answer, but they probably want to talk to me too.'

He skids into the other lane – no oncoming traffic – and I gasp before he corrects us into the right lane and fishtails for a second.

'It's okay.' His voice quavers. 'We're okay.'

'We're not driving back in this,' I say. 'Once we get to your house, we're spending the night.'

'The electricity is still off.'

'We have the fireplace,' Joey pipes up from the back seat.

'Yeah, you still have the fireplace.'

Chris peeks in the rearview mirror again, his expression mixed, but resignation is definitely present. 'Fine.'

We make it the rest of the way without incident and pull into the gravel driveway.

'Be careful on the ice,' I warn Joey, opening the back door for him and Hank to jump out. Hank sniffs around a bit before tainting the snow yellow.

Snow covers the old house like an eerie Narnia. Each individual tree branch is encased in silvery ice, which would be beautiful if the smaller trees weren't bending with the weight. Streaks of ice claw at the windows like they're trying to scratch their way in.

I duck and cover for the front door Chris is already opening, slipping a bit myself. Snow falls over the top of my shoes and sinks into my socks.

Inside, the stale air feels crisp and fragile. It's only been four days since I've been inside with Dominic, but maybe because of the cold, it seems longer. If there's a shred of evidence left behind by whoever did this, I'll find it.

Chris stomps off the snow and ice from his boots. I search for what he's feeling, but either by coincidence or intention, his face stays hidden. He jangles the house keys before pocketing them and moving out of the room.

A rush of memories must be flooding over him – the good of all the years past and the bad of that night – at least, they do for me: the years we spent playing hide-and-seek in the nooks and crannies, the forts we built in the attic, sliding down the wide railing of the stairs. I only have a fraction compared to him. More to give him privacy than anything else, I open the door wide to call for Hank while Joey slinks in.

Being back in this house is a reminder that it's not about me. Yeah, an invisible, silent monster lives in my brain, but I'm still here, and Julie's not. Right now, I can't do anything to get rid of the tumour growing in my head, but I can do something for her: bring justice against those who invisibly and silently tried to kill her.

Here, I text Mom. The best part is she doesn't have Sierra's or her mom's number since they haven't met yet. All that will change at the recital, so if there was ever a time to lie, it's now. I'll worry about it coming up in conversation later.

Chris returns from downstairs. 'The circuit breaker isn't working. The power company hasn't turned it back on.'

'The storm could've taken the power out.' I can't verify my suspicions with the other houses being so far away.

'Great.'

'Let's get the fire going,' I suggest.

'Yes, please,' Joey says, curling himself into a ball on the couch. Hank jumps up next to him, something I know Aunt Julie would never allow. As much as I want to honour her, thinking of her – walking in, taking our coats, and offering cocoa – makes the words stick in my throat. Plus, Joey's arm is already wrapped around him, and I don't have the heart to break them apart.

Chris must be thinking the same, because he opens his mouth when he sees Hank, but closes it and runs a hand along the fireplace instead.

'The lighter's in the cabinet next to the microwave,' he says, heaving a few logs from the decorative metal bucket next to the fireplace. 'Newspaper's in the garage.'

I gather both, but when I test the lighter, it doesn't flicker. Out of fluid. Shoved in the back of the cabinet is a small box of matches, so I grab those instead. Even with grey clouds covering the sky, enough light reflects off the bright white of the snow with the blinds open.

'I've always been jealous of your house.'

'Why? Is it the creaking floorboards? The stained grout on the kitchen floor?'

'You have a fireplace. They're romantic, a place to actually hang your stockings.'

Chris opens the flue before building the fire. 'My mom never let us have fires in this thing.'

'How come?'

He strikes a match. 'Insurance liability.'

And just like that, the reason I'm here comes rushing into the room like the blast of cold air from the flue.

Someone killed Aunt Julie and tried to kill Chris and Joey too. We thought it was Blake, but if he's dead, who else is out there, right now? More importantly, what can I find to prove I'm right?

'What're you thinking about?' I ask Chris.

'Huh?' His head whips up from searching the floor. 'I'm worried the mice might think this is a nice place to get out of the storm too.'

Joey's eyes sweep the floor as if the rodents might appear upon being summoned. But I'm not so sure that's all Chris is worried about.

'We're going to need some blankets,' I say.

'In the laundry closet.' Chris stokes the fire with a poker.

Down the hall, the closet doors remain open, the hidden door to Joey's playroom concealing the old disconnected dryer, where I discovered it with Dominic – no, I'm not thinking of him.

The house is uncomfortably quiet without the hum of a refrigerator or furnace, like the blood running through its veins stopped when the electricity was shut off. A shiver runs up my spine as I reach for the blankets.

If anyone out there did want to hurt us, being alone in this house might be the perfect opportunity to strike. Right now, the only thing I can protect us from is the cold.

23

January 6

I pull a stack of three heavy quilts from the closet shelf above the detergent and lightbulbs, but before I walk back to the living room, I linger. Unlike Chris, I'm not looking for mice. What secrets might be here that the police missed? I evaluate every item on the shelf. A screwdriver. A flashlight. Dryer sheets. Nothing out of place. Nothing out of the ordinary.

The pieces are all here. I can feel it. I only need to put them together.

'Where's Chris?' I ask Joey when I walk back into the room, draping a blanket over him and Hank. Joey scratches the dog's ears, but a creak tells me Chris is on the stairs, probably getting the stuff he wanted from his room.

'I'll be right back,' I say, but instead of following Chris, I move to Julie's bedroom. I adjust the shades to let more light in, but even with that, I bring out the flashlight on my phone. I'll have to be careful with my battery if I have any hope of it lasting all night.

The halo of light catches on the few framed pictures on her dresser, Julie and her boys at the beach last summer, standing by the Christmas tree a few years ago, Chris cradling Joey as a baby in the hospital.

I steady myself with a breath. I'm doing this for her.

Her dresser is cluttered, but no sign of a diary or journal. She probably wasn't disciplined enough to keep one daily.

I open her jewellery box. Is there a piece that doesn't belong? Something I don't recognise? Nothing stands out, so I open a drawer. Someone else has been through them. My lip curls in disgust at the thought of an officer rifling through her clothes, her underwear, digging their hands in her things without care.

But if there was anything to be found, they would have found it already. I shove the drawers shut, too forcefully.

I grab a candle off the dresser. We can light it from the fire.

In the nightstand drawer next to her bed, there's a stack of envelopes right on top. The first one is a bill from a bank, a foreclosure warning on the house. Julie must have been further behind in her bills than I realised.

The next one is from a different bank, but Julie wrote a note on the back. It's hard to decipher her scrawl. If I squint and tilt my head, it might say '*Give $10k.*'

Ten thousand dollars? Who would Julie be giving that kind of money to? There's nothing else of interest in the drawer.

I repeat the words on my way back to the living room, wrestling with the possibilities, massaging my temples.

Sierra sends a text: *how are you feeling today*

Rather than answer that question, I say, *If anyone asks, I'm at your house tonight.*

k but you're feeling okay?

New diversion needed. I snap a picture of the envelope. *Found this in my aunt's room. What do you think it means?*

your aunt's room? i thought the police were investigating

I thought you agreed Blake's death was too much of a coincidence.

but why does it have to be you that finds out?

I don't respond. Sierra thinks I can leave it to the police, but Chris is right: sometimes we have to make things happen. We can't just sit around and wait for others to believe us. Too many people won't believe it without proof.

I'm going to give it to them.

'Chris,' I call, leaving Sierra's question unanswered and bringing the envelope under the light.

He enters the room and I stick out the envelope.

'Does it mean anything to you?'

His brows scrunch almost immediately, but he doesn't answer.

I point to her words. 'She doesn't say *pay ten thousand dollars*. She says *give*. Could she have been planning to give the money to Blake? Was someone . . . blackmailing her or something?'

'Blackmailing her? For what?'

'I don't know. I'm just tossing out ideas.'

'We don't even have ten thousand dollars to give.' Chris flips over the envelope and opens it, pulling out a bank statement. I lean over his shoulder.

'According to that you do.' The bottom dollar amount is a little over ten grand.

'No,' Chris says, flipping the paper over, checking the envelope again. 'That's not even our bank.' He points to the logo.

'Your mom's name is on the statement.'

'That doesn't make any sense. If she had all this money, why didn't she spend it? You've heard the mice. Once the snow melts, the kitchen ceiling is going to leak again, and obviously we needed a new gas tank. This place is falling apart.'

The house I always dreamed of – with the old-fashioned fireplace and unique floor plan, the walls that have been painted fun colours every time Julie had a whim – isn't as glorious as I made it out to be.

'Maybe she was planning to.'

'My mom couldn't plan ahead enough to finish painting a wall. You think she could plan far enough ahead to replace a roof? She always said we didn't need our dads around because we didn't need their child support. But we did. That's why I've worked since I was a freshman. That's why I never made plans to go to college – I have to work full time as soon as I can. Anything around here that needed to get done, I did.'

I never had to consider finances like Chris is talking about. I've wanted a job for something to keep me busy and my own spending cash, but never because I had to contribute to the family budget. 'Did she ever ask my dad for help?' I ask, suddenly ashamed I never considered she might need it before.

'She did.' Chris rubs the back of his neck and becomes absorbed in examining his shoelaces. 'At Thanksgiving.'

My jaw drops. They had a fight after dinner. I didn't hear it, but the tension was obvious. 'Did he turn her away?'

'Not exactly. He . . . he said he wasn't sure how much he could help because you guys would be having new bills coming in soon.'

Medical bills. My medical bills.

Chris shifts. 'I . . . I know about your brain tumour.'

His confession fills the room and swells like a balloon pressing me against the wall until all the air has squeezed out of my lungs.

'H-how?'

'I overheard you talking to your mom the other day in the kitchen. I was in the living room, and I tried not to listen – I swear. I put my earbuds in when I realised you two were arguing, but then you said those words and I don't know – I – I froze.'

He knows. I believe what he says about trying not to overhear and being stuck. It's exactly how I am right now. I haven't moved a muscle since he said it. Haven't blinked.

He's not crying or upset. He might've when he found out. I don't want to know. I don't want to be responsible for someone else's reaction.

But Chris has known for days, and he hasn't treated me any different. He hasn't tried to protect me from every danger in the world because I already have one inside me. He even asked me to help him in Blake's office. He knows what I'm still capable of.

'I found out a little over six weeks ago,' I whisper.

I've kept this secret because I was afraid people would treat me differently. That I might catch them looking at me with a mix of nostalgia and hope and pride the way Mom does. Or like Sierra, who thinks she's treating me the same but is too nice. I'm not so fragile that no one can fight with me. Chris has had no problem arguing about Blake or stealing my pizza rolls. It explains why he wasn't surprised about picking me up from the doctor's office.

'Why?' I ask, my voice papery.

'Why what?'

'Why haven't you treated me any differently?'

'You did the same for me.'

His answer surprises me. Since Julie died, I've been trying to treat him and Joey the same, because they are still the same people for me, and they always will be.

We're both messed up right now, our lives leaning precariously over the edge of a cliff without any warning of what's below.

Through it all, Chris has believed me. When the evidence wasn't there, when everything seemed contrary, Chris believed me.

'I'm sorry I didn't tell you sooner.'

'You don't owe me anything.'

Chris has been trying so hard to keep himself together, and

he doesn't owe me an explanation any more than I owe him an apology. But sharing isn't about debts.

'It seemed like I should be able to figure things out on my own.'

'Yeah. I get it. Remember this?' He pulls up his pant leg to reveal a four-inch mark crawling up the back of his calf.

I better remember it. I'm part of the reason he got it.

'Julie cleaned it up. She said you were tough and could handle it.'

'She taught us both to take care of things ourselves.'

If Mom thought I could endure the migraines, we never would have found the tumour in the first place. It would have grown bigger and bigger until it was too late.

'You probably should have gotten stitches,' I say.

Chris jiggles his pant leg down. 'What's done is done.'

'I'm sorry my parents couldn't help when you needed it.'

'It's not your fault.'

'But it still sucks.'

'Yeah, it does. Mom never wanted to ask your dad anyway. I made her because otherwise it fell to me. I was the one who paid the difference when the mortgage went up. Same house. Same property. More taxes, and I paid the difference. Everything fell to me.'

I don't know what to say, but something tells me there's more that Chris isn't telling me. He's known about the bills for months, but those circles under his eyes haven't been there that long. He's hiding something.

'That's why this doesn't make any sense,' Chris continues, smacking the bank statement across his palm and pulling my attention back. 'If we had the money, why didn't she use it?'

If I had an answer, I'd give it to him.

But Chris has a secret, and he's not sharing it with me either.

January 6

By dinnertime, I've finished searching Julie's room and the main level, while Chris packs and tries to round up more flashlights from the basement and Joey quietly drives his truck over the pillows.

It's strange because this is Julie's house, the place where I've spent countless hours, but after listening to Chris, it feels like a shoe from the summer that's now half a size too small. The unfinished murals, intended to cover up scratches and holes in the wall, seem a different shade, darkened by a new way of seeing Julie.

She helped raise me when it mattered and she raised Chris. She was fun and loving and cared for us all so much . . . but was it for the best?

It took Chris a long time to see Blake for the villain he was, and while Julie isn't anywhere on the same level, there are shades of her I haven't wanted to see either.

It's hard for Chris to see the faults in people he cares about, which is why I don't think he's ready for me to bring up my theory about someone else being involved again. Not yet, but maybe—

'What was that?' I ask, not sure if the sound I heard was really anything. A mouse?

Joey's eyes grow wide.

Nothing.

Chris and I agreed to conserve our phone batteries. I don't know what time it is.

'What was it?' Joey asks.

'I don't know . . . a scratching.' It comes again, more distinct. 'From outside.' I hop beside him on the couch and pull back the blinds. It's dark. The sleet has given way to a light dusting of snow, but the ice sparkles against slivers of moonlight flashing through the clouds. It really would be quite beautiful if it wasn't so sinister.

But there's nothing moving out there besides the softly drifting flakes.

I heard it, right? This isn't like when I was locked in the shed. I'm not panicked. I'm not imagining things.

Am I?

Crunch.

'What was that?'

We both freeze. Joey hugs himself.

Crunch. Crunch.

'Wait,' I whisper.

Crunch.

Breaking ice shatters the silence of the night and sets Hank off like an alarm.

Joey scampers to the narrow window next to the door. 'I see something!'

I pull back the blinds. But there's nothing moving in the softly falling snow. The tree branches don't even sway in the wind, encased in ice.

'I don't see anything,' I say. But if I heard something and Joey saw something, then I'm not imagining things.

The envelope. Could whoever Julie was planning to give the money to have come looking for it on their own?

Wait. Don't jump to conclusions. It could be an opossum or raccoon. Something harmless.

Hank growls, hackles raised, snout pointing at the door, at Joey.

'It was there. It – wait, look.' Joey presses his index finger against the glass. 'In the snow.' His whispered breath fogs the window, but I see them.

Footprints.

Big footprints, like those of a grown man. They come in off the road and run right up to the front window, then disappear around the side of the house.

Almost like someone outside was looking in. Trying to see inside.

Watching us.

'Where are they?' I ask, looking for a person.

Joey lets out a whimper in response and curls into the corner of the couch. His heartbeat might be pounding in his ears like mine.

Because there is no excusing it away now. The noise isn't just in my head. It can't be if we both heard it.

And the footprints prove it.

Someone is out there.

24

January 6

Scraaaaaape.

I gasp and Joey buries his head in a pillow.

Hank barks loudly.

'Shhh, Hank.' I pull his collar to me and he circles around us, snorting and grunting. 'Shh,' I tell him again.

The noise comes from the east side of the house. I imagine one of the icy branches scratching against the siding like a long fingernail against a chalkboard.

But what would move the branch? Or who?

The firelight flickers in the living room, our shadows stretched out along the carpet.

A light swirls in through the window above the sink.

'Down!' I whisper-yell, dropping to the floor and pulling Joey beside the couch. My phone sits on the table, in direct sight of the kitchen window, too many yards away for me to grab without being seen.

If I call out for Chris, whoever is outside that window will hear me, giving away our position.

Staying low, I lunge for the fire poker, clutching the long metal rod like a bat.

The shadow moves.

If only I hadn't lied to my mom about where we were going . . . I wish she knew where I am. I wish she was expecting me home tonight and worrying that I'm not there right now. I wish someone, anyone, knew that a stranger was outside trying to get in.

The back door jiggles. Hank goes wild. He races out of my grip and charges at the back door, barking like mad. The flashlight sweeps around the room again, but I can't see who's holding it.

A knock.

Hank jumps against the back door, but whoever knocked isn't scared away.

'*Stay*,' I mouth to Joey.

I peer around the corner of the coffee table. If it is an intruder, they wouldn't knock. If someone was trying to break in, they'd leave when confronted with a dog.

The handle rattles again.

The figure stands outside the door, a dark silhouette against the white of the snow blanketing the ground, a silhouette I know.

'It's Dominic!' I say.

'Dominic?' Joey squeaks.

The halo of flashlight reveals the mustard yellow of his Carhartt and the point of his red-tipped nose.

'Down, Hank,' I say, but my command does little to settle my relentless dog. I grab his collar and flip the back door lock.

Dominic steps in, bringing a rush of icy air and a snow shovel with him.

My ferocious guard dog stops barking immediately and wags his tail, whining for attention. Dominic stomps off the snow from his boots and complies with Hank's wishes.

'What are you doing here?' I ask, the fire poker at my side.

'I saw the smoke when I was out clearing the driveway. I drove the snowmobile over to check it out, make sure no one was looting the house or something. I didn't want to drive right up without knowing who was here, so I parked at the edge of the property and walked.' He falls to his knees to scratch Hank's ears.

'No looters here,' I say. 'But Chris is going to lose it if he sees you.' If the hockey puck in his window wasn't enough, Chris might be worried I'll tell Dominic about our stunt in Blake's office. Blake might not be able to stand trial for that evidence, but if our actions are ever discovered, maybe we could for planting it.

'Where is he?'

'Downstairs. He could come up any minute.' I raise my hand to move him back towards the door.

'Wait. Can we talk? Upstairs?'

I look towards the basement to where Chris is still packing, but besides that, I would rather avoid talking to Dominic, even if it means admitting Sierra is right about my tendencies.

'Please?' He pouts just enough to be genuine without overdoing it. Is he the guy I think he is? Or the one Chris tells me he is? Someone else entirely?

'Talk to him,' Joey says, climbing back on the couch. I roll my eyes and laugh at his advice. If Joey thinks he's worth it . . .

I sigh. 'Fine.' I point to the stairs, and Dominic follows. I whisper-yell to Joey, 'Cover for me.'

Hank circles up on the couch, plopping down next to Joey, as if declaring he'll stay with the kid. The fact that it means sitting on the couch next to the warm fire is purely a coincidence, I'm sure.

Joey gives a thumbs-up, and Hank barks. 'Guess that means challenge accepted,' Dominic whispers, following me up the stairs.

He must know that things between us have changed, shifted, since the other night. I'm aware of his presence all the way up, of how close we are in the stairwell.

'Ella, I—'

'Shh.' I know the ventilation in this house, and sound carries right down the grand wooden staircase.

Dominic reaches for a door.

'Don't—' But Dominic opens it to a blank wall before I finish, 'bother.'

He raps his knuckles on the exposed drywall. 'A door to nowhere?' he whispers.

'Another quirk. I think there used to be a set of exterior stairs that went up the side of the house.'

'This house is weird.'

'One of the reasons I love it.' Or loved. Nothing here is the same.

I point to a string dangling from a ceiling in the hall.

Dominic looks sceptical but doesn't argue. Would he if he knew I was using this opportunity to find more evidence connecting Aunt Julie and Blake to someone else who might want them both dead?

It would be so easy to tell him my mission to find something in the house to prove it, but not after last night.

He pulls on the string so the ladder unfolds and waves me up first. A gentleman.

The attic is musty and freezing. I shiver, rubbing my arms and wishing I hadn't removed my coat by the fire. Joey's old crib is in pieces against the wall, and a Christmas tree is stashed in the corner with a variety of decoration boxes, dust disturbed from being put away recently, maybe even the day Julie died. The care Aunt Julie must have used to protect those ornaments for another year when she won't get to celebrate again . . .

A pile of old tablecloths shoved in one corner with a few snack wrappers signals that Joey makes a habit of playing up here, whether he is supposed to or not.

I move to the middle of the room before I spin to face Dominic.

'So why are you here?' I shiver and cross my arms.

'I told you. I wanted to make sure no one was here who wasn't supposed to be. Last year my dad didn't hear from old man Latters for a while, and by the time he went to check, there was a guy who'd been living in his house for . . . I don't know, days. The coroner said Latters had been dead close to a week, but no telling how soon that squatter moved in. He just . . . walked around his body in the living room like the corpse was an old chair and—'

I hold up a hand. 'Why did you really come?'

Dominic pulls a worn leather coat off a hanging rack. 'Here.'

'You came to give me a coat?'

'You have goosebumps. I can see them up and down your arms.'

'I can take care of myself.'

'I never said you couldn't.'

'Not in those words.'

'So I want to help you. That's why you're mad at me? Should I not have helped you when you were banging on the shed doors?'

'That was different.' He left when I most wanted him to stay.

'You shouldn't have to be in danger to let people be nice to you.'

'Are you here to lecture me? Because I—'

'No.' He sighs. 'I came here to talk to you about something. But first, I need to apologise. Which I realise is not going very well.'

I clench my jaw. 'I don't—'

'Need my apology? I know, I get it. That doesn't mean I don't still want to give it. I'm sorry I left like that the other night. I shouldn't have.'

My stubbornness can last for record-breaking lengths of time, but something in his voice makes it harder for me to dig in my heels. It's not like a text where I can make up the tone in my head.

Dominic lifts the coat again, a peace offering. I reach out, a begrudging acceptance. But he ignores my hand, instead draping the coat around my shoulders, pulling it tight when we both become aware of how close we're standing. A piece of hair hangs over his gentle brown eyes. His hands don't move from the edges of the coat, even while his knuckles brush my stomach through my shirt.

'Better?' he asks, his voice almost a whisper, an invitation to step closer, step into the warmth of his arms and chest and breath.

My insides perform a swoop so intense I'm vaulted back to reality: he held me close outside the shed yet didn't believe me.

'Yeah,' I say, stepping back and freeing my thoughts from whatever hormones took over. I pull the jacket tighter and immediately look around a stack of cardboard boxes.

My goal is to find something to convince everyone this didn't end with Blake, which means I need to forget how much I wish his hands could have found my sides.

I mumble, 'Thanks,' and dig through a stack of old artwork.

Dominic blows out a breath and runs a hand through his hair. 'No problem.'

He's trying, which counts for something, but not everything.

'So what did you want to tell me?'

'It's about Chris.' He stops, as if gauging my reaction.

'I wanted to ask you about him too. How come you didn't tell me you broke his car window?'

'Because I didn't.' He crosses his arms, but he's not upset by the accusation, not even surprised. He's almost detached, bored.

'Then why does he think you did?'

'I guess because he found a puck in the back seat.'

'Not many neighbours around. You play hockey. Makes sense.'

'But it's not the only explanation that makes sense.'

I wait, but he doesn't offer. I raise my brows to prompt him. Still nothing. 'For example . . .' I roll my hand forward, to pull an answer out from him.

'Plenty of things.'

I exhale through my nose and brush past him towards the stairs. 'Seems like you would have a suggestion if you wanted to clear your name.'

'People are going to believe what they want about me,' he says, stopping me in my tracks. 'It's not my job to change that.'

'You really don't care if someone believes a lie? If they don't know the truth?'

'Not everyone. Some people aren't ready for the truth.'

'Am I one who's ready?' The question sparks between us like a live wire, like we're both afraid to touch it. But he does.

'I hope so.'

I swallow, and his eyes flick to my throat. Suddenly the coat feels too heavy and warm.

'What do you think I believe?' I ask.

'That Chris is right and I locked you in.' The challenge is in his face, but right underneath is hurt.

'You saw my panic, but you were calm. Too calm. Like you knew right away there was nothing to be afraid of.'

'So because I was calm, you think I might be guilty?' It's as if every block he tears down from my wall goes towards building up his.

I lean against an old end table that looks like it's from the nineties and give him my full attention, assuming he wants to take it.

'If you want to explain, I'm listening.'

25

January 6

He studies me, and I push every ounce of patience into my countenance. As frustrating as he is, he's equally intriguing. It's so obvious he wants to be honest, but he tries to hide it at the same time. The war is being fought in his tense shoulders, the crease of his brow, the way he runs his tongue over his lips.

I try to focus on him instead of how badly I want to brush that piece of hair from his face and trail my finger along his jawline.

'Remember how I told you about my mom?'

'She struggled with alcoholism.'

'Yeah. My parents tried to hide it from me. Which, I was a kid, I get why they thought it was best. Except I think only my dad was trying to protect me. My mom . . . she tried to hide it from everybody – making excuses, dismissing comments. She kept acting like it wasn't a problem.'

'But it was.'

He picks at his thumbnail. 'It's not easy to block out irrational screams when you're a kid. She was so . . . erratic.' He chews his cheek, and it takes everything in me not to tell him it's okay, not to interrupt him. This is about more than me listening and understanding. It's about him saying it out loud. 'It's hard to describe. But that night at the shed . . . I think I was calm because I had to be growing up. I didn't have the chance to freak out. I grew up learning how not to throw gunpowder on a lit stick of dynamite.'

My face crumples. Am I the dynamite for him? Am I the irrational, uncontrollable . . .

'I'm . . . I'm not trying to make comparisons between you and my mom. I'm trying to explain me. My reactions.' Again, it's the sincerity in his voice that lowers my defences. 'Seeing you upset, worried . . . when I get stressed, I mellow way out. It's not a choice. It just . . . happens. A lot of other people at Alateen have said the same thing. But yeah, that night, I was freaked.' His eyes reach mine again. 'Because seeing you so scared brought up those old instincts.'

So he wasn't trying to avoid me. I took my own insecurities and saw everything through that light. If I look past that, if I only focus on him, I see a boy who's been hurt by one of the people who is supposed to love him most in the world.

'I get it.'

'You do?' He's so hopeful, but his words are laced with doubt.

'Do you know where your mom is now?' I ask, thinking of what Sierra said she found online.

'I got a postcard from out west a few years ago. I threw it away.'

So he knows.

More than anything, it's nice that Dominic feels like he can lean on me rather than offering a support for me to lean on him. He's trusting me to handle this, to not judge his mom or his past, to only listen.

The knowledge of what I'm hiding hovers beneath the surface, so close to breaking through the water of my fears. In some ways, I wish Dominic could guess the truth on his own or stumble upon it like Chris, so I wouldn't have to actually voice the words.

I've wondered what it would be like if I collapsed in the middle of a semester exam and an ambulance rushed me to the hospital. It could be easier that way, if everyone knew at once.

Instead, I have to decide in quiet moments like right now if I can trust him with this piece of me.

He hasn't moved or blinked. He's waiting patiently.

'You know I have migraines.'

'Yeah.' But he says it like that's not at all that he expected me to say.

'I've been getting them for months, and at first we thought they were inconvenient, random, or related to my diet. Teachers were accommodating for a while, but as we got closer to the end of the semester, some of them lost their patience. They didn't believe the migraines were really that bad. Even the first doctor we went to was quick to brush me off.'

This is the part I've never said out loud. Not to Mom, not to Julie, not to Sierra.

'It messed with me. I felt like I was overreacting, like they really weren't that bad and I should be able to do more despite having them. I should have been able to fight them off. But then we went to a different doctor, and she found the cause.'

My throat closes over the words I've been hiding from him, but I've come this far. There's no going back, and I don't want to.

'The scans showed a brain tumour.'

I brace myself for raised brows or a dropped jaw, even a little gasp of surprise. Incredibly, Dominic doesn't flinch. He doesn't ask me questions. And he won't, I realise. He won't ask me anything I'm not willing to give. Maybe it's that freedom that unhinges my jaw and loosens my tongue. Maybe it's the chance to have a choice of what to share without obligation that makes me want to elaborate.

'It's not cancer. I'm not dying. Not right now, anyway. They've been monitoring it for growth.' I've been trying to convince myself I'm fine for too long, and I can't do it anymore. 'It's interfering with school, my social life and dance, so I need to start treatment.'

'That must be hard.'

The absence of '*I'm sorry*' isn't lost on me, and neither is the relief of not having to convince him '*It's okay*,' because it's not okay.

Instead, I say, 'Yeah, it is.'

'Are you scared?'

The temptation to dismiss his question almost wins. I've been pretending the answer is no since I got my diagnosis.

'Most days. It feels like someone else has taken control of my life, and I don't get a say in my future anymore. I've been afraid of telling people because I don't want them to . . .'

'Look at you differently?'

'Yes.' My shoulders relax without the tension I didn't realise I was keeping there, the weight of my secret pressing on me. I never would have guessed Dominic had so many obstacles in his life or how they still affect him today.

'Thanks. For telling me,' he says.

'You trusted me first.' I take a step towards him, then another. 'I shouldn't have iced you out before.'

The left side of his mouth quirks. 'Pretty easy to do in this weather.'

'Does that bad joke mean we're . . .' I take one more step towards him and stop, but reach for his wrist, rubbing my thumb over the soft spot on the inside. 'Okay?'

He closes the gap between us and lifts my chin with his finger until I'm staring directly at him. 'Does that mean you forgive me?'

'Yes,' I whisper against his lips right before they brush mine.

He is warmth and comfort. We're slow at first, savouring the new taste and texture of someone else, but then I open my mouth, and the kiss intensifies. He shifts closer, and I do the same, amazed at how quickly my concerns can disappear and only focus on the feel of his palms against my hips.

The leather jacket falls to the floor, but instead of shivering in the cold, a heat burns across my skin. I thread my fingers through the hair on his neck, pulling just enough to let him know I want him closer.

'Chris could come up here,' I whisper, but oddly the idea of him catching us only makes me lean against Dominic more, and when my lips find his again, his tongue parts them and a little sigh escapes the back of my throat.

Hank barks like mad, and I jump, laughing at myself for being startled and for the intensity of what just passed between us. I'm breathing heavily. An interruption may be for the best, because I shouldn't be trusted in a room alone with Dominic.

'We should go downstairs,' I say. 'I have a theory I want to run past you.' He'll have to slip out the back door the same way he came before Chris sees him, but it won't take long for me to convince him whoever killed Blake must be involved in Julie's death too.

He tugs on my hand, and I stumble back, where he catches me and gives me a quick kiss. I don't resist – for a second. Then I pull back, exhaling deeply.

'Downstairs.'

'You keep saying that, but you're not leaving.' He laughs against my cheek and breathes into the side of my neck.

Yes. This is definitely dangerous. Intoxicating.

But the intensity vanishes like smoke in the wind when Chris's words fill the attic.

'What are you doing here?'

26

January 6

'I – he came by to check on the house. I let him in.'

Chris stands on the stairs, only visible from his torso and above, but suspicion covers his face, so I add, 'He didn't lock me in the shed.'

This time, Dominic doesn't cross his arms in defiance or try to stand firm against Chris's accusing stare. He says, 'It's true. I pulled up as her message came through and ran when I heard her pounding on the door. I just came over to make sure everything was okay.'

'As you can see,' Chris says, 'we're fine, so you can be going.'

'You're not planning on sleeping here, are you?' Dominic asks me. 'Come to my house.'

'Do you have power?' I ask.

'The storm knocked it out, but at least at our place there's a chance of it coming back on.'

'We're fine, thanks.' Chris waves a hand in front of him, directing Dominic to leave.

'Chris, if this is about my dad—'

'Shh!' Chris says, hand up. 'Do you hear that?'

'Hear what?'

'Shh,' Chris says again. 'You don't hear that?'

The wind howls, whistling over the chimney just above the attic roof. I strain my ears.

'I swear I heard something,' Chris says. 'A scratching.' He disappears down the steps.

I follow him.

'Ella, wait—'

But I ignore Dominic and trail Chris down the stairs, alert for any sounds over the creaking. Dominic comes behind me.

It's dark outside the glow of the fireplace when we enter the living room. Joey and Hank simultaneously raise their heads. Chris's hunt for flashlights must have been successful because two wait for us on the coffee table. Chris grabs one and waves it around.

'I don't hear anything,' Dominic says.

'Maybe it was an animal?'

I quiet my breathing, but the scratching is gone.

'It was coming from the second floor . . .' I move back towards the stairs.

Dominic's hand wraps around my arm as I pass. 'Ella, there's something else I want to talk to you about, can we . . . ?'

'If you two want to make out, just go to his place.' Chris feeds the fire with another log, sending a fresh wave of sparks glowing in the stone before they burn out.

'That's not – we weren't—'

'Seriously, I'm fine here.'

'No, Chris, I'm not leaving you. We can all go.'

I look to Dominic but he hesitates.

'He doesn't want me there,' Chris says.

'That's not true. Right?'

Dominic says nothing.

'We should stay together,' I insist.

'Why? What's the big deal?' Dominic asks.

I resist the urge to fidget with my hands. I wanted to keep this theory quiet until I had proof, but if I can convince them, they can help – or at least be focused on a goal other than scowling at each other. Joey waits expectantly on the couch, arms wrapped around Hank.

'I've been thinking, and I don't have all the answers yet, but there must be more to this story than only Blake.'

'What do you mean?' Chris's question is quick.

'Yeah,' Joey echoes. I hesitate in front of him, but he should be aware, like all of us. On guard.

'I think there's another person out there, a partner of Blake's who double-crossed him.'

There's a beat before Chris says, 'You don't think he was working alone? Who else would there be? Nicki Davis?'

'You think they were working together?' Dominic says slowly. 'Why would she kill Blake before he's collected the money?'

'I don't know . . . there's something else we're not seeing. Joey and Chris were listed first on the insurance forms, so maybe they need to tie up loose ends.'

'Loose ends, like killing us?' Joey asks, checking outside. His face pales in the fading light. I don't want to scare him, but I don't want us to be lulled into a false sense of security either.

Were all the noises outside from Dominic or an animal, or is there someone else out there . . . someone looking to finish what they started . . .

'What if someone is trying to get in the house?' I ask.

Chris tenses, muscles ready to react. Dominic's brows knit together. He puts his hands in his pockets. 'I don't think anyone else is out there.'

'How do you know?'

'They'd have to be out of their mind to be out in this.' As if to support Dominic's point, sleet hits the window in a sloppy, icy mess.

'You were,' Chris quips.

Dominic ignores him, and Joey presses his nose against the window.

'See anything?' I ask.

He shakes his head, and even Dominic's footprints have been filled, revealing only a slight shadow in the dips. 'Someone was trying to kill your mom and Blake, and now they need us gone too. We know too much.'

The information keeps fitting together, tighter and tighter. It all makes sense. This is the only logical explanation.

'So you believe the same person who killed your aunt killed Blake?' Dominic asks carefully.

Chris's eyes dart to Dominic and back to me.

'What evidence is there to support that?' Dominic asks.

'There's a connection with that house in Springtown . . .' I'm pacing now; the energy of pieces fitting together is electric. 'But nothing ever came out about Blake or Nicki being listed on that guy's life insurance. The police would have seen the pattern, so there's someone else involved. And the message. What if that threatening message I got was never from Blake at all? What if it was someone else trying to scare me away, just like they're trying to scare us away right now? They'd only be doing it if we were close.'

I stop pacing to face them, and the look they exchange isn't tainted with suspicion or anger or anything else that's been battling between them.

But then Dominic asks Chris, 'What do you think?' and I hear the suspicion in his voice: I'm overreacting, imagining things. He probably thinks I'm tired again and need a nap.

Stress might be triggering his calm reaction, but at what point does it become denying a dangerous truth?

'I'm not paranoid, Dominic.' My tone is measured, matching his. I can make him believe me if he doesn't hear any panic. My theory is as logical as anyone else's, and certainly more than anyone who says it's all an unfortunate coincidence.

'I never said you were.'

I stand tall, even if it means I'm still several inches shorter than him. 'You didn't have to.'

Chris and Joey watch us like a ping-pong match.

'Look, I'm not trying to fight—'

'I'm not either. And it won't be one if you can take me seriously.'

'I'm taking you very seriously.'

'But you still don't believe me.' I cross my arms.

'I just don't think there's someone else out there.' He looks at me, like he's trying to convey another meaning, but I can't quite grasp it. 'Between the shed and the noises, something else could explain everything . . .' He trails off.

'Wait,' Chris says. 'Do you mean . . .' Chris's jaw drops in disgust. 'Wow, man, low blow.'

'Wha—' Dominic says.

'You told him, didn't you?' Chris asks me while keeping his eyes on Dominic. 'About your diagnosis. He knows.'

'I, yeah, but . . .' Then it hits.

The tumour.

Dominic thinks this is all in my head, but not because I'm tired. He thinks my judgement's impaired by the growth in my skull.

'No,' I shout. 'No. That's not what's happening.'

It's not. I know it's not. This isn't connected to my diagnosis at all. I'm right. I know I am. Not everything is because of this stupid tumour!

I'm not sure how my face contorts – into rage, surprise or betrayal – but Dominic knows the instant I realise what he's implying.

'I didn't mention anything about your diagnosis—'

'You didn't have to.' Revulsion lines Chris's face.

'Ella,' Dominic says. 'Take a deep breath and think things through.'

There's nothing to think through. It's right here in front of me. After trusting him with everything – from my medical stuff to my theory – after kissing him and opening myself up, after all of that, he only sees one thing.

And just like Dr Mullins, he doesn't believe me. Just like my teachers, he doesn't hear anything I say without thinking of the tumour. Just like my worst fears, he can't look at me without seeing a girl with a brain tumour.

'You need to go.' I point to the door.

Dominic plants his feet. 'Ella, I want to help.'

'No!' I shriek. I should be able to laugh him off or shut him down but his doubts scream: *I'm not worth listening to. I can't do things on my own. My ideas aren't worth considering.*

Chris reaches for Dominic's upper arm. 'Time for you to go.'

Dominic shakes him off. 'Get your hands off me, man.' He shoves Chris back, and he stumbles. Hank jumps off the couch and barks.

'What are you doing?' I scream, reaching to help Chris off the floor.

'Ella, I—'

'LEAVE!' I shout, but he doesn't move. 'Go!' I get in his face, but he only stares at me, and I can't read him, but he won't listen to me and he won't move. I push him, and he lets me, and it's wrong and I know it, but I need him to listen and he won't. 'Get out of here! You don't believe me and I don't want you here anymore! GET AWAY FROM ME!'

He shuffles back and Chris picks himself off the floor.

'LEAVE!' I scream again.

Chris pulls the door open against the frigid cold.

And this time, Dominic listens.

His gloves are on and he's out the door into the icy white once more.

27

January 6

Joey's frozen on the couch. Chris skirts around me. Neither says a word.

Minutes – minutes – after I tell Dominic about the tumour, he uses it against me.

Tears prick, but I have to pull myself together. I won't fall apart.

Turning my back on the boys, I march to the pantry, releasing a huff when I open the door. I grab the peanut butter and try to rip off the lid. It doesn't budge.

'Come on.' I beat the plastic against the edge of the counter. 'You.' *Bang.* 'Stupid.' *Bang.* 'Piece of—'

'Ella, Ella.' Chris reaches for the jar.

'I got it.' *Bang. Bang.*

Sierra would probably tell me to give Dominic the benefit of the doubt, but she hasn't been dismissed and doubted, or kept herself hidden and then had her weakness used against her as a weapon.

At least I was right. I never should have told anyone.

Chris's hands find mine, gently pulling the peanut butter from my grasp. 'Let me.'

I relinquish my hold and am rewarded by seeing him struggle too.

Looking for any distraction, I grab my phone before I remember I'm supposed to be conserving the battery. The 10 per cent warning of doom flashes at me. I grumble and tuck it in my pocket.

'Mine already died,' Chris says quietly, like he's a little scared I might explode again. He pulls open a drawer and grabs a butter knife, wedging it between the lid and edge of the jar before the lid finally twists off and he hands it to me.

'Thanks. Don't you have a charger in the car?' I latch onto the change in topic but spread the peanut butter more aggressively than strictly necessary. The bread rips and falls to pieces.

'I have one, but not a ton of gas. Better to have no battery at night when we probably won't need it. We can charge in the morning as we're driving home.' He pauses. 'You call that a sandwich?'

I look at the mangled pile of bread and peanut butter sitting on the plate and laugh through a sniffle. Chris pulls me into a side hug.

'He doesn't know what he's talking about.'

I step out from his arms, wiping my nose, and huff. 'Yeah.'

'You were right to kick him out.'

'If that's true, shouldn't I feel better?'

Chris makes himself a sandwich – one that's actually edible.

'Not always. Sometimes you have to do what sucks because it's best in the long run.'

That's true. I know whatever treatment plan I choose for my tumour will be awful going through it, but it's the only way I'll have a future. A little pain for a lifetime of... well, any life at all.

But right now, it doesn't feel that way with Dominic. I don't know who I'm more angry with: him or myself.

I was stupid to trust him, to think I could tell someone and have him treat me the same. An idiot. A fool.

Chris and Joey had to witness it all.

I try to hide how much it bothers me while we finish eating. While we spread blankets on the couches. While I lie with my feet curled up across from Joey's. While I pretend to sleep. While my mind races in circles.

I'll prove Dominic wrong.

The truth is hiding here, somewhere. I can find it. Julie's funeral is tomorrow, and she deserves to be laid to rest. I'm going to find the proof no one can deny. I'll make sure everyone believes me.

I wake to Hank growling. It's still dark. The fire is mostly embers. The clock on my phone reveals I haven't been asleep very long, but my battery is fading fast.

An extra stash of meds are in my bag, but a headache didn't wake me.

Hank growls louder.

'Shh!' I tell him.

Joey stays motionless on the other end of the couch. I strain my ears for what's drawn Hank's attention, but it's an old house. It creaks all the time.

The shadows cast by the fire waver with the flicking of flames, like someone is breathing them in and out.

No one is trying to get in. No one is out th—

Creeeak.

Hank growls again. 'Chris?' I hiss, rolling over. 'Did you hear that?'

He's gone.

A cast-aside blanket lies across the sofa where Chris was sleeping.

Another floorboard creaks, and Hank's bark rips through the quiet.

'It's just Chris,' I whisper to Hank, careful not to wake Joey when I slip out from under the blanket. Chris is gone, so he's the one creaking the floor.

Right?

Hank spins in circles when I stand.

I'd call out for Chris, but Joey's sweetly sleeping face stops me. Instead, I walk in that direction, using the pale moonlight reflecting off the snow as my guide. Hank pads quietly next to me.

I'm not one to believe in ghosts or souls being left behind, but even if it's not a spectral energy in the house, the weight of knowing she died here lingers like the smell of smoke and ash.

A shadow flashes. I spin and gasp, barely stopping a scream.

Wait. The shadow is gone.

Was it there at all? Was it like the one I saw the other night outside the shed? My pulse pounds in my ears.

Breathe. Just breathe. I'm tired. That's all. I have to stop freaking myself out.

A beam of light bounces from Aunt Julie's room.

'Chris?' I whisper-call, reaching the doorway.

'Son of a – Ella.' Chris nearly drops the flashlight when he startles. He's standing at Julie's dresser.

'What are you doing in here?'

Chris's body should relax now that he knows it's me, but it's like every muscle has forgotten how. His shoulders remain tense. His brows scrunch. So much has been weighing on him for so long, and in the dim moonlight, I can see it better than ever before.

He holds something small between his fingers, but I can't see it until he places it in my palm. 'It was Grandma's ring. After Grandpa died, she gave it to my mom.'

'I never saw her wear it,' I say, examining the purple gem in the centre of the thick gold band while Chris steadies the flashlight.

'She said she didn't trust herself not to lose it. It was too special, one of the few things that made Grandma smile.'

Dad never talks about his parents much, but apparently Julie did, to Chris anyway.

'She said she never wanted us to grow up in a house like she did,' he continues. 'Always clean. Always serious. Stifling, she'd said. She didn't want us to feel that way.'

'Did it work?' I ask.

'I don't think anyone can escape life without feeling trapped by something.' Chris's face is masked by the dark, but his voice says more than his words. It's like glass, cracking, almost imperceptibly, but on the brink of shattering.

'I regret telling Dominic about my diagnosis, but I don't regret telling you. We trust each other.'

He's silent, like he's battling how much to share, a battle I recognise.

'She tried so hard not to be like her mom,' he says. 'And I tried not to be like mine. I hate being late. I turned in my homework even when I wanted to work and pay the bills on time instead.' He pockets the ring and sits on the bed, looking around the room. 'It would be better if this was all gone. If I never had to come here again. If I was gone.'

I'd almost forgotten what he said in the car about leaving. It's selfish for me to want him to stay, but with Julie's absence so fresh, I can't stand the thought of saying goodbye, even if it won't be forever.

I step in front of him, waiting for him to break away from whatever ghosts haunt him in this room. 'We have to do what you said. We take life in our own hands and try to make it better.'

But Chris doesn't nod. He doesn't get up and wander back into the living room. He doesn't move at all.

I wait with him. His secret is close, and once he releases it, I'll catch him when he falls.

Trust me, I beg.

Finally, he says, 'I was so angry at Blake, and I wanted to make him pay.' His voice is rough, fractured, the cracks growing. 'I wanted justice. I should be glad he died.' His volume grows, the last words escaping like a plea, like if he could somehow muster relief from hearing that Blake died, then all might be right in his world. 'But his death doesn't change anything. I should have seen what he was doing. I should have stopped it. And now I have this weight around me . . . I killed someone.'

'No, Chris, no. This wasn't your fault. Blake did this. He wanted you to blame yourself.'

'You don't understand.' Even in the dim light, his eyes glow, red and wide, full of fear and self-loathing.

'Remember what he said to me in the station?' The words fly, desperate to shield my cousin from the blame he's wielding like a weapon against himself. 'Remember how he suggested Julie's death was my fault? He wants you to feel like I'm responsible or you're responsible, because it would mean he's not. But you're not a killer, Chris. You didn't kill your mom.'

'No, but I killed Blake.'

28

January 6

Chris's words echo against my skull, pushing against every piece of truth I know about him. That can't be true. Chris isn't a murderer.

'Wh– how?'

His hands tremble, eyes glassy. 'I went over to his house.'

I sink onto the bed next to him, but my body feels like it's floating above us, unanchored. 'When?'

'After Peterson and Langdon left.'

He was so upset. I let him leave. I thought he needed time and space.

'I just . . . I had been trying to deny the truth for days. Blake kept telling me it was an accident and not my fault, and I wanted to believe him, but it was *his* fault. And I could finally see it. So I went over there that night.'

He rakes his hands through his hair.

'What happened?' I'm not sure I want the answer.

'I pounded on his door and pushed my way in.' He sucks in a shuddering breath, like it's playing before him, an unwanted horror rerun. 'Blake – he'd been drinking. He tried to wave me off. He threatened me . . . and you. He said if the message you got on your phone didn't stop you from snooping around, he would have to make good on it.'

'He actually said that?' Blake was the one threatening me. I was right about that too.

'I . . . I couldn't take it. He was so casual about it, like he didn't see what he'd already taken from me. I just . . . I . . .'

'What did you do, Chris?'

'I . . . I don't know.' He pops off the bed, pacing at the foot of it like he can't stop moving any more than he can stop the words from pouring out. 'My anger just . . . just took over, and I charged him. Ran straight at him and slammed him into a wall. His drink fell out of his hand. I think the glass broke. His head and back put a dent in his drywall. A big one. I let go, and he slipped to the floor . . . but he was conscious. He was breathing and his eyes were open. He was dazed, but he looked at me. I pointed at him. I said something, I don't even remember what, something about staying away from my family. He threatened you, Ella. I couldn't let him . . . not after . . .'

Chris is always so protective of his family, and now he might have killed Blake over it. If Blake hadn't died, would he have come after me? Would I still be here now?

'He laughed,' Chris says. 'That's what I remember. He laughed at me, and he was still laughing when he tried to get up and I slammed the door on him and left.'

'But . . . that doesn't sound like you killed him, not if he was awake when you walked out.'

'Head injuries can show up hours later. He could have had a concussion. He was drunk. That would make it worse. I looked it up after the police left.'

Chris twists his hands together and then shoves them under his arms, like he can't sit with the truth, like it's been preying on him since that night.

And it has, I realise. He was so determined the next morning to plant evidence, but not tortured. He didn't know Blake was dead then, only that he'd threatened me and laughed at him when he tried to protect me. It wasn't until that night, when Officer Varden told us about Blake's death, that he changed, that the shadows appeared . . . now I know why.

'You weren't trying to kill him. You didn't go over there to hurt him.' The police had already called wanting to question him. He can't hide this.

'No, I went over there because I knew it was all his fault and I wanted him to admit it. I wanted him to hurt like I was hurting, but I – I don't feel better about Mom being gone, and shouldn't I feel worse about Blake being dead? I don't. What kind of person am I?'

'This isn't your fault,' I say, but he could still go to prison. He's an adult now, and his entire life could be ripped away.

'It doesn't matter! I might have killed him, Ella!' He stops abruptly. 'You can't tell anyone.'

Desperation coats his voice like thick syrup, and his plea drips on me, sticking between my conscience and my loyalty. I want to say yes immediately and full-heartedly. I want to promise I'll take his confession with me to the grave if I have to. We're family, and he'd do the same for me, so of course I don't want to see Chris go to prison, not for trying to protect me, not for hurting the man who killed his mother, not when he didn't mean to kill anyone.

But his eyes are bloodshot. His hands are trembling. This secret's tearing him apart. People drive themselves insane with this kind of guilt. It might not even be his fault, but he's convinced himself it is, and he doesn't deserve this torture.

For the first time, I understand why Mom's been pushing me to talk to people about my tumour. She's watched me hurting, even when I didn't want to admit to myself how much.

That's what I want for Chris right now. I'm not qualified to get him through this, but I don't want him in trouble and—

'Ella, promise me.' Chris's desperation jerks me back to the present where Chris stands, waiting.

'I promise.' I don't even know if it's a lie. My heart hasn't committed. He can't keep living like this, and if telling someone can get him the help he needs, betraying his trust would be worth it.

Right?

Chris lets me take the flashlight from his hand.

'We're in this together,' he says.

Chris waits for my confirmation, its absence ballooning in the space between us. All I can muster is, 'Let's go to bed.'

Wordlessly, he follows me back to the living room couches, the warmth of the fire not strong, but better than his mom's room. I tuck myself into the covers without waking Joey, but sleep isn't an option.

'Ella,' Chris whispers. His hushed voice reminds me of when we were kids and he spent the night. Except his next words feel like a hand reaching from under the couch to grab my ankle: 'You promised.'

I'm quiet for so long, he might think I've fallen asleep, or that I'm faking it. He doesn't try to convince me, doesn't try to persuade me. He might not even be looking for acknowledgement, because it's done.

I promised.

'Let's talk about it in the morning,' I say, drawing the quilt up to my chin.

Chris doesn't say anything else, and after a bit, steady breaths signal he's out.

Blake is dead.

Chris may have killed him.

Someone else might still be out there.

Chris wants me to keep his secret.

And even though the house is still and we're all together in the living room with the fire breathing its warmth over us in this tight circle, I can't ignore the feeling –

But, no. No one is watching us, surely.

January 7

When I awake in the morning, it feels like I've hardly slept at all.

Julie's viewing is in a few hours.

Joey stirs by my feet on the other end of the couch. The blanket's encased around him like a cocoon he hasn't crawled out of.

It's way too early for him to be up, or at least the heavy weights on my eyelids suggest it's earlier than anyone has any right to be awake.

None of that can distract me from my conversation with Chris last night.

Someone might have seen his car outside Blake's house that night, or the police might get a warrant and be able to track his movements somehow. If he's honest with a lawyer, he'll be able to explain what happened, that he's not the same as Blake, that it wasn't premeditated.

That has to count for something, doesn't it?

I don't want him to be arrested, but keeping his secret won't necessarily prevent that. It might only make things worse for him. The events of that night – of this whole week – will haunt him for the rest of his life.

But I don't have to betray him at all if I can convince him to tell the police himself, or a lawyer, or at least my parents. Someone.

'Hey,' I whisper to Joey, 'have you picked out any more toys to bring back to my house? We're going to leave here as soon as the roads are safe.'

Joey walks away rubbing his eyes. He's not the same kid he was, and I can't expect him to be, but something else has changed since we've returned to this house. For all of us.

Nothing will ever be the same.

Hank stands on alert, staring at the doorway.

'It's okay, boy.' I scratch behind his ears until he circles around. He's been on edge since we got here too, and I don't blame him.

Without notice, Hank jumps to his feet and scampers up the stairs after Joey.

Chris rolls over, giving a stretch. 'What time is it?' He folds the blankets and pokes the black and grey stubs left in the fire.

'Time to get going. The roads out here won't be great, but once we get closer to town, it should be better.'

My phone's weather app still warns of icy road conditions, but if the salt trucks were out all night, it must be safer than it was. Before I get to click on any specifics, the red light flashes. My battery is nearly dead.

A message comes through. Chris pauses his folding while I read, like he can sense what's coming.

'It's from my parents. They've been trying to reach you.'

'My phone died yesterday.'

I keep reading. 'They said the police are at my house. They want to talk with you.'

Chris pales. 'They know. They must know.'

'It's okay, it's okay. You can tell them the truth.'

'No, I can't.' He ties his shoes. 'Tell them you haven't seen me, I'll leave.'

'You can't leave. What about Joey?'

'What about him?'

'He's lost so much already. He can't take his brother leaving him too.'

The mention of his brother stops Chris in his tracks. His brow draws tight in confusion, like he's not sure how to fix his problem at hand and protect Joey.

Finally he says, 'Just . . . just buy me some time. Tell them I left to go . . . to go . . .'

Chris must see eerie dread spilling over me like an egg cracked on my skull, dripping with the blood draining to my feet.

His voice changes from panic to curiosity. 'What?'

'Did you take these pictures of me?'

'What pictures?'

'These. On my phone.' I swipe through a series of five or six photos so Chris can see. I'm asleep in all of them. The pictures are from different angles, some getting close. Very close. Hovering right over me.

'They're all from last night.'

The images change, and there are a few of Chris, also sleeping on this couch, also disturbingly close.

My screen goes black. I tap the buttons on the side, but nothing happens.

Dead.

All three of us were asleep, and Chris's phone is dead. If we didn't take these, then . . . the only possibility hits me like a wave, knocking me off my feet and scraping me on the sand all the way back to shore.

'Did someone get in the house?' I should be looking at Chris when I ask, but instead, my head whips over my shoulder, like the intruder will jump out of the shadows with a knife.

Chris takes the phone from my hands, but there's no juice left. 'Who would do that? Why?'

I lower my voice. 'Just to mess with us? Freak us out because they can?'

Judging by Chris's face, he doesn't believe it either.

'They broke in to steal stuff?' I offer, still quiet.

'Someone breaks in to loot the place, sees us on the couches and decides nah, I'll leave and just take these pictures of them sleeping instead?'

'Okay, then what do you think?' The pictures were so close. Chris's eyes were closed, face relaxed, defenceless. Whoever took them would have been standing right over us in the dark, breathing on us.

Chris jumps to look out the front window before jogging to the back one. 'There aren't any new footprints outside. So no one came in or left last night.'

The doors are still locked, reinforcing that theory.

The answer is staring us in the face and smacks us at the same time, but I say it first.

'They've been inside the whole time.'

Chris's jaw drops, arm outstretched.

Instinctively, we come together in the centre of the living room, checking over our shoulders, dropping our voices to a whisper, afraid to speak.

'Could someone have been living here, moved in after the police?' My voice sounds scratchy, not my own. 'A . . . what did Dominic call them? Squatter?'

'Maybe.' Chris raises the fire poker over his shoulder. 'Or they're trying to scare us off.'

'We might be overreacting,' I suggest, trying to be calm and rational the way everyone says I'm not lately. My skin tickles like a spider disappeared in my bed.

'Do you' – Chris rotates to face another doorway – 'think they're watching us right now? Listening?'

The vents line the living room. They're in the walls, on the floor. What kind of crawl spaces do these old houses have?

I gulp. 'Once, I read a book where there was an old woman and her son who were living in the basement and the family never knew. The woman would come out at night and talk to her little stepsister. Oh—'

'What?'

The nest in the attic. The tablecloths and wrappers I assumed were Joey's doing.

'Chris. Could someone have been living here before you moved out? Could someone have set that gas leak to kill your family and get rid of all of you?'

He licks his lips, like he's tasting the theory, rolling it over his tongue, trying to swallow it as a possibility.

Could someone secretly have been living in this house for . . . who knows how long? Someone deranged? Someone who tried to kill him and his brother, who successfully killed his mom? Someone who did Blake's bidding?

'We have to get out of here. Now.'

29

January 7

'Get the car ready,' I whisper, muscles on edge. 'We'll meet you there.'

'Ella.' Chris extends the fire poker for me to grab. 'Hurry.'

'Joey!' I whisper-yell and race up the stairs. We have to get out of here, before we don't have a chance.

A flash of movement catches my attention, too big to be Joey. I dodge behind a corner, holding my breath.

Ka-shhh. Ka-shhh. Ka-shhh.

What is that?

I need to get Joey and get out of here. I grip the fire poker and flee down the hall, but when I open the door to Joey's room, no one's there. Only toys. The weird noise comes from a red box in the back corner. I dig around and find a robotic astronaut lighting up.

Ka-shhh. Ka—

I hit the power button, and the toy stops. The room settles into an eerie silence.

'Joey?' I double-check under the bed and in the closet.

If he's not in here, where is he?

'Joey!' I call, panic setting in as I fly from the hall closet to the spare room until – 'There you are! What are you doing?'

Joey stands in the corner, a dirty grey heap at his feet. His body is relaxed, his face empty, tired.

'I found it.' His voice is even, steady. That's when I recognise the grey heap as the body of an opossum.

'Oh, Joey,' I say, reaching for his hand. He pulls away, a violent movement I'm not expecting.

'I didn't kill it,' he says.

'I know you didn't. Of course you didn't.' This animal isn't playing dead, not with the way its stomach curves in under its ribs.

There's no telling when it died. It's possible it got into the house while it was empty, the cause of the scratching we heard.

Or it's possible whoever is in the house killed it. And we might be next.

'I know you're scared. We're all scared. But we're leaving, okay?' My voice shouldn't be this steady. 'Someone wants us gone, and we're going to listen.' I won't let anyone hurt Joey. Not when he hasn't done anything to deserve this, not when he might stand a chance of having a bright future. I slowly grab Joey's hand and this time he lets me, even if he won't stop staring at the carcass. 'We're going to keep you safe,' I say, pulling him to the doorway. 'Come on.'

I call for Hank, but he's already at my heels, ready to leave.

Any crack in my voice might reveal to Joey how scared I am. 'I've got him, Chris!'

Chris pops up at the bottom of the stairs. 'You've got him?'

Hank bounds to his side, and Chris grabs his keys off the coffee table. 'I've got your stuff. Let's go.'

We sprint for the door.

I carefully skate my way to the car. It's slippery. Really slippery. The car is encased in a thin layer of ice. I crush my fist against the door handle, and the ice cracks, falling off in chunks. I move up to the window, hitting it twice until the ice splits like glass. I wipe it away in shards.

'Kick the door so you can open it.'

Joey doesn't move and Chris hesitates before he kicks, icicles breaking off.

'I just saw someone!' Joey shouts. 'Upstairs. In the window.'

A sudden urge to talk to my mom rushes over me. To hug her, to tell her I'm okay and I'm sorry for being bitter when she tried to protect me.

I will not let anyone hurt us.

'Let's go! Hurry!'

'Get in! Get in!' I throw the door open and wait for Hank and Joey to scramble inside, but when I reach across to open Chris's from the inside while he smashes at it with his fist and elbow, nothing works.

'Come on!' Chris shouts, whether to me or the door.

I twist on my back and kick out, both feet smashing into the door until it pops. The ice cracks and splinters again when Chris slams it shut and he jams the key in the ignition.

We can't even reverse out of the driveway without fishtailing.

The tires squeal against the ice, throwing us more to the side than straight back.

'We have to call the police,' I say as Chris throws the car in drive and struggles to get forward momentum. 'Where's your charger?'

'I thought it was right there.' He flips open the centre console and nearly slides off the road.

'Chris!'

He wrenches the wheel back with two hands, releasing the gas pedal until we coast in a straight line, fields flashing by on both sides. It's like driving on an ice rink.

We both breathe heavily, afraid to make any sudden movements. Chris's knuckles are white against the wheel, shoulders tense. Hank whines in the back.

'This was a bad idea,' Chris says.

I ignore him and rifle through the centre console, the glove compartment, feeling under my seat.

'There's no charger.'

He lets out a curse and shoves the wheel. 'I forgot I let Alex borrow it.'

I slump in my seat, my useless phone a brick in my hand. No calling for help. No alerting the police.

'Who was it? Back there?'

'I didn't see them.'

In the back seat, Hank pants wildly, whining to get in front. Joey stares at his shoes behind Chris.

'Buckle up,' I tell Joey, and he obeys. 'We should stop

somewhere and call.' The police might not take me seriously after the shed, but if Chris calls . . .

'Where?' Chis says. 'There aren't any gas stations between here and your house.'

'There's that one Dollar General—'

'If they're even open.'

The radio's emergency tone cuts through our conversation announcing that the county is still under a state of emergency and no one except emergency personnel should be on the roads.

We seem to be the only ones dumb enough to risk our lives, which at least means the odds of us hitting another car are drastically lower.

Still, I can't help but imagine the car's body wrapping around every pole we pass or crunching into any fence.

'We should turn around and go to Dominic's,' I say.

'He doesn't have any power either. His phone is probably as dead as ours. We'll take it slow. We'll get to your house. You can tell your parents what happened.'

He says the directives simply, like he's comforting himself with the plan, convincing more than just me and Joey that everything will be fine.

'Once we get there, I can show them those pictures.'

'What pictures?' Chris says, still pale. He swallows like it takes conscious effort. He turns down another road.

'The ones someone took on my phone.'

He shakes his head.

'I showed them to you right before my phone died.'

'I . . . never saw any pictures.'

'What are you talking about? I showed them to you. And they were of us sleeping.'

I showed him my phone and he said we were both sleeping, and that's when I realised someone else must be in the house with us. That's how it happened, right?

Right?

'Ella . . . you look pale.'

My breaths are fast, sharp.

'Take deep breaths,' he says. 'You're panicking.'

'We were both panicked. At the house. You saw the pictures. I showed them to you.' We're both terrified, still coming down from the adrenaline. That's all. I showed him, but in the frenzy, he's forgotten.

'I – I don't know anything about any pictures, Ella. You said you thought someone was in the house, and then you raced upstairs—'

'Yeah, *after* I showed you the pictures. After you saw them on my phone. I went upstairs to get Joey, and—'

Chris's head whips to me. If I'm pale, he's the snow. The dark circles under his eyes make the whites pop. 'What do you mean *to get Joey?*'

Hank barks, and I have to force him back from between the two seats. I almost expect Joey to be crying in the back or curled in a ball, but he's sitting, hands folded, placid. Still as a statue. 'He was upstairs, so I had to get him without being seen by . . . whoever was back there!'

'Ella, who's in the car with us?'

'What do you mean? It's us and Hank, right?'

I lean around the seats, for a split second worried someone else is in the car with us, somehow hiding and waiting to pop out and wrap their hands around our necks or mouth or—

No, no. That's ridiculous. Chris is being ridiculous. He isn't making sense – forgetting the pictures is one thing, but suggesting someone else is in the car . . .

We skate around another corner.

'Maybe I should drive,' I offer.

Chris watches me with the same uncertainty I give him. 'What happened when you woke up this morning. Exactly.'

'I woke up and Joey was already awake, and—'

He frowns. 'When did Joey get there?'

'What do you mean? He came with us to the house.'

Chris speeds up again, both hands on the wheel. 'I'm going to bring you back to your parents. Everything's going to be okay.'

'You're not making any sense. Joey was asleep in the back seat when you picked me up from my appointment. Right, Joey?'

'I've been here the whole time.' His innocent voice is barely audible over the slush thrashing the undercarriage of the car, but it's distinct. Chris turns in his seat.

'See? Watch out!'

Chris whips forward and spins the wheel, the car fishtailing into the other lane before he corrects himself.

'Slow down!' I'm clutching the handle above the window, but he doesn't slow. He speeds up.

'I'm going to get you home.'

'You're scaring Joey!' His soft whimpers come from the back.

'Ella,' Chris says, his voice quavering. 'Joey's not back there. He's—'

'CHRIS!'

Too late. His arms jerk with his focus on trying to control the car, but we're off the road now and a tree is right in front of us, and he yanks on the wheel again, trying to avoid it.

With a crunch and splintering of glass, we hit head-on.

30

January 7

When I wake up, I hear the hissing first. Constant and high-pitched.

Gas.

I startle. I'm in the car. My ribs hurt. My head aches. I move, and glass tinkles off, showering the ground with more shards.

Hisssssss.

It's not carbon monoxide or gas. It's from the engine. Smoke or steam or something pours into the car through the broken glass. The air bag is deflated in my lap, white powder caked around me.

I touch my head and wince. My fingers come away with blood, bright red.

A tree. I can see it through the smoke and powder. We hit a tree.

Chris is in the driver's seat next to me. His head rests on his shoulder. Blood speckles the air bag. He's not moving.

Is he dead?

The thought doesn't quite reach my core, or it must not,

because if I saw my cousin dead in the seat next to me, I would be sad or scared or try to help him. But I don't feel anything. Numb.

Joey. Where's Joey? I can't twist to see into the back seat.

I reach for my seat belt and have to stop. It hurts. Everything feels like I'm filled with sand and even stretching my fingers requires too much effort.

Click.

The belt releases, and something inside me releases too. I was in a car wreck. We hit a tree. Chris isn't moving beside me. A pounding builds in my ears. Blood. My heart is racing.

Where's Joey?

I can't see him in the back seat.

'Joey?' I call, but my voice isn't nearly as loud as I expect it to be. I cough and sputter. 'Joey!'

He doesn't answer. The door groans when I push it open, and I practically fall onto the crunchy snow. The rear passenger window is gone. Bits of glass mix with the broken ice scattered all around.

Hank whines in the back seat, lying still, slowly blinking.

But Joey isn't here.

Was he thrown from the car? Was he not wearing his seat belt? No, I checked. I saw him buckled. 'Joey!' I call again. But there's nothing here, or anywhere. He's not outside the car.

No footprints. No tracks except for our tires careening off the road. Joey's not here.

He's not here.

Chris's words right before the crash come back to me: *Joey's not back there. He's—*

But he has to be. He was in the back seat with us. I blink and wipe my cheeks, like I can clear away the sharp and clear picture before me, like I'll open my eyes again and Joey will be sitting in the back seat safe and sound and whole.

But only Hank is there, whining. The seat belt isn't fastened where I saw Joey buckle. The door isn't open. No footprints mark the snow.

But he can't have just . . . disappeared. That doesn't make sense. It doesn't make sense.

'Joey! Joey!' I scream again, but my voice floats into nothingness, and from the depths of my subconscious, a whisper of truth escapes.

He was never here.

Joey was never in the car . . .

No. That's not true. That can't be true. Because if he was never here, then . . .

Dr Gupta's voice comes back to me, an unwanted answer to my calls for Joey.

She listed other possible effects of the tumour: *seizures, short-term memory problems, hallucinations . . .*

'Joey!' I scream again, not wanting to believe it. I stumble around the car, looking for missed footprints, ones I know can't be here because Joey isn't here. *No!*

'JOEY! JOEY! JO—'

I collapse to my knees, my voice dying as the truth swells to life.

Joey's not in the back seat of the car because he was never in the back seat.

But I saw him there, vivid and real. He was crying in his bed the first night after the gas leak. He was at the counter when I made him dinner. He was in his room picking out toys for me to bring home. He was lying on the couch when Chris and I went to sleep.

But he wasn't.

I remember sitting beside him at the hospital, waiting for Chris to wake up, putting my hand on his knee like it wasn't there. When the blanket fell to the floor, my brain told me he stood to hug his brother.

But Chris never hugged him back because he was never there.

Joey was never there.

He wasn't standing over the opossum, cold and distant. Joey would never. He's warmth and light and joy.

So that means . . . he was never at the house. Dominic never spoke to him. When I made a joke about Joey covering for us going to the attic, Dominic thought I was talking to Hank on the couch.

I thought Joey was just being quiet. Around the house. I replay the conversations with Mom. At the doctor's office, she said, *'And what about Joey? It always seems harder with someone so young.'* I thought she meant losing a parent, but she could have meant . . .

It's harder when someone so young dies.

Joey is . . . dead?

My stomach churns and I double over, heaving. Julie and Joey both died on New Year's Eve. My little cousin is gone.

Joey is dead.

Joey who wanted to be a pilot will never board a plane. He'll never play checkers with me or giggle playing Connect Four. He won't run and tackle Chris on the couch . . .

Chris.

I call his name while I stand on trembling legs and throw myself back into the car. He doesn't move. 'Chris!' Blood's smeared down the side of his cheek from his temple. I want to shake him awake, but I'm afraid to touch him. What if I hurt him more? Paralyse him?

Hank tries to get up and reach me, but he collapses as soon as he puts weight on his front right leg.

My phone sits on the floor, battery still dead.

I reach for Chris's phone at his feet. It's as shattered as the windshield. When I press the power button, it blinks coloured stripes and goes black. Nothing.

I have to get out of here.

Chris needs help. I can't lose another family member. I won't.

Home isn't far. I can make it on foot.

'I'll be right back,' I tell Hank, and Chris, though I know he can't hear me.

I stumble, my legs rubbery. I brace myself against the car for a few steps, get my bearings. We're near the road, but we went down an embankment; the car's not visible from the road.

I have to get home.

I have to get to Mom and Dad.

I have to get help.

My house is over that hill, one street over. I can make it. I start slow, picking up the pace the closer I get. There aren't any other cars around. My chest still hurts. And my head. It's not the agonising ache I'm used to, but sharp, like an echo of pain radiating from my skull every time my foot hits the ground.

Chris. I have to save him. Keep walking for Chris . . .

But Joey is gone. My little cousin . . .

No one else is on the roads. No one else can help.

I can save Chris. I can save him—

But I couldn't save Joey. I didn't. I can't believe he's—

I pound against the pavement anyway, limping. My house is in sight. I'm almost there. I'm going to make it.

I go in through the back door, the closest entrance.

'MOM! DAD!' I race through the kitchen. 'MOM!' I cry again. I'm out of breath. I can't breathe.

'Ella? What's wrong?' Mom and Dad both come in from the living room. The worry on their faces is immediate. They're at my side in seconds. Detective Peterson hovers in the background.

'Chris. He needs help.'

Their responses tumble together.

'What do you mean? Where?'

'What happened?'

'We slid off the road,' I pant. 'Around Hosmer Street.'

'I'll call it in,' Detective Peterson says, lifting a radio to his mouth.

'I'm going to him,' Dad says, grabbing his keys from a hook and racing out to the garage.

'We went to Chris and Joey's, but someone was there. We thought.'

Was the nest in the attic actually from Joey? What about the pictures on my phone? What's real? What was in my head? The room shifts. I sway to compensate. Mom clutches my shoulders.

'You're bleeding. Are you okay?'

Dad's questions slam against my own while Detective Peterson's voice hovers in the background relaying information to dispatch.

'No, I'm fine. It's Chris. I shouldn't have left Chris. I shouldn't have left him. Hank's hurt too.'

I lunge towards the door, to do what, I'm not sure.

Mom pulls me back. 'Calm down. It's okay. The ambulance will get him,' she says, but her face betrays her, eyes white and red. She's imagining what I am: a delay in the funeral so we can add another casket.

'What's going on?' Joey's little voice cuts through the panic. He's standing in the entryway, wearing his Spider-Man pyjamas, still too short for him. His big brown eyes blink behind his mess of hair.

'You're not real,' I tell him, trying to look away, to ignore the face I now know is dead, to block out the voice that's been haunting me for days without being aware of it.

'Ella, honey.' Mom's more concerned than before.

How can I tell her? How can I admit that I'm sicker than I thought, that I wasn't okay, that everything she worried about must be coming true and the tumour is affecting my brain, affecting *me*, who I am?

Does this mean I'm dying?

My chin quivers. 'I – I've been . . .'

Joey stands in the doorway, ghostly in his stare, like he's seeing me for the first time just like I'm seeing him.

He's opaque, solid, full. I blink and shrink away.

Mom glances to the doorway and back at me.

'Ella, what is it? What's wrong?'

'Ambulance is on their way,' Peterson says.

'What's wrong, Ella?' I stumble back at Joey's voice. Exactly as I remember. Exactly as if he were alive. He reaches out a hand.

'Don't – don't touch me!' I screech. 'You're not real. You're not real!' I fall to the ground, back pressed against the door.

Stop!

I scream the word in my brain. I don't want to see him alive. I don't want to miss him. I don't want to think I can reach out and touch him or ruffle his hair or hug him. Because he's gone and seeing him means I'm hallucinating, that I can't trust myself, that my brain is broken, that my mind doesn't work, that the tumour is worse, that I've lost control and—

'Ella!' Mom is next to me, trying to pull down my arms, but I keep clawing at my hair, scratching at my scalp, digging at my skull, getting at the thing buried deep inside, the cluster of cells torturing me with the memory of my sweet, innocent cousin.

'He's dead!' I scream. 'HE'S DEAD!' I have to believe it. If I believe it, it will stop. He'll go away. I won't see him anymore. If I believe it, it will go away. He has to go away. He has to . . .

Mom's calling my name over my shrieks. 'Who's dead? Ella. Ella.' Her voice is firm, level. 'The ambulance is going to Chris. It's going to be okay. It's—'

'Not Chris!' I sob, wrenching my hands down into fists. 'YOU!' I scream at Joey, at the figment of Joey my imagination has created. 'YOU'RE DEAD!'

The panic in Mom's voice doesn't compare to the horror and fear that flash across Joey's with tears in his big brown eyes.

But then my world goes black.

31

January 7

Wee-oo, wee-oo, wee-oo.

Sirens scream. Nearby. My body jostles. I'm moving. In a car. Voices. Strangers.

Something's wrong. I'm not at home. Where am I?

'BP one-ten over seventy.'

My eyes flutter. Someone's face hovers over me. I don't recognise him. It was his voice speaking.

Something's on my face. I try to move it off, but my arms aren't moving. Something's on top of them, keeping them at my sides.

'Ella? Ella?' he repeats. I focus on the stranger, his face. He has a straight nose and clean-shaven cheeks. 'You're on your way to the hospital,' he says. 'You were unconscious, but we're going to take good care of you.'

I blink in response.

The hospital?

Unconscious?

I'm in an ambulance on my way to the hospital. Why was I unconscious? What happened? I was . . . driving down the road.

No, someone else was driving. I was in the passenger seat. Chris was driving and Joey—

Joey.

I try to say his name, but the mask muffles it. I reach to pull it off again, but my arms are strapped to my sides.

Joey's dead.

He's gone. He opened his last Christmas present without knowing it. He got his last hug from his mom.

But I got to skate around the rink with him one more time. I got to tickle him and hear his laugh. I got to tuck him in and talk to him like he was still here.

'Shh, Ella.' Julie's voice drifts to me as if from afar, but when I turn my head, she's there. Next to me. Sitting on the bench next to the EMT. 'You don't have to be afraid.' She reaches for my hand. I see it enclose mine, but I don't feel it. I squeeze.

Nothing.

She's not here. She's not real.

'You're stronger than you think, Ella. You can get through this.'

Tears sting my eyes. No. No, it's not real. I'm not strong. I can't do this.

'I'm right here, Ella.'

I squeeze my eyes shut to make her disappear. She's not a ghost. She's in my head. I should be able to make her go away. If I was strong enough, she wouldn't be shredding my heart, because it hurts. It hurts so much to see her alive when I know she's not. I know she's gone. I know I couldn't save her.

'I tried,' I whisper, so softly no sound comes out.

'I know.' But this time it isn't Julie's voice.

Joey. He sits next to his mom, legs dangling over the seat.

'You tried to save me,' he says, his voice as soft and sweet as ever.

My voice cracks. 'It wasn't enough.'

'I know you tried.' Joey's still wearing his Spider-Man pyjamas. I told myself Mom wasn't making him change. When she said she was shopping for something he could wear at the funeral, I didn't know she meant while he was lying in the casket.

'I'm sorry I couldn't do more. I'm really going to miss you.' The mask is still over my face. I'm not saying the words aloud. But it feels like I am. Just like it feels like he's here with me. With her.

'I know,' he says. Julie wraps an arm around him, her hair falling across her face like an angel, and her beauty hurts because she should still be here. She should be hugging her son for real, and I have never in all my life wished for an afterlife more, for the hope that they really are together, that whether I can see them or not, this moment is happening up there, somewhere, for real. That even though I will never feel her hugs again or see his smile, they can be together forever.

'I wanted to watch you grow up.' The Joey I'm hallucinating now will always be the Joey I remember. He'll never grow another inch or become a pilot. He'll always need help tying his shoes and want someone to sing him 'Twinkle Twinkle Little Star' before bed.

Once I finish radiation, I'm not going to see him ever again, only in his little casket when I tuck Mr Brown next to his shoulder so he won't be afraid of the dark.

As if confirming he's only in my head, reading my thoughts, he says, 'Even if you can't see me, it doesn't mean I'm not with you.'

I give a watery smile.

'Don't cry. I get to fly now.' He stretches his arms like a plane.

'We'll always be with you, Ella,' Julie says. 'And you don't have to be strong all the time. It's enough to know you will be eventually.'

Even though I know those aren't really Julie's words or Joey's voice, what they're saying is true. Julie wasn't perfect, and if I hadn't idolised her, I might have seen when I needed to ask for help instead of avoiding it or being in denial. But I don't have to pretend those pieces don't exist. I don't have to ignore the side of her I didn't want to see.

I can still love her as I learn to accept the worst parts of life, because I'm never really alone.

Julie and Joey will always be with me, whether I see them here or not.

Wee-oo, wee-oo, wee-oo.

The sirens keep screaming.

'We're almost there, Ella,' the EMT says, placing a hand on my forearm, strong and warm.

When I open my eyes, he's the only one on the bench.

Julie and Joey are gone.

32

January 9

Beep . . . beep . . . beep . . .

The rhythm comes to me first. My body feels like I was hit by a truck. Heavy. I should open my eyes. It seems to be taking a lot of effort.

I'm in the hospital. I know it when I roll over on the firm mattress and the too-soft pillow collapses under me. The antiseptic stinks, void of anything like home.

'Rick, she's waking up. Ella, honey?'

Mom's hand is on mine. Her face is tired but smiling. Tears bloom at the corners of her eyes. Dad hovers over her shoulder, assessing.

The room is small, bland, with no bright colours. The harsh light comes from the ceiling, washing out any soft glow of sunshine that might come through the skinny window in the corner.

A noise escapes my throat, but it's not the '*Where am I?*' I say in my head.

Something hard and plastic covers my index finger like a chip clip, but it doesn't hurt. There's a needle taped to the back of my hand. That doesn't hurt either. Nothing hurts. But it feels like it should. I don't feel much of . . . anything.

Bits and pieces come back to me like strokes of a paintbrush creating a clear image.

Stroke one: I came here in an ambulance.

Stroke two: before that I was at my house, hyperventilating.

Stroke three: I was in a car crash. With Chris.

Stroke four: Joey has been dead for a week.

'Chris?' My voice sounds raw and scratchy, huskier than usual. Or maybe my ears are the problem, like they're filled with cotton.

'Here, have some water.' Mom raises a cup and moves the straw to my mouth. It's lukewarm but tastes better than any water in my life. I suck it down greedily.

'You're here,' I whisper.

Dad chuckles. 'Of course we're here. Sean should be getting in any time. He said he was looking for parking when he called a few minutes ago.'

'Where's Chris?'

'He's fine,' Dad answers. 'A little banged up, but the doctors checked him out and he was released yesterday.'

'Dominic came by to visit but had to go,' Mom says, releasing my hand and offering the straw with water. 'He said he would be by later. His dad came by too. We got to meet him.'

'Very nice family,' Dad says.

My shoulder hurts, and the right side of my head. That must mean the pain medication is wearing off. That could be why I woke up. I still feel heavy, like I could lie here for days.

Or I already have been.

'What day is it?'

'Monday.'

Two days. I've been here that long. I've been here longer than I thought.

'The funeral,' I mutter.

'We delayed it,' Mom says.

'I'm going to call your grandma. She's going to be so happy to hear you've woken up. She's been calling for updates every few hours.' Dad pulls out his phone and walks towards the hallway but stops in the middle of Mom's next question.

'Do you remember what happened?' she asks.

'Yeah . . .' I sit up.

'Stay put,' Dad says. 'I'm going to get the doctor.'

'I remember all of it. I always have . . . sort of.' I remember everything so clearly. I don't think I have any periods of lost time.

A man enters the room with a nurse and introduces himself as Dr Gardner. He's tall with a blonde beard. 'Ella, good morning. How are you feeling?'

'Tired.'

The little hospital room is crowded with all four of them, the nurse moving around to the pole connected to my arm with a tube.

'I'm glad you're awake, and you seem more alert.' He waves a little light, asking me to track his finger.

'You have some bruising on your ribs from the air bag, but the other injuries are superficial from the crash. Your regular doctor sent over the results from your previous scans yesterday. Your tumour is pressing against the optical path of the temporal lobe, which explains why you were having hallucinations.'

So it's as I thought. Judging from the lack of reaction from Mom and Dad, they've heard all this before. 'I was delusional.'

'Delusions are a very specific term used when there is no physiological explanation for a false reality. What you're dealing with is a different diagnosis. You're anchored in reality, but the tumour pressing on your optical path has allowed you to see things that aren't there. Many patients report seeing shadows in their peripheral vision.'

'I've seen those,' I say, remembering as I walked to the shed and several times around Julie's house. I thought someone was there, or I was only being paranoid.

Dr Gardner says, 'In your case, your hallucinations have been primarily taking the form of your younger cousin.'

I'm too tired to be embarrassed, too exhausted from grief pressing down like a heavy blanket over my bones. It's like my subconscious has been processing while I was sleeping in this hospital. I'm not scared anymore. I want answers.

'Why him?'

'There could be a variety of reasons for this,' Dr Gardner says, 'but after hearing from your parents and Chris, my first instinct is to think his image was providing some kind of comfort when your world was flipped upside down with the loss of your aunt, particularly when you entered her house again. He became a coping strategy, appearing when you needed him most.'

'What about hearing and smelling?' I ask. 'Would those be affected?'

'While it's possible the tumour is affecting your other senses, it would be unlikely.'

I tell him about being locked in my shed and smelling rotten eggs, hearing the hissing of the gas.

'Our brains are experts at playing tricks on us.' Dr Gardner rocks back on his heels. 'We automatically fill in the gaps we want to see or expect to see. Magicians and illusionists rely on it. Our brains can especially trick us when we are afraid. After a house fire, a victim may hear the smoke alarm and see or smell smoke. While there isn't any external stimulus creating smoke, their brains fill in what they expect to experience, or what they did experience the last time a smoke detector went off.'

Dr Gardner continues. 'In the same way there are optical illusions, there can also be auditory illusions. In your anxiety, you were afraid, particularly afraid of gas leaks. I'm not entirely surprised to hear you smelled it and heard it, but in all reality, you likely didn't hear or smell anything external.'

'So . . . it was all fake? I was imagining the gas in the shed?' And not because of the tumour. Anxiety.

'You said someone had to open the door for you. I can't explain how you were locked in, so it seems that reality is pretty easily verified.'

I was imagining things . . . but not everything. How am I supposed to know the difference? How can I trust myself? What else have I been imagining?

'What about Chris's house? We heard noises.'

'It's an old house,' Dad says. 'In an ice storm, there were bound to be some creaks or wind whistling.'

Mom adds, 'The police said there were no signs of anyone else there.'

So the nest in the attic really was from Joey. But it doesn't explain everything.

Chris walks into the room, his foot in a black medical boot, giving him an uneven gait. A bruise covers the side of his face, but it's tinged green around the edges. A chunk of his hair is shaved, with what appear to be stitches across the gap.

'You're okay,' I say, trying to take in the sight of him.

'Better than you.' His mouth twists in a sad smile.

'But – I don't understand. Chris, you thought someone was in the house too.'

Chris rubs the back of his neck. 'I wasn't sure what to do. I kept wondering if you were right. I guess I got caught up in the hysteria of it, but once we were in the car, I had a chance to think things through a bit more, but you were making less and less sense.'

'What about the pictures? Of us sleeping. On my phone.'

I pull my phone from the table where it's plugged in and charging.

'You mentioned those in the car, but I never saw any pictures.' Chris exchanges a glance with my parents.

'No, they were—' But there are no new photos on my camera roll, no images of us in his house.

I imagined them too? 'What about – Chris, at night when I got up and found you in your mom's room, you said—'

Chris is already shaking his head slowly. 'I don't know what you're talking about. We went to sleep around eleven, and I didn't wake up until morning, when you started panicking.'

That whole time was all . . . in my head? The memory is so clear, so distinct. Sitting on Julie's bed . . . Chris holding the ring, confessing to killing Blake.

'But . . . how did Blake die?'

'They're still investigating,' Mom says, and Chris frowns with concern. 'Detective Peterson hinted there's a warrant out for someone's arrest, but they can't speak directly about it yet.'

Chris is innocent. Of course he is. He never confessed to killing Blake. A wave of shame rushes through me for even thinking my cousin could be guilty. I should have known then my mind couldn't be trusted.

That conversation never happened. Just like every conversation I've had with Joey.

'You've been through a lot, Ella,' Dr Gardner says. 'Between your diagnosis, the emotional trauma of losing someone close to you and a car accident, it's going to take some time to adjust, long after your body feels ready. You've got a strong support system here. Trust them to help you through it.'

Doctors have told me plenty of things I don't want to hear, but this is the first time relying on others feels like a comfort.

'So it was all an accident, then. The gas leak?'

'No, the police said Blake seems to be at fault for that. Julie's insurance policy was changed in the last month to name him as beneficiary, and it's too convenient to be ignored. The police are still investigating his death, though.'

'What about the note for Julie to give ten thousand dollars?' I ask, remembering the envelope and my certainty that it was somehow connected to a bigger plot.

Chris clenches his jaw while Dad answers. 'She'd been planning to give that money to Chris once he graduated. She's been saving for years, avoiding repairs on the house wherever she could, scraping off grocery bills. She's dreamed of trying to repay him for all he's sacrificed for the family.' He claps a hand on Chris's shoulder, while Chris moves his hand in a way that could be scratching his nose or wiping his eyes.

'We're just glad you're both okay,' Mom says, stepping in front of Chris as if to give him privacy. 'I told Dr Gardner you'd need some time before your treatment. You don't need to think about that right now. Take a few days to rest and—'

'No. I don't want to put it off. And thank you, Mom.'

She looks surprised.

'For worrying about me.' As hard as all of this has been, if she hadn't believed me from the beginning, if she hadn't taken me to doctor after doctor until we got answers, I know I would be worse off than I am.

She falls into a hug, and Dad gives me a tight-lipped smile over her shoulder. They must have been terrified when I stumbled into the kitchen, bleeding and without Chris. Then watching me the last few days in the hospital . . .

But I can't let that guilt consume me. Sometimes tragedies simply happen and no one's at fault.

'Excuse me, I have some other patients to see,' Dr Gardner says. 'Mrs and Mr Forrester?'

Mom gives me one more squeeze before she and Dad follow him into the hall.

Chris shifts his weight, the only one left in the room.

'I can't imagine what it would have been like for you, to have me losing it—'

'It's not worse than what you're going through.' Chris traces the bruise around his cheekbone, moving back to the stitches on his skull. 'I'll still make fun of you for beating the crap out of that peanut butter jar, but would I be a good cousin if I didn't?'

He laughs, but it's forced, like he knows that's what he's supposed to say. Not even his usual banter can distract me from the weight that's settled in my stomach.

Maybe that's okay. Maybe the longer I sit in these uncomfortable feelings, the better I'll be at navigating them.

A small woman in heels almost passes the door before she skids to a halt, popping up from behind a bouquet of droopy carnations.

'Ella Forrester?'

'Yes.' The woman looks familiar, but I can't quite place her.

'These' – she extends the flowers – 'are for you.'

Her hair is pulled back, but pieces fly free. One side of her collar is flipped, and there's a drop of something that looks like toothpaste on the edge of her jacket. Her speech is as flustered as her appearance. 'I probably shouldn't be here, or at least you probably don't want to see me, but, well, I feel awful about everything that's happened, and I wanted to extend my sympathies when I heard you and Chris were in an accident.'

At this, I look at Chris, who steps forward.

'Oh, you're here too. I—'

'Who are you?' Chris asks.

'Nicki.' She struggles to remove a glove and extends her hand. 'Nicki Davis.'

'Blake's girlfriend.' The words tumble out before I can stop them.

Chris takes a step back, and Nicki splutters, 'Girlfriend? No. No, no. I'm not his girlfriend. I'm Blake Bartnicky's sister.'

'Sister.' I nearly drop the flowers. The kiss on the cheek was familial, not romantic. Blake wasn't cheating on Julie.

'You were my mom's insurance agent,' Chris says.

'Yes, but that's also why I'm here.' She flicks her gaze back and forth between us like a nervous mouse before settling on Chris. 'I wanted you to know I had nothing to do with my brother's relationship with your mom. I didn't even know they were together until the police told me, and then I reviewed her policy and saw the changes. I never approved them. I can only assume Blake stole my information somehow.'

Her purse slips down her arm and a tube of ChapStick and a ring of keys clatter to the floor. She collects the items, but not before three more things fall from her purse. It's not a stretch to imagine her leaving passwords on a sticky note and assuming she misplaced it.

'I'm cooperating with police, sharing all my files and information, whatever they need to prove what really happened. I don't think your mom ever suspected.'

'Do the police know how Blake died?' Chris asks. His voice is tight, and while I can't read his expression, I imagine the feelings that must be warring inside him at seeing this woman whose incompetence aided Blake in his scheme to collect on Julie's life insurance policy.

Nicki pauses and slowly rises from her kneeling position on the floor. I expect her to fight off tears at the mention of her brother's death, but her voice is clear when she says, 'Not yet, which is frankly maddening considering I've already told them who did it.'

'You did?'

'I knew those gambling debts would get him in trouble. The house was found in a mess like there'd been a struggle. He didn't fall on his own, did he? He called me over to his house a few days ago asking me to help him pay them off. He wouldn't tell me the details, but he seemed to hint someone might be after him, that money he was counting on didn't come through. I've told him for years to stop messing around with that and get some real help, but Blake never would listen to his younger sister, would he? Pretty obvious whoever he owes broke in and killed him since he didn't get Julie's insurance sum and couldn't pay.'

Aunt Julie and Joey died so Blake could collect on her life

insurance and pay off his gambling debts. Only, when Chris survived, his plan fell through and, at least according to Nicki's theory, his collectors ran out of patience.

Nicki fails another attempt to tame her hair out of her face. 'Blake never saw himself as the problem. Always had some excuse why it was someone else's fault. He truly believed he was innocent – got pretty good at convincing other people too.'

She checks the clock and curses. 'Is that the time already? I'm running late. Right. Well.' She pulls her gloves on. 'I know an apology for my brother's behaviour does nothing. He needed more help than I could give him. After the life he lived, maybe he deserved the end he got.' She turns, bumping into the doorframe, and leaves.

Chris slumps into a chair, head in his hands. Mom and Dad return, hovering near the door.

'He lied to everyone,' I say, and then, when Chris doesn't look up, I add, 'There was nothing you could have done to stop it.'

'Do you think she's right?' Chris asks. 'That he deserved to die?'

Does anyone deserve to die? Is any death 'fair' or 'just'? Can one death ever make up for the loss of another life?

'I don't know if he deserved to die. But I'm glad he did. Blake was a liar, a cheater, a greedy, despicable man who preyed on others. And he murdered two people.'

The atmosphere in the room shifts. They all share a look.

'Something's wrong,' I say. Mom clasps her hands and Chris swallows. Dad dips his head. 'Tell me. Mom?'

'We wanted to explain things in pieces, not to overwhelm you.'

The heart monitor next to me picks up pace. 'Tell me. What else?'

Dad takes a deep breath. 'Blake didn't . . . murder two people.'

My mind races. Who else did he kill? Sierra? Dominic? But I've talked to them both since Blake died.

Unless . . . unless those were hallucinations too, and—

'Blake killed Julie, but Joey is alive.'

33

January 9

'Wait. What?' I'm not sure the words even come out of my mouth. This can't be real. The blood pumping in my ears beats like a deafening wind. 'Dr Gardner . . . he – he said—'

'Yes.' Mom sits on the edge of the bed and grabs my hand, waiting until I look her full in the face before continuing. 'Dr Gardner explained you were having hallucinations, caused by the tumour, but exacerbated by losing Julie. When you went to her house, when you and Chris got snowed in, you hallucinated Joey. He wasn't at the house with you.' She waits, lets the words settle before taking a deep breath and confirming. 'But, Ella, he's alive. You saved him on New Year's Eve, and he's been living with us since. On the night of the snowstorm, he was with your dad, safe at home.'

At some point while Mom was talking, Chris left the room. He comes back now, holding Joey's hand.

Joey. He's wrapped in a fuzzy superhero blanket, hair dishevelled, brown eyes wary.

My throat is dry, closed. Thoughts careening.

'This can't be real.' My head shakes like a blender. 'This is all a hallucination. None of you are real. Joey died in the gas leak and none of you are here. I must still be sleeping – or you all left with Dr Gardner and this is another hallucination and—'

Mom squeezes my hand harder, repeating my name over and over, calmly, slowly. 'Focus, Ella. Shhh. Do you feel my hand?'

'It's not real. This can't be—' But her hands are both wrapped around my one, warm and steady.

Tears stream down her cheeks. 'We're here. It's real.'

Dad rests a hand on my shoulder. It's heavy. He smells like his green soap he's been using since I was born. The details feel real.

Chris steps forward, ahead of Joey. I can't look at him. I can't trust myself. I can't trust he's there. But the rest of them – Chris, Mom, and Dad – they're so sure, so calm.

'Say hi,' Chris gently tells him. Joey ducks half a step behind Chris before peeking out from behind his brother's leg, and something about that expression proves what they're all saying.

'Hi, Ella Bella.'

A ridiculous burble of laughter escapes me, and it's contagious. Mom and Dad are crying through smiles. Joey steps out fully from behind Chris, still wary.

'You're alive. You're real. You're here.' I suck in a shuddery breath, tears and snot streaming down my face. 'But then – after the accident—' When I saw Joey in my living room, when I collapsed against the wall and screamed at him that he was dead . . . I must have been terrifying. 'I'm so' – my voice cracks – 'so sorry.'

He crawls up on the bed and wraps his arms around me, and my soul aches. I thought I lost him. I thought he was gone. My Joey. My fingers run through his hair, cradling his head against my shoulder. I scared him, but he's real.

He's here.

He's alive.

He's safe.

'I can't believe I was so wrong about both my cousins. I should have known something was wrong.' I lock eyes with Chris over Joey's shoulder, trying my best to show him everything he means to me and how thankful I am he's okay.

Chris must be as emotional as I am, because he ducks into the hallway. I give Joey another squeeze.

'Ella Bella,' he squeaks. 'You're squishing me.' We all fall into laughter, but I can't let go.

I will never let go.

I nap for most of the morning, and when I stir, someone else is in the room.

'Ella?' Dominic's voice is gentle and warm, like a sweatshirt I want to pull over and hide in. His hand finds mine, and I squeeze it. He squeezes back, warm and sure.

I blink, but Dominic stays. He's really here. I'm not imagining him.

'Hi,' he says. And he sounds real. 'I brought you something.' He pulls out a tray of half a dozen custom cupcakes: some brown with chocolate and drizzled in caramel, a pink one topped with a single slice of strawberry, a white one with a luscious raspberry perched on top.

And in the corner, a chocolate one with bright green icing, complete with a cheap plastic ring like you might find at a kid's birthday party.

He must be real because I couldn't have imagined such a perfect gift.

'And look who I found already waiting in the lobby.'

'Sierra!'

She rushes over to me and throws herself in my bed, nudging me until there's enough room.

'They kept me in that waiting room for hours, you know.'

'I was starting to . . . never mind.' The truth is I was still wondering if she was real or imagined too. She and I became friends when my migraines began. The funny (not funny) thing about being told you've hallucinated someone is questioning everything after.

'Wait . . . it's Monday. Aren't you supposed to be preparing for the recital?'

'Yeah, I am.' She gives me a hug then, and there's no doubt she is here and she is real. I need her as an anchor now more than ever.

'I'm sorry for getting so annoyed with you. It's not that I don't appreciate you. It's just . . .'

'Please. I know you.' She pouts. 'I know avoidance is your self-medication of choice.'

'From now on, I'm telling you everything up front.'

'You know I'll hound you if you don't.'

'I need to thank you both,' I say. 'I feel like such an idiot.'

'You don't have to be embarrassed,' Sierra offers.

'Really? Because I yelled at Dominic and got frustrated with you, and—'

'I know how much you hate people to take it easy on you, so if it will really make you feel better, I'm sure we can come up with a list of ways for you to make it up to us. I've got a Jeep that needs to be cleaned. Inside and out.'

She stares at Dominic expectantly.

'Oh, right,' he fumbles. 'I . . . have a hockey stick that needs to be taped?'

'That's all you've got?' Sierra clucks her tongue and counts off on her fingers. 'I've got laundry to get done, a locker to organise, college essays to be proofread . . .'

'All of it!' I laugh. 'I'll do all of it and more.'

Sierra gives me another hug and then looks around the room. 'What do you have to drink around here? Nothing?' She surveys the room before settling on Dominic and hopping off the bed. 'I'm going to sneak down and get you a pop to go with your snack.' She winks at me, and I hope it's only obvious to me that she's implying the snack is not a cupcake, but Dominic. 'But you're not getting rid of me that easy. I'm going to be here all day long whether you like it or not. Now you two behave while I'm gone.'

She sizes Dominic up and down while she backs away, but as soon as he turns back to me, she pretends to swoon against the door before stumbling out of the room.

'How are you feeling?' he asks.

'Better. I think.'

'Good, because my dad wants you to come over for dinner as soon as you get out of here.' He takes a seat in the one chair in the room, and suddenly I'm thankful everyone left me to rest while they went for lunch. His voice is softer, serious. 'I want to apologise, especially if my actions or words did anything to make it worse.'

'Thank you,' I say, accepting the cupcakes and putting them on the table next to me. 'But you don't have anything to apologise for. The truth is you were gentle and kind, patient with me when I was . . . not.'

Thinking back to the other night, how I shouted at him . . . and now knowing I was paranoid for nothing . . . I'm embarrassed. Worst of all, when Dominic tried to help me see it, I screamed at him to go. I pushed him.

He was right all along.

'I should be apologising to you,' I say.

'You were being rational for you, though.' He pulls his chair closer. 'I can't imagine how . . . disorienting that would be, to be told what you perceive as reality is . . . not.'

'It's a lot to process.'

I let my hand fall to the side, and Dominic takes it.

'I'm here to answer any questions you have.'

'Actually, I do have one, but it's not related to any of . . . this. What really ended your friendship with Chris?'

Dominic leans back and exhales loudly. 'Freshman year, after wrestling practice, I walked into the coach's office and saw Chris with a bunch of fundraising money. He turned bright red and told me how things weren't going well at home and he wasn't using the money for a new video game system or anything. I convinced him not to steal from the team, but after he handed me the money, the coach came in. Chris immediately said he'd walked in on *me* stealing the money.'

'And you didn't defend yourself?'

'I was holding the money. I looked pretty guilty and I didn't want to get Chris in trouble.'

Just like he let me think he stole my cupcake all those years ago. 'You don't care when people think the worst of you.'

He winks. 'Not if I know I'm doing right.'

'So then . . . why does Chris not like you? Shouldn't it be the other way around?'

'Oh, trust me, he hasn't been my favourite person for a long time, but I always felt bad for him. I think he was mad because I told my dad the truth, and when he heard about why he was stealing, he went over to offer his mom some help. I don't think that went down well either.'

Julie always could hold a grudge and didn't like people thinking she couldn't take care of herself, and especially her kids.

'It didn't help when he found my puck in my car – a puck I gave Joey months before by the way. He's the one who broke the windshield, not me. But it never seemed like Chris could get ahead of the money,' he says.

'Don't worry about Chris.' The insurance money will probably be tied up in legal stuff for a while, but Dad says that bank account money will transfer easily.

'I keep looking back on everything and wondering . . . was it real or in my head?'

'Sounds like a party game.' Dominic leans back in his chair but doesn't release my hand. 'Let's play.' He must see my confusion. 'No, seriously, let me help you. Ask me a question from the last week, and I'll answer based on what I know.'

'Okay . . . Joey was on the couch when you came in from the storm.'

'I never saw him. We went upstairs to the attic until Chris came in, and then you both thought you heard something so we came down, but I still never saw anyone besides the two of you.'

'On the day you showed me the gas lines in the furnace, we were in the basement and someone called my name.'

'I think so. Technically, I didn't know Joey was with you, and I never heard him until you ran up the stairs and he was standing in that back room.'

So he wasn't a hallucination every time I was at the house, only the day of the storm.

'We went ice skating.'

'Yes.'

'Joey was with us.'

'Skated on the opposite side of the rink from us, but yeah, he was there too.'

In some ways it's at least comforting to know my brain wasn't lying to me the entire time, but sorting back through everything, seeing it all through this lens, is exhausting.

'Any other questions?'

'Umm.' I search for the hundreds of questions that have been flooding my thoughts since I woke. 'The threatening message telling me to stop investigating? Real?'

'At least the screenshot you sent me looks real. But I don't know who sent it.'

'Some rando on the internet?'

'The account is gone now,' he says, pulling out his phone. 'They could've sent out tons of random messages and got reported.'

It's an odd coincidence, but coincidences still happen in life. No one else saw the pictures of us sleeping, so I must have hallucinated those, but I sent Dominic that message. It existed. Even if it's not connected to the gas leak or Blake or anything else, I'm oddly comforted by the knowledge it's real, that something gave me a legitimate reason to fear.

'The drive we took to Blake's house?'

His face grows serious.

'Real.'

'The pinky promise we made?'

He leans forward, scooping my pinky into his.

'Real.' His eyes sparkle again, a mischievous glint in them.

'The kiss we shared in the attic?'

He leans in closer, slowly, asking permission before I close my eyes and his mouth touches mine gently. He pulls back, still close enough that I feel his breath on my cheek when he whispers, 'Very real.'

34

January 9

Later that night, I'm discharged with notes for monitoring at home and a plan for treatment. The doctor gave me strict orders for rest and reducing stress.

It feels good to be home. Hank greets me too. The vet said he has some bruised ribs, but as long as he doesn't run and jump too much, he should recover just fine. How he plans to keep a dog like Hank from running and jumping is beyond me.

He can't take the stairs, but Dad finagled a ramp for him to claim his favourite spot on the living room furniture, and Mom didn't even argue.

Sometimes I still can't fully believe how wrong I was, how much I had convinced myself that Blake was working with someone else. Trusting my own judgement might have a longer recovery time than radiation.

Dad's due home from work and Mom ran out to pick up an order of butter burgers and cheese curds, which sounds like the ultimate recovery meal.

Until then, it's me, Joey and Hank.

The trauma of the last few days lies thick and heavy on my skin, which I wash away in a long – really long – and hot shower.

I won't ever be able to pretend none of this ever happened, but I can still put it behind me and move forward.

If I weigh the life of Julie next to Blake, he certainly deserved to die more than she did. Blake made choices, and there are consequences for those choices, but it feels wrong to be glad he's dead.

I'm glad we have answers, and I'm glad all of this is finally, finally ending and Julie can be laid to rest. Except I wish Blake had to face what he did, to admit all the lies he told, to own up to his cruelty.

The truth is, no one will ever suffer enough to make amends for the wrongs of this world, and others – whether from tragic accidents or unforeseeable illness – will suffer more than they deserve.

Life isn't fair, and we can't change that. We can only change ourselves. There's more power in that than we want to admit.

I finish my shower and pull on a pair of sweats from my drawer. A bag from the hospital sits on my bed, and I throw away the clothes from the accident. Even if they can be salvaged, I don't want them.

It feels like weeks ago, not days.

Joey hovers near the doorway of my bedroom. There's an instant where I wonder if it's really him or a hallucination like I had in the ambulance, but now that I'm aware of it, it's easier to tell the difference. I flash a bright smile, hoping he didn't pick up on my hesitation.

'How's Mr Brown doing?' I tug on the ear of the bear in his hand. Another reason I should have known it wasn't the real Joey at the house or in the car with us. He never would have gone to sleep so easily without his bear.

He shrugs.

If hallucinations can change what I know to be true about a person, how will I ever trust myself again? If Blake could fool Julie and Chris, how can we trust anyone?

But the alternative is existing alone.

Maybe the trick is to never only trust one person, but to have a group you can go to. Not an army, not even a team. But if I can let a handful of people in, it's okay if one is busy or doesn't respond the way I expect. If I trust all of them, I don't have to depend on any one of them. And I don't have to depend on myself either. I don't have to pretend to be strong when I'm buckling. I don't have to put on a smile when I'm crumbling. I don't have to trust everyone all the time, but I can keep learning who to trust some of the time.

As easy as it would be to offer to play a game or paint a picture, sometimes it's better to tackle things head-on.

'Things have been kind of scary around here lately,' I admit to Joey. 'It's hard when we don't know or understand everything.'

Joey nods and steps into the room.

'Do you know where Chris went?' I ask. 'I think my mom's going to be home with dinner soon.'

'I don't know. My mom used to check where he was using something on her phone.'

Chris is an adult now so he doesn't need anyone checking on him, but I still want to. I don't think I've seen him since he ducked out of the hospital room after I realised Joey was alive.

Hank barks downstairs.

'Is someone here? Chris?'

As we descend the stairs, I can see it's Dominic's car parked in the driveway, not Chris. Joey opens the door while he walks up the path and Hank runs out to greet him.

'Hey.' Dominic ruffles Joey's hair, and Joey immediately grabs onto his forearm. Dominic lifts, and Joey's grip tightens while he rises into the air. He shuffles forward before dumping Joey at my feet. 'Did you order a package? If not, I think we can return this one to sender,' he says, tickling Joey before he can reattach himself around Dominic's leg.

Just as I'm leaning over to join their laughter, something rolls out from Joey's pocket. Something gold and shiny. It spins on the floor and falls flat.

A ring. A gold ring with a purple stone.

Dominic and Joey fall quiet as I lift the ring.

I know this ring. It was Julie's. But I never saw her wear it. I saw it in her bedroom. The night at the house. When I woke up and Chris was upset in Julie's room. I saw this ring right before Chris confessed to killing Blake.

But no.

That didn't happen.

It wasn't real.

Chris said it wasn't real.

And yet, here's the ring.

Wait. Am I clutching a ring? Is it really here, or in my head?

'Ella?' Dominic asks. 'Are you okay? You just got really pale.'

'Wh-what am I holding?' Please let them see it. Please let it be real. *Please.*

'A ring?' Dominic says. Joey nods.

My hand trembles.

'Where did you get this?' I ask Joey. It came out of his pocket, but they said he wasn't at the house, so how did he get it if he wasn't—

'I found it in Sean's room next to Mr Brown.'

'You didn't take it from your mom's jewellery box?'

'I promise I didn't. I found it in an envelope. I didn't take it—'

'You're not in trouble,' I say, recognising the panic in his voice. 'Can you go get the envelope?'

Joey scampers up the stairs and Dominic steps closer.

'What's wrong?'

'I've seen this before, I think.'

I had held this ring in my hands. Until Chris put it in his pocket. So he must have woken up with it and brought it home. But that means . . .

That whole conversation was real.

It happened.

He confessed. Chris killed Blake. He told me.

'I—' No, wait. Maybe it is all in my head. Maybe Dominic isn't even really here. Maybe I'm home alone. Maybe—

'What is it?'

'I . . . I don't want to say. It sounds . . .'

'You're not crazy.'

'I have hallucinations, and I can't tell what's real.'

'That means you need help. Nothing else.' He cups my face. 'I'm real. Right here. Right now. Can you feel me?'

He is here, real, present. With his warm hands and brown eyes.

But I still can't say it out loud. I close my fist around the ring until the stone presses into my hand so far it might bleed.

It's real. The ring is real, and it's in my hand.

Chris killed Blake.

'No one . . . no one will believe me,' I whisper.

'Just because you've had hallucinations,' Dominic says, 'just because you were wrong about one thing, doesn't mean anything. People get sick. Sometimes people can control factors that make them sick and sometimes they can't. Sometimes people can make choices to make themselves better, and sometimes they can't. But no matter what you've been through or are going through, it only means the rest of us can step up to help. If anything, it means we need to listen more. Really hear you.'

'What if I'm wrong? What if it's like the shed and it's all in my head?'

'Do you trust me to listen?'

I nod.

'Will you listen to the facts?' he asks.

I didn't listen to reality before I kicked him out of Julie's house. I got angry when he tried to show me the truth. 'I'm sorry.' A hot tear slides down my cheek. 'I'm sorry I shouted at you.'

He presses his forehead against mine. 'I know. Will you tell me? Tell me what you were thinking when you saw that ring.'

I want to tell him, I want to trust he'll listen to me, but . . .

'If you tell me, I can help you figure it out. We'll do it together, decide if it's real.'

His hand slips into mine and squeezes. I squeeze his back. I slip the ring on my finger.

They're real. It's all real.

And everything Chris said that night was real, and I can't keep it inside.

'Chris took this ring out of Julie's jewellery box in the middle of the night when we slept at the house.'

'Okay,' Dominic says patiently, inviting me to continue.

'But in the hospital, he said that never happened. He said we went to sleep and stayed asleep until the morning when I woke up and panicked.'

'I'm listening.'

I tell him everything Chris said that night: how he went over to Blake's because he saw him for who he was. How Blake threatened me, and Chris attacked him. How he shoved him against the wall. How Blake laughed when Chris left. How Chris didn't feel bad about hurting Blake, but still felt terrible for not seeing it sooner, for not protecting his mom, for her still being gone.

Joey's feet pound down the stairs and he arrives with a white envelope in his hand as Dominic says, 'I believe you.'

Those words shudder through me just like they did after Dr Gupta listened to me say my migraines needed more than a prescription. It's relief that someone is listening, but laced with terror because it means whatever comes next will reveal something I'm not ready for, something I never really believed could be true.

Joey hands me the envelope.

Chris's blocky scrawl is across the front. It only says two words: *Remember us.*

'What?' Dominic says, leaning in to read the message. Joey does the same, even though he's already seen it.

He doesn't understand what it means, but I do.

Julie is already dead, and it was her ring.

Chris had it when he said everything would be better if he was gone.

At the time I thought he wanted to move, but now, with the ring left behind . . .

Remember us.

Is Chris planning to join his mom?

'What is it? What's wrong?'

I pull out my phone and dial before I remember Chris's screen was shattered in the accident. Does it still work? Did he get a new one while I was in the hospital? Will it have the same number?

It's ringing.

'Come on,' I mutter. 'Pick up. Pick up.'

We're too late. He's already done it. He's—

He picks up on the fourth ring.

He's still alive.

'Chris! Are you okay?' I practically yell it into the phone, turning my back on Joey. He shouldn't hear this. Dominic must understand, because when I glance back, he's ushering him into the living room.

'You know the answer to that—' Chris's voice is resigned, but it's not too late. He's still alive.

'I've got your mom's ring.'

'She'd want you to have it.'

'Chris, where are you?'

'I need to get away.'

'Chris, are you thinking about suicide?' I learned in school to be direct, to not be afraid of the word. But I'm terrified of his answer.

Silence.

'Do you have a plan?'

He swallows, sucks his teeth.

'Chris, I want to get you some help.' He needs a professional. With trembling fingers, I switch to speaker and Google a hotline. 'Can you stay on the phone with me while I—'

'I'm leaving, Ella. You don't know what I did.'

'I know more than you think, Chris.'

He did kill Blake. The pain and fear in his voice that night was real. I didn't imagine it. It's been eating away at him ever since.

'If you knew,' Chris whispers, 'you'd want me gone.'

'Whatever it is, we'll figure it out together.'

'We can't.'

The line goes dead.

'Chris! Chris!'

35

January 9

I hit redial as I walk into the living room, but Chris doesn't pick up.

'I need your car,' I tell Dominic, already pulling on my coat. 'Give me the keys.'

'Ella, wait.'

'Can you stay here with Joey?'

'I'll take you wherever you need to go. You're still recovering from the accident.'

'I can—'

'Ella, I believe you and want to help you, but I also want you to be safe. *Please.* Let me drive you.'

Listen to the facts. That's what Dominic asked me to do. I have to trust him too.

'Fine. Let's go.'

'Where?'

What else had Chris said that night? *Everything would be better if* this *was all gone.*

This.

'Their house. Back to Chris and Joey's house.'

Five minutes down the road and Chris still won't answer.

'What do you think he's doing there?' Dominic asks, driving down another street. The roads are clear of ice, but it's already dark.

I don't want to answer him with Joey in the back seat. Chris left the ring behind, the only thing he took from the house, the only thing his mom valued. He blames himself for not seeing what Blake did.

As much as I know I'm right, I'm secretly, desperately, pleading to be wrong.

'Ugh!' I don't wait to hear the voicemail before I hang up.

I call another number instead, someone who might be able to help.

An answer.

'Detective Peterson?'

'He's not available,' the deep voice on the other end of the line says.

'It's an emergency.'

'Who is this?'

'Ella Forrester. Detective Peterson's been working with my family. My cousin—'

'Yeah, I answered a call at your house a few nights ago.'

Officer Varden. I recognise his voice now.

'It's my cousin. I think he might be in danger.' I should have seen it earlier. All the signs were there, and now we might be too late. 'I need you to get out here and—'

'Whoa, slow down.'

'You have to go! Or send someone! Please!'

'Are your parents with you?'

'No, they're – it doesn't matter. My cousin is in trouble! I know it!'

'Uh-huh. Is this the cousin you thought was dead?'

'No, I—' I can almost hear the eye roll in his voice, and it takes everything in me not to scream. 'I think Chris might be trying to hurt himself!' Joey's fearful gaze in the mirror reinforces why I didn't want to say it in front of him. I hate traumatising him more than he's already been, but I need Varden to take me seriously. 'I think he might try to kill himself.'

'Of course. Why don't you give me his name and number, and while we look into it, you can make another call to your doctor.'

I hang up with a low scream.

'What happened?' Dominic says, calm, controlled. But I know now his stress is through the roof, like mine. 'What did they say?'

I don't answer. I call the other number on the card, Detective Peterson's private line. No answer, but when the automated voice prompts me to leave a voicemail, I speak calmly and clearly. 'This is Ella Forrester. Chris left me an important item that he'd never part with unless he was planning suicide. I think he's at his house. He's lost everything else in his life, but he's not going to lose me. So believe me, or don't, but he's in trouble, and I'm not going to let him die.'

I hang up and dial Chris again, hoping and begging and praying he answers.

Dominic speeds us over the bridge. We're only a few minutes away. We'll make it in time. I can't pull another body from that house. I can't—

'Do you remember when I said I didn't think anyone involved was outside the house?' Dominic says, not taking his eyes off the road. 'I said it because . . . well, I thought someone *inside* the house might be.'

'Wait – you thought Chris might have been the one who hurt Blake?'

'No, I never suspected anything about Blake, but I thought Chris was lying. I didn't bother bringing it up after the crash, because it seemed obvious Blake was at fault and all the loose ends were tying up. I wasn't sure how you would take it. I didn't know if you were ready to hear something bad about him.'

Because I took Chris's word for everything. I trusted him.

'So what made you think Chris was lying?'

'I talked to Alex, Chris's friend.'

The one he spent New Year's Eve with.

'It was small, but when I talked to him, he said he didn't even know Chris was gone at first. He came back from upstairs and Chris was just gone.'

But that would mean—

I can't right now. We're here.

There's no car out front. I don't even know how Chris got here, but as soon as Dominic parks in the driveway, I throw myself out of the car, shouting at Dominic, 'Stay here with Joey!'

The part I don't say is I'm not sure what I'll find inside. I race up the front steps knowing I might be too late. He might already be gone.

'Chris!' I shout, flinging open the door. 'I'm here. Don't do it!'

He's not in the kitchen or living room. Julie's room is clear. 'Chris!' I call again, taking the old wooden stairs two at a time, my hand sliding along the wobbly banister and pulling me up as much as my legs.

I reach the top hall and stop dead in my tracks. Chris is in his room, his back to me in the open door.

'Go home, Ella. It's better for everyone if I'm gone.'

The smell of gas hits me, but not from a leak. Gasoline. His hand holds a red container with the yellow nozzle sloshing another splash on his wall.

'Don't do it!' I can't think of a more horrific way to die than in a house fire.

'Trust me, if you knew what I've done, you wouldn't want me around.'

'I know you went over to Blake's house. I know you killed him.'

'Then you also know I lied to you about it.'

He did lie. I'd been so confused about whether that night was real, and then panicked about the message Chris left and why he'd leave the ring behind, that I skipped over what it meant.

He let me think I was hallucinating more, made me unable to trust myself, took advantage of my diagnosis to keep himself safe. And that means . . .

'The pictures. You took them.'

'I could tell you weren't going to keep your promise. I tried to scare you like the message and then I tried to cover it all up by blaming it on your hallucinations, but then . . . when I saw you hugging Joey in the hospital, I could only think about how I helped put you there, that I was willing to lie to save myself. I have to face that, Ella! And that means I can't stay here.'

He drops the container at his feet, some of the gas spilling. I launch myself back as he removes a box of matches from his pocket.

'Why burn it all down? The insurance won't pay out. Joey won't get anything.'

'This isn't about money anymore.' He opens the box. 'The house has to go just like I have to. I failed to fix the roof. To pay the mortgage. To see Blake for who he was. To save her!' The last two words claw their way out of his throat like they're ripping him apart.

'You set the gas leak.'

The words escape me as a whisper, but it's true. He was blaming himself when he woke up in the hospital, and I thought it was the same guilt I felt for not being able to pull them out in time, but now I know the truth.

'They weren't supposed to be home,' he cries. 'Nobody was

supposed to be home. I didn't try to kill her. I told you I never wanted to murder my mom or my brother. I tried to save them!'

'You left your phone home on purpose on New Year's Eve so there'd be no record of your movements, no parent app tracking you.' Based on what Alex told Dominic, he planned to be back before Alex noticed.

He brings a match out of the box.

'Chris, no! Don't do this.'

'You don't get it.'

'You were trying to explode the house, like Springtown.' Chris was telling me truths all along. Nicki Davis's client tried to collect on insurance money but died in the process, and Blake told Chris about it. Chris, desperate and wanting to help his family, thought they could execute a better plan to collect the house insurance and rebuild.

I overheard part of his conversation with Blake in the police station.

'You remember what I said?'

'It's no one's fault. It was an accident.'

'That's right. Now you keep repeating that to yourself over and over until you believe it.'

I thought Blake was comforting him, but he was trying to make sure Chris didn't crack.

Blake had other plans. He intended to have the three of them die in the explosion and for him to collect Julie's life insurance money.

That's why Chris didn't want to believe Blake was behind it for so long. That's why he felt the betrayal so deeply after Peterson and Langdon left that night.

'Blake said it'd be easy.'

'You sent me the threat because you didn't want me to find out you were involved.' Chris's hanging head is confirmation enough. He fiddles with the box of matches. 'Blake was in on it with you. You helped him.'

'He said he'd get us the money, that I only needed to make a hole in the furnace line and come back to explode the house.' His voice trembles, weak, unstable. 'But he disconnected the dryer. He released more gas than we planned. He killed her. He tried to kill me. He was guilty.'

'Wait. Did you—' I wouldn't have thought it possible, would have quickly dismissed it as delusional. But now I know that the ugliest pieces of truth can't be swatted away. 'Did you kill Blake on purpose?'

Chris spins the red-and-white box in his hand. 'He wouldn't return my calls. I drove to his place to confront him. He shoved me up against the wall when he thought I was going to cave. I shoved him off.'

'You said he threatened me again.'

'He did, and he really was alive when I left. I wasn't trying to kill him! I never tried to kill anyone! But it doesn't matter.'

'It does matter! You can tell the police the truth.'

'They won't believe me because it's my fault!' he cries out.

His chest heaves and those words are true, but it's obvious

he hates himself for them. He hates himself for everything he's done.

'She's never coming back,' I say. 'There's nothing you can do to change it.'

'Don't you think I know that?'

'You can't keep trying to escape, Chris. That's what you've been doing this whole time – trying not to face it while Blake takes the fall.'

'That's where you're wrong, Ella. I do have to face it. I've had to face bills and work and being an adult before I should have. I have to face that I trusted Blake, that I believed I could take an easy way out and blow up my house. I have to face that I was cruel enough to lie to you, to trick you, to lie to everyone who's ever cared about me!'

No sirens wail, no lights flash through the windows. Help isn't coming. I'm all he has.

'You can't run from this,' I say.

'You should hate me, Ella. I'm the reason no one will believe you. This could all be a hallucination.'

It's not. I know it's not. And if Detective Peterson gets here in time, he'll know too.

'I thought if I didn't take care of my family, no one would, but I was wrong. Your parents will take care of Joey. He doesn't need me. No one does. I've got nothing to tie me here. There's nothing to connect me to what happened.'

I helped make sure of that. I planted the evidence in Blake's office. Blake was pulling the strings on Chris, just like Chris pulled the strings on me.

Until now.

His voice is the growl of a wounded animal, one who's cornered and prepared to bite rather than let anyone release him from the trap he's stepped in.

'Come home—'

'I don't have a home anymore!'

'Come back to my parents' house,' I correct. 'We'll figure this out.' I don't know what to do. He doesn't deserve to walk away. He killed a man, a terrible man, but he's lied about it. He lied to me and threatened me, whether he meant to follow through or not. He shouldn't be out in the world.

But he's still my cousin.

He's not that little boy anymore, though. He made his choices, and it might not matter why he made them, because the results are the same. He didn't mean to kill anyone, but he did mean to lie to me, to gaslight me, to use my illness against me. I don't know what it means, but I don't want him to die. 'You can't kill yourself.'

'I don't want to.' He opens the box of matches and removes one. 'But I need them to think I am.'

'What?'

'Let them find the house burned to the ground, let them believe I died here. I'll never come back. I'll start over.'

'But then—' That really has been his plan all along. He wanted Joey to remember his mom and himself, but only because he was never planning to come back, not because he was joining her in death. 'Give me the matches. I'm not leaving you and we both know you're not going to hurt me. You protect your family, Chris. It's why this all started.'

He cared about me and wanted to drive me safely home to my parents where I could get help. I remember his voice in the car, telling me we were almost there. It had to be true, at least a little.

Or I'm in denial.

He manipulated me and lied to me every bit as much as Blake manipulated him. It makes me hate Blake more, but it doesn't excuse what Chris did. He had time to step back, time to evaluate, time to change.

The cold chill in the air brings silence. No sirens coming to the rescue.

And with a shiver I realise Chris is right. Detective Peterson must have assumed from my call begging for help that it was all in my head, just like Officer Varden had. He's not coming at all.

'I have to protect myself first. Just go. Get out of here. They'll think I'm dead, that I burned in the fire, and I can leave.'

I reach out towards him. Towards the match. 'Stop. Think about this. They'll know you're still out there.'

'Not if you don't tell them. Walk away. Get out of here. I hurt you before. I don't want to do it again.'

'Chris, don't—'

He strikes the match. 'Go!'

'They won't find a body! It won't work!'

The flame eats away at the match in his hand, and he can't look away, like it's hypnotising him. 'It has to! It has to!'

'I called the police.'

'You what?' In the instant he's distracted, the fire reaches his fingers, and he drops the match.

The room ignites in a blaze.

The rush of heat is so overpowering, I have to shield my face with my hands and back away, but then Chris's screams tear the house apart.

His pants are on fire and some piece of my brain registers that he must have gotten gas on himself, but the how doesn't matter. Nothing matters except flames ripping across his body, eating his flesh.

He pitches forward but there's nowhere to drop and roll. I yank his arm and push him to the floor in the hall. He rolls and I take off my coat, patting the flames. I pull under his armpit like I did on New Year's Eve, desperately trying to save him, and I don't know why except that I still love my cousin who rode bikes with me as a kid and introduced me to scary movies as a teen. I love Joey's brother who tried to take on the responsibility of a dad he never had, and I love Julie's son who did everything he could to help, even when the thing he should have done most was trust others to take care of themselves.

So I pat down his legs under my coat, and the flames disappear from his body, but the hall is full of smoke. The fire's already eaten through the wall of Joey's room.

'Come on!' I call, coughing into my arm. I don't know how badly Chris's legs are burned, maybe badly enough to not feel the pain right now, or maybe the adrenaline pushes him forward, but we move down the stairs – until he slips.

Or the banister gives out, or he slips because the banister gives out.

But he's falling over the side of the stairs, black smoke pouring above his head. Flames cover the ceiling, eating straight through the floor. It's loud. The fire roars. Something crashes, and the ceiling caves in.

'Chris!' I scream, racing down the steps.

A heavy block of wood from the stairs lies across his back. He's trapped.

'Go,' he shouts. His voice raspy, firm. 'Get out!'

Not a request. An order.

He still wants to save me. Still thinks he knows better than everyone around him what's best, still doesn't trust me to decide for myself, and he won't ask for help when his life depends on it.

'Ella!' Dominic's voice screams from outside followed by 'Chris!' in Joey's littler one. They can't come in. No one else needs to be in danger.

It would be easy to run to the door, to run into their arms, to leave Chris behind, to give him his last request.

'Leave me!' Chris shouts again, and I could. I could race out of the house and call 911 again and let the firefighters and medics come and either save him, or more likely, fail to get him out in time just like his mom because there's nothing that can be done when the enemy is time and they aren't notified with enough of it. I could even pretend there's nothing I could do, that after all he's done, he's getting what he deserves.

But he's not the hero he's trying to be. He's still the scared kid who doesn't know how his family's going to pay for heat. He's still my cousin and he deserves a lot, but dying here, now – with the smoke choking him and flames hovering around his head while I turn my back on him and walk out of the house – I'm not convinced he deserves that.

'You don't get to die a hero,' I say. He's not saving me by telling me to get out. He's not dying at all. I won't let him. I won't let Joey lose someone else. I won't let the boy who grew up beside me die when I have the power to save him.

The beam is smoking, not on fire, but hot. Instinctively, my hands yank back at the first touch, but I wrap my fingers around the wood, bend at my knees, and heave. I cry out in strain, pushing my muscles past the point of what should be possible for me, a girl who's spent days in the hospital, but right now no one else's opinion of my strength matters. No one's expectations of what I'm capable of matters. All that matters is shoving this over Chris's head and freeing him from its weight, and I do.

I fall to the ground next to him, coughing. The left wall of the house sways, and the ceiling caves in more. The flames devour Julie's murals along the walls. We're not far from the door, almost exactly where Chris was on New Year's Eve.

I scramble to my feet, Chris's legs a mess of charred clothes and raging red welts. I want to shout for him to come on, but sucking in air is too hard and the roaring is too loud. There's another crash and glass breaking. I can barely keep my eyes open against the heat, and I imagine my lashes must be singed off, so

I don't yell, but I grab under his shoulder and pull him along, the front door only feet away.

It flies open and Dominic ducks under Chris's other arm, stepping in to take his weight. We cross the threshold as another crash of glass rings through the house.

Fresh air. I suck in a breath and collapse in the snow, coughing and crawling away from the house. Dominic and Chris fall beside me. Joey hovers by the mailbox, obviously wanting to come forward and terrified to leave the spot where Dominic must have told him to stay.

A police car lurches to a stop in front of the house, and Detective Peterson rushes to pull us away.

He believed me.

'Fire trucks are on their way,' he says. We're in the snow with the frigid January air at our backs, the intense heat and glow of the fire reflecting in our eyes. The second floor collapses.

The house is gone.

But we're alive.

36

April 16

Dominic and Sierra finish setting out chairs next to Mom and Dad. Sean's home too and sitting in the front row. He hung twinkle lights over the pergola on the deck for the occasion. I stretch next to the shed, pulling at my costume and slicking back stray hairs.

Mom and Dad found a counsellor who's helped me work through all the anxiety about what's real or not. I know how to stop the spirals. Sometimes. I'm not great at it, but I'm getting better at asking for help.

The radiation treatments have made Dr Gupta very optimistic. The tumour is shrinking, and I haven't had any hallucinations in months. I've even gotten better at resting, at not measuring myself by my productivity or avoiding being alone with my thoughts.

When the funeral arrived, Aunt Julie was beautiful, but in a different way than I remember. Seeing her devoid of life and spirit convinced me the viewing was for us to say goodbye, as she'd already moved on. She wants us to find new reasons to smile.

'You almost ready?' Sierra asks, handing me a bottle of water and adjusting her camera settings to film.

'Yeah, almost. Is the music set?'

'Ready when you are, babe.' She blows me an exaggerated kiss and takes her spot in the back. The yard swells with people: neighbours, classmates, friends of my parents. On the left are Steven and Kate, two others I met at my teen illness support group. Turns out, one of the most helpful things to do when faced with a major life-altering event is to talk to people who don't even need you to explain.

At first I wasn't so sure about the idea of a performance to help raise money for medical bills, but once I told people the truth about my diagnosis, the difference their support made was undeniable. Even people at school I'd barely said hi to shared stories of themselves or family members going through similar hardships. There were some stares and whispers and even a rumour or two that I was faking it, but by then, I had no interest in proving to people what I knew to be true.

'I brought you these!' Joey says, brandishing a bouquet of fresh tulips and irises.

'You did?' I gasp, taking them in my arms.

'Well, he helped pick them out,' Dominic whispers, sidling up behind me.

I twist until I'm facing him. 'Not willing to let him take the credit, huh?'

'I'm working on being honest with people's perceptions of me, remember?'

'Mmm, thank you.' I inhale the sweet scent. 'Both of you. Will you keep these safe for me until after the performance?' I ask Joey, handing back the bouquet.

He clutches them to his side and bounces away to sit by Sierra's mom, who has let him tour plenty of planes in the last few months.

'Is your dad here?' I ask Dominic.

'Right next to your parents.'

He gives me a kiss before I shoo him away so he can fill the seat next to Joey. Hank sits in the aisle, fully healed and enjoying the head scratches from all the guests.

I exhale a deep breath and wait for Sierra's signal. There's one face missing from the crowd, but I don't think I'd want him here anyway.

Chris is awaiting trial, and I can't decide what I hope the verdict will be. I've given his lawyer and the police the truth. All of it. What happens as a result isn't for me to decide – including the consequences I could still face from planting evidence in Blake's office. I can't control every aspect of my world, my thoughts, my body. But I can control some of it, and that's the part I need to focus on.

He spent weeks in the hospital's burn unit. It was even longer before his letter arrived. At first I didn't want to read it at all. As much as I knew I didn't want Chris to die that day in the fire, when Detective Peterson shut the door of the ambulance on Chris's gurney, my anger took hold and wouldn't let go.

My relationship with him was the one thing I never believed

could be fake, but his betrayal proved once again I can't trust myself to know what's real. With my counsellor's help, I eventually opened the envelope.

Ella,
You deserve this apology to be spoken to you face to face, but you also deserve to never have to see me again. I made so many mistakes, and I don't really know how to begin making them right. I guess the truth is, I never will. I thought I could escape what I did and the people I hurt, but I'll never be able to undo the damage I've done.

I've spent the last few months alone. Stuck. Last night, I remembered what you said to me, that it's okay not to be okay. So I talked to my mom, and I told her everything I did and how sorry I was for taking her away.

I don't know if she forgives me, or if she can, but I'm not apologising for forgiveness. I'm apologising because I need to acknowledge how wrong I was and who I hurt.

Which is why I'm writing to you now. I'm sorry, Ella. For everything.

I'm sorry I wasn't honest with you. I'm sorry I didn't trust you enough to talk about what I was going through. I shouldn't have tried to pull you away from Dominic. I'm sorry I sent you that message. When I finally told the truth about Blake, I wished I could take it back. At the hospital, you realised so much was in your head, so I lied to make it seem like my confession was too. I'm sorry I let you believe your tumour was to blame.

I should have taken better care of you when I realised you were hallucinating.

I was so scared about what would happen to me if the truth came out, but it did anyway.

I don't deserve your forgiveness. I'll never earn it. But I can make a promise to live a different life, to be a different person from the one who hurt you.
Chris

A prison sentence may not change anything. Even if a jury decides he wasn't at fault for his mom's death, he'll still be on trial for Blake's murder. Intentionally or not, Chris has a lot of blood on his hands. He'll have to live with what he did to me and to his own family for the rest of his life.

In a lot of ways, it feels like a worse punishment than anything the state could give him. I respect him for not using that as an excuse to avoid the consequences of what he's done, but I haven't forgiven him. I don't know when I will.

With time, I will heal from this tumour, I will heal from the trauma and I will heal from the broken relationships.

Forgiveness doesn't mean trust. I can give one without the other.

There will always be scars, but there doesn't have to be pain. We don't get what we deserve in life. If we did, what did I do to deserve this tumour? I've made plenty of mistakes, but I try to live a good life. Does it matter? Did that stop a tumour from growing?

So if good things don't happen to good people, then bad things don't always happen to bad people. And sometimes it's too complicated to decide which is which.

Especially alone.

I cue Sierra to play the music, and the crowd hushes almost immediately.

Learning to accept the bad in the world also means learning to accept the bad we create for ourselves. Sometimes the world isn't fair, but sometimes we're making the world worse, even if our intentions are to make it better. We have to learn to cope and accept, not control. We definitely can't control other people.

Dominic showed me that. He learned early on that he couldn't control his mom, and it still hurts him, but he doesn't stop his life for it, and that's what I'm learning too. Thinking of what Chris did to me, the lying and manipulating, still hurts. For now. But I can't let it stop me from living my life any more than I let my diagnosis.

I take off my shoes. I let my toes burrow into the cold grass. I grin at the lights flickering with moths and the lightning bugs skating on the breeze.

And I dance.

Acknowledgements

Before I ever signed a publishing contract, I'd heard how hard second books were. Despite the warnings, nothing could have prepared me for reality. For this reason especially, I want to give glory to God for His faithfulness and my thanks to all the people who believed in this book even when I didn't.

Thank you to:

My incredible agent, Molly Ker Hawn, whose honesty, humor, and wisdom have saved my sanity and my confidence. May all your roads be forever free of ice.

My US editor, Kelsey Horton. This book would not exist without you, and I'm so glad you could see beyond the pages and to its potential. May you never be trapped in an ice storm without power.

The team at HarperCollins UK, especially Tom Bonnick, and everyone who has had a hand in helping this story spread across the world. May your New Years always be safe and go according to plan.

The team at The Bent Agency, including Martha Perotto-Wills and Victoria Cappello, for all you do behind the scenes. May your house never smell of rotten eggs, but if it does, may it only be a sign you need to clean out the fridge.

There or Square, the writing group that feels like home (if home had questionable taco gifs and microwaved chicken). Sana Z. Ahmed, Elle Desamours, Christine Arnold, K.A. Cobell, Emily Charlotte, Valo Wing, Lally Hi, Sul, Laurie Lascos, P.H. Low and (always) Aimee Davis. I never want to find out what writing is like without you all in my life. May you never encounter a constipated nutcracker.

Former students and current friends, Allison Pinion and Allison Tinsley. Thank you for sharing your experiences and answering all my medical questions. Your testimonies are inspiring, and I pray you never have a cupcake stolen, at a birthday party or otherwise.

Detective Johnson, for once again putting up with my inquiries about all things concerning the law. May your phone battery never die, especially in an emergency.

Critique partners: Paula Gleeson, the best pantser mystery writer I know; Morgan Watchorn, whose fantasy career is taking flight; Anna Mercier, whose Turning to Story podcast helped this story as much as her notes; Kayla Rundquist, librarian extraordinaire, social media star, and writing inspiration; and Kimberly, whose stories I *will* one day hold. May you always win at Connect Four against any and every six-year-old.

Overbooked Book Club: Tana, Amanda, Sabrina, Kay, Kendra, Ashley, and any others who've joined since writing this. Thanks for the laughter and hype. May all your peanut butter jars open with ease and hockey pucks stay far away from your windows.

My friends, who are too many to name, but whose prayers, encouragement, and trust have kept me going. May you never run out of Oreos or Twizzlers.

My husband, who keeps me grounded and focused on what matters, and my kids who only complain a little when I talk about my books and make cringey videos. I pray you always trust in something greater than yourself.

And finally, my readers, especially you, teens. Thank you so much for spending your precious time on Earth in these pages. Every comment, post, message, and smile mean more to me than you'll know. May your friends always be real and your words believed.